TREASONS, STR␣
SPOIl

By

H A Culley

Book six about the Anglo-Saxon Kings of
Northumbria

The man that hath no music in himself, nor is not moved with concord of sweet sounds, is fit for treasons, stratagems and spoils.

William Shakespeare
From the Merchant of Venice

Published by

Orchard House Publishing

For Aliina and Henrik

First Kindle Edition 2017

Text copyright © 2017 H A Culley

TABLE OF CONTENTS

List of Kings and Principal Characters

Historical characters are shown in bold type

KINGS OF NORTHUMBRIA

Ceolwulf – 728 to 737. Deposed briefly and restored in 731.
Abdicated to become a monk at Lindisfarne. Died 764, later canonised
Eadbehrt – 737 to 758. Abdicated to become a monk. Died 768
Oswulf – 758 to 759. Son of Eadbehrt. Murdered
Æthelwold Moll – 759 to 765. Origin disputed. In this series of novels
he is portrayed as the bastard son of King Osred I
Alchred – 765 to 774. Married to Osgifu, daughter of Eadbehrt and
brother of Oswulf
Æthelred – 774 to 779. Son of Æthelwold Moll and his queen,
Æthelfryth. He was eleven when he became king and was a puppet used
by powerful nobles until he became sixteen. He was then deposed
Ælfwald – 779 to 788. Son of King Oswulf
Osred II – 788 to 789. Son of King Alchred. Deposed and exiled
Æthelred – 790 to 796. Restored. Murdered
Osbald – 796. Usurper. Reigned for 27 days before fleeing into exile
Eardwulf – 790 to 806. Deposed. Restored in 808. Married a
daughter of the Emperor Charlemagne. The end of his reign is not
recorded and may have been in 811 or 830

KINGS OF MERCIA

Æthelbald – 716 to 757
Beornred – 757. Usurper
Offa – 757 to 796. Nephew of Æthelbald

KINGS OF THE ISLE OF MAN

Heartbehrt – 716 to 740. Brother of Æthelbald of Mercia
Thringfrith – 740 to 755. Youngest brother of Æthelbald and Heartbehrt. Descended from King Penda of Mercia's brother, Eowa. Otherwise no historical records exist

KINGS OF THE PICTS

Óengus mac Fergus – 732 to 761
Bridei mac Fergus – 761 to 763. Óengus' brother
Cináed mac Feradaig – 763 to 775. No known relationship to Bridei
Alpín mac Feradaig – 775 to 778. Brother of Cináed
Talorcan mac Óengus – 779 to 785. Son of Óengus mac Fergus
Conall mac Taidg – 785 to 807. No known relationship to previous Kings of the Picts

KINGS OF STRATHCLYDE

Eógan mac Muiredaig – 733 to 740?
(Conquered by Óengus mac Fergus in about 740, amongst the kings who ruled as vassals, subordinate to the Kings of the Picts was **Rotri** – 750 to 754)
Áed Find – 768 to 778
Fergus mac Echdach – 778 to 781
Donncoirce – 781 to 792

OTHER CHARACTERS
(In alphabetical order)

Acca – Bishop and Abbot of Hexham
Æthelwold – Bishop of Lindisfarne 721 to 740
Beorhtmund – Ealdorman of Dùn Barra
Bleddyn – A Welsh slave boy, servant to Seofon's sons, who becomes his agent and assassin, later called Anarawd

Cerdic – Captain of Seofon's warband

Cynwise – Octa's wife

Cynewulf – Bishop of Lindisfarne 740 to 780

Eafa – Octa's son

Octa – Seofon's eldest son

Eafa – The son of Octa and Cynwise

Eanbald - Archbishop of Eoforwīc 780 to 796

Ecgbert – Archbishop of Eoforwīc 735 to 766, brother of King Eadbehrt and uncle of King Oswulf

Eochaid – Ealdorman of Alnwic, Ulfric's cousin

Ethelbert – Archbishop of Eoforwīc from 767 to 780

Higbald – Bishop of Lindisfarne from 780 to 803

Hilda – Eoachaid's daughter. Later married to Seofon

Renweard – Ulfric's younger son, Seofon's brother

Osoryd – Octa's daughter

Otta – The late King Aldfrith of Northumbria's middle son, actually named Offa but the name has been changed to save confusion with King Offa of Mercia

Seofon – Ulfric's elder son

Seward – A Mercian slave. Seofon's body servant

Sicga – The noble who murdered King Ælfwald. In the novel he is portrayed as the Ealdorman of Hexham

Torhtmund – The man who slew Sicga. In the novel he is Beorhtmund's nephew and successor.

Ulfric – Ealdorman of Bebbanburg until 762. Great-grandson of the first Ealdorman of Bebbanburg

Uuffa – Seofon's younger son

Uurad – Captain of Ulfric's gesith

Place Names
(In alphabetical order)

I find that always using the correct place name for the particular period in time may be authentic, but it is annoying to have to continually search for the modern name if you want to know the whereabouts of the place in relation to other places in the story. However, using the ancient name adds to the authenticity of the tale. I have therefore compromised by using the modern name for places, geographical features and islands, except where the ancient name is relatively well known, at least to those interested in the period, or else is relatively similar to the modern name. The ancient names used are listed below:

Alba - Scotland

Bebbanburg – Bamburgh, Northumberland, North East England

Bernicia – The modern counties of Northumberland, Durham, Tyne & Wear and Cleveland in the North East of England. At times Lothian was a subsidiary part of Bernicia

Berwic – Berwick upon Tweed, Northumberland

Caerlleon – Chester, Cheshire

Caer Luel – Carlisle, Cumbria

Cantwareburg – Canterbury, Kent

Dalriada – Much of Argyll and the Inner Hebrides

Deira – Most of North Yorkshire and northern Humberside

Dùn Breatainn - Literally Fortress of the Britons. Dumbarton, Scotland

Dùn Èideann - Edinburgh

Eoforwīc - York

Elmet – West Yorkshire

Frankia – The territories inhabited and ruled by the Franks, a confederation of West Germanic tribes, approximating to present day France and a large part of Germany

German Ocean – North Sea
Glaschu – Glasgow, Scotland
Loidis – Leeds, Yorkshire
Luncæster – Lancaster, Lancashire
Lundenwic – London
Mercia – Roughly the present day Midlands of England
Bernicia – The modern counties of Northumberland, Durham,
Tyne & Wear and
Cleveland in the North East of England and Lothian, now part
of Scotland **Pictland** – The confederation of kingdoms
including Shetland, the Orkneys, the
Outer Hebrides, Skye and the Scottish Highlands north of a line
running roughly from
Skye to the Firth of Forth
River Tamsye – River Thames, which flows though London
River Twaid – The river Tweed, which flows west from Berwick
through northern
Northumberland and the Scottish Borders
Strathclyde – South east Scotland

The Carolingian Empire of Charlemagne:

1. At the time of his accession to the throne:

Aquitaine – South-western France
Burgundy – South-eastern France and Switzerland
Frisia – Belgium and the Netherlands
Neustria – Northern France
Swabia – Part of Eastern France and Southern Germany around
the upper Rhine and lower Danube

2. Conquests:

Lombardy (in Northern Italy) - 774
Thuringia (in Northern Germany) in 774
Saxony (in Northern Germany) – 777 – 97
Bavaria (in Southern Germany) – 788
Carinthia (in Austria) - 788

Glossary

Ætheling – Literally 'throne-worthy. An Anglo-Saxon prince

Birlinn – A wooden ship similar to the later Scottish galleys. Usually with a single mast and square rigged sail, they could also be propelled by oars with one man to each oar

Brenin – The Brythonic term by which kings were addressed in Wales, Strathclyde and the
Land of the Picts

Bretwalda - In Anglo-Saxon England, an overlord or paramount king accepted by other kings as their leader

Ceorl - Freemen who worked the land or else provided a service or trade such as metal working, carpentry, weaving etc. They ranked between thegns and slaves and provided the fyrd in time of war

Cyning – Old English for king and the term by which they were normally addressed

Gesith – The companions of a king, prince or noble, usually acting as his bodyguard

Heræswa – Military commander or general. The man who commanded the army of a nation under the king

Knarr - A merchant ship where the hull was wider, deeper and shorter than that of a birlinn

Palliasse - A bag made of strong, stiff material such as canvas, linen or sackcloth. This is then filled with material such as straw, horsehair, wool or feathers to make a mattress

Seax – A bladed weapon somewhere in size between a dagger and a sword. Mainly used for close-quarter fighting where a sword would be too long and unwieldy

Thegn – The lowest rank of noble. A man who held a certain amount of land direct from the king or from a senior nobleman, ranking between an ordinary freeman and an ealdorman

Settlement – Any grouping of residential buildings, usually around the king's or lord's hall.
In 7th century England the term city, town or village had not yet come into use

Weregeld – In Anglo-Saxon England, if property was stolen, or someone was injured or killed, the guilty person would have to pay weregeld as restitution to the victim's family or to the owner of the property

Witan – The council of an Anglo-Saxon kingdom. Its composition varied, depending on the matters to be debated. Usually it consisted of the ealdormen, the bishops and the abbots

Villein - A peasant who ranked above a bondsman or slave but who was legally tied to his vill

Vill - A thegn's holding or similar area of land in Anglo-Saxon England which might otherwise be described as a parish or manor

Prologue

737 AD

Ceolwulf of Northumbria shifted his body uneasily as he sat on his throne in the king's hall at Eoforwīc. He had never been comfortable as a ruler. He was well aware that even his closest friend, the Venerable Bede, had expressed some reservations about his suitability as king. Ceolwulf was a man with deep monastic interests and little suited to affairs of state. Bede had dedicated his History of the English Church to the king in 731. A year later Coelwulf was deposed for a short while and fled to Iona.

Bishop Acca of Hexham supported the usurper, a supposed descendent of one of the many sons of Ida of Bernicia, the first King of Bernicia. The usurper lost his head and Acca his diocese.

Coelwulf had been persuaded to return but now, five years later, he had called a meeting of the Witan – the council of senior churchmen and nobles – to inform them that he was going to abdicate and retire to the monastery on the Holy Island of Lindisfarne where he would spend the rest of his days as a monk. As he was only forty one his retirement was likely to be quite a long one.

He cast his eyes around the motley assortment of men as they chatted amongst themselves, waiting for the meeting to be begin. Some, mostly the younger ones, were dressed in bright colours and wore tunics and trousers tied around the calf with ribbons. Often the three colours chosen for these items of apparel clashed, making the young nobles stand out even more against the sombrely dressed older ealdormen and the clerics.

Both wore robes that reached the ground, the ealdormen in a variety of colours varying from crimson to dark blue, and the churchmen in black habits for the Benedictines and a dark cream for the rest. The bishops were only distinguishable from the abbots by the shepherd's crook or the crosier they carried. All were tonsured, of course, and all wore a crucifix of some sort on their chests.

'My lords, bishops and abbots,' Coelwulf began is his slightly high-pitched voice. 'Thank you for coming to this special meeting of the Witan. As there is only one item for us to discuss, I have decided to preside myself.'

There was a buzz of interest at this. Normally the bishop or ealdorman hosting the council would act as chairman. The king waited patiently for the hubbub to die down.

'As you know I am not married and therefore I have no children; nor do I intend to marry.'

'That doesn't mean you can't have children, Cyning. King Aldfrith was a bastard. For all you know you may have sired a few already,' one of the younger nobles called out.

A pained expression crossed Ceolwulf's face at this sally. He knew he had no children because he was still a virgin. When the laughter had died down he continued.

'The succession will therefore have to be decided sooner or later and I have decided that it should be resolved now.'

A fresh tumult greeted this statement. This time one of those present decided that, if the king wasn't going to bring the Witan to order, someone had to do it.

'Silence, silence I say,' Eochaid of Alnwic, the hereræswa, yelled above the noise. 'Let the king speak.'

'Thank you, Lord Eochaid.'

He smiled at the elderly commander of Northumbria's army to convey his thanks. Eochaid had been an ealdorman for over forty years and had taken over as hereræswa when his friend Swefred,

Ealdorman of Bebbanburg, had done what Coelwulf now proposed to do and retired to Lindisfarne. Eochaid hadn't been called upon to display his military skills in all that time as the kingdom had been at peace, mainly thanks to Swefred's efforts to defeat their northern neighbours, the Picts, decades earlier.

'There is a need for urgency I fear as I have decided that I am a poor ruler but a devout Christian and I need to devote more time to the great love of my life – scholarship.'

Instead of the uproar he'd expected, his announcement was greeted by a stunned silence. Anglo-Saxon kings had abdicated and become monks before, but usually they were forced to do so as an alternative to being killed.

Then everyone started talking at once. Eochaid shouted to restore quiet again but this time he was ignored. He stalked out of the hall and came back with half a dozen members of his gesith. They banged their spears against their shields and this time the Witan slowly became silent.

'You can protest all you like,' Coelwulf said quietly, 'but my mind is made up. Your task now is to choose my successor because tomorrow I will start the long journey north to Lindisfarne.'

With that Coelwulf got up and walked out of his hall for the last time.

Chapter One – The Killing of Cousin Eardwine

745 AD

I was born at a time when Northumbria's golden age was coming to an end and chaos and strife were about to descend upon the kingdom. My father was Ulfric, Ealdorman of Bebbanburg. He ruled over the shire that surrounded the gaunt fortress standing on top of a tall outcrop of basalt rock on the coast of the German Ocean in what had been the Kingdom of Bernicia; an area which had been conquered by an Angle called Ida two centuries ago.

My parents named me Seofon because I was the seventh male child to be born to the House of Catinus. He was my great-great-grandfather and the first Ealdorman of Bebbanburg. I had a brother a year younger called Renweard, but no sisters. He and I were near enough in age that we thought of ourselves as twins and we were a lot closer than most brothers. Even when we were old enough to realise that I would inherit eventually and my brother would have to find his own way in the world, we didn't allow that to come between us.

I was eleven when this story begins and my father was two years short of forty. I had known vaguely that I had a great-uncle called Eadwulf who had been King of Northumbria for a few months before the boy king, Osred, took the crown from him. Now Eadwulf's son, Eardwine, was challenging the present king, Eadbehrt, for the throne.

I found it all very confusing until my father explained it to me. The descendants of Ida – the man who had built the original fortress of Bebbanburg – were æthelings, meaning throne-worthy. Ida's grandson, Æthelfrith, had united the kingdoms of Bernicia and Deira to form Northumbria - literally the land north of the River

Humber. His sons and grandsons had ruled Northumbria until the last king of his house, Osric, had died.

That was when the problems started. There had been a couple of usurpers before this - my great-uncle Eadwulf being one of them - but now there were a number of nobles descended from one of Ida's many sons who had a claim to the crown. The strongest of them, Eadbehrt, had been elected by the Witan when the previous king, Coelwulf, abdicated and became a simple monk on Lindisfarne.

Both Renweard and I were at the monastery on Lindisfarne being educated at the time and the former king was a great curiosity to us boys for a while. However, novelty is short lived and soon he became just another member of the community.

When I left there at fourteen to return to Bebbanburg and join other boys my age to be trained as warriors, I found out that Eadbehrt had been a controversial choice to succeed him. One of the original royal family, Otta, was still alive in exile. It was also whispered that Osred had raped a nun when he was thirteen and that the bastard born of their sacrilegious union was now the Ealdorman of Berwic, which lay at the mouth of the River Twaid to the north of Bebbanburg. His name was Æthelwold Moll and he was a great friend of my father's.

Like his brother, King Osred, Otta had the reputation for being an irreverent wastrel and had been passed over in the past. Now he was said to be a reformed character and many thought he had a better right to the throne than Eadbehrt. Privately I thought that Ealdorman Æthelwold probably had a better claim than any, if the stories were true, but I kept my thoughts to myself.

However, it was Eardwine who first challenged King Eadbehrt in the spring of 745.

'This is bad news for our family, boys,' my father told us one night in the hall at Bebbanburg as we sat around the central hearth watching the smoke – or most of it – curl lazily upwards to be sucked out of the hole in the roof by the strong easterly wind off the sea.

'Your grandfather, Swefred, allowed his brother, Eadwulf, to become a monk and escape King Osred's justice after he was defeated by him, something the boy king never forgave him for. As you know, Eadwulf reneged on his sacred vows and became a warrior in Ireland. He married and had a son, my cousin Eardwine. Eadwulf died in some minor war but his son landed in Cumbria a month ago with an Irish warband.

'We have to tread very carefully. We have always been loyal to the king appointed by the Witan, but many will believe that we are tainted by our relationship to Eardwine. What is worse, we are likely to be the losers whoever wins: Eardwine because he blames Swefred for defeating his father and sending him into exile and Eadbehrt because he doesn't trust us. Needless to say, my cousin's revolt will have made matters far worse.'

I was now a trained warrior and a member of my father's gesith – the companions who formed his bodyguard – whilst Renweard was in his last year of military training. We realised at that moment that what had at first seemed of little relevance to us up here in the North, remote from the politics of the court at Eoforwīc in the south of Deira, was likely to have a significant effect on our lives.

'What do we do, father,' Renweard asked whilst I was still trying to make sense of all this in my mind.

Instead of replying, he turned to me.

'What do you think, Seofon?'

'Well,' I replied slowly after thinking through the options. 'There is little to be gained by siding with Eardwine. He will want revenge on us whatever we do. However, if we support Eadbehrt then, hopefully, he might well regard you as a loyal subject from now on.'

'I couldn't have put it better. Well done. Go and tell Uurad to call out the fyrd. In two weeks time we march to join the

muster at Hexham.' 'Even me, father,' Renweard asked
hopefully.

'No, your mother would never forgive me if I took you to war
before you've finished your training. However, I have an important
job for you. I want you to stay here and help your mother and the
reeve to prepare to defend our home.'

~~~

I felt immensely satisfied with life as I rode behind my father
and Uurad on the road to Hexham. The weather was fine but there
had been enough rain in the past week to keep the roads from being
too dusty. As we travelled down the old Roman road to Alnwic the
sheep on the hillsides looked incuriously at us and the cattle carried
on eating grass. It was an idyllic pastoral scene and it seemed
inconceivable that we were off to war.

I was in charge of the Bebbanburg banner and that made me
extremely proud. Of course it was furled and kept in the baggage
wagons during the journey, but it would be unfurled so I could
carry it for the last few miles to let King Eadbehrt know that the
men of Bebbanburg had arrived.

We weren't alone. Æthelwold Moll had ridden down from
Berwic and when we reached Alnwic, their ealdorman - Eochaid -
joined the column. Eochaid complained to my father that he was
too old for this sort of thing now, but if that was the case he could
have stayed at home and let his eldest son take his men to the
muster. He was approaching sixty, twenty years older than my
father so the king would have understood.

I was slightly in awe of his sons, although I would never have
admitted it. Acwulf was twenty five and Bryce was four years
younger. There was also a daughter – Hilda – who was about five at
the time. It caused quite a stir when she was born because his wife,
my aunt Guthild, was over fifty and had shown no sign of being

pregnant. Everyone accepted Hilda as Eochaid's and Guthild's daughter but it was rumoured that her birth mother was, in reality, one of the slaves that worked in the hall.

The elder son helped his father to rule the shire whilst Bryce was captain of his gesith. Both teased me, not unexpectedly as I was the youngest member of Ulfric's gesith, but they had known me since I was a baby and it was all good natured. To be honest I enjoyed the attention.

The king's encampment looked enormous to me, about four times the ground covered by the settlement below the stronghold at Bebbanburg and that had a population of four hundred. Of course, here there were leather tents of various sizes instead of huts and instead of the thegn's hall there was a large tent in the middle of the rest. Obviously it belonged to the king and that's where my father and the other two ealdormen headed whilst the captains led the men off to find somewhere to camp.

The three ealdormen rode up to the king's tent with their banner bearers so I was lucky enough to be present at the meeting.

The king wasn't alone in the tent, apart from a few servants another man was sitting with him. They looked so similar that I would have known him for his brother, Ecgbert, Archbishop of Eoforwīc, even if it hadn't been for the cleric robes and the large gold pectoral cross. One of the last acts of the previous king, the saintly Ceolwulf, was to persuade the Pope to raise Eoforwīc to be an archdiocese. It hadn't pleased the Archbishop of Cantwareburg overmuch as it challenged his position as the Metropolitan of All England; nor had the creation of a fourth diocese in Northumbria – that of Whithorn in Galloway – pleased the Bishop of Hexham as he'd lost Cumbria from his see.

'Welcome.' Eadbehrt said. 'I'm glad you've chosen the right side, Ulfric. I half expected you to support your wretched cousin.' As a greeting it could have been warmer.

'I don't know the man, Cyning, and our fathers hated each other. This branch of the family has ever been loyal to the true King of Northumbria. I can't think why you thought otherwise.'

It was as close to a rebuke as my father dared to go.

'You won't be aware of the latest developments,' Eadbehrt said, scowling at the riposte. 'The Picts have decided to support your cousin.'

This clearly puzzled my father. He'd told me some time ago that their king, Óengus mac Fergus, didn't want war with Northumbria.

'How do we know this, Cyning?' he asked.

'Because a party of my scouts has reported them streaming over the River Kelvin heading for Lothian,' he replied impatiently.

'Surely that's more likely to be the Britons from Strathclyde? If it was Óengus and his Picts they would have had to cross Strathclyde territory to get there.'

From the ruddy hue of his face it was evident that the king was close to losing his temper.

'Brother, I think Ulfric may be correct,' the archbishop said softly before Eadbehrt could say anything more. 'It does make more sense. Why would the Picts aid Eardwine? What do they have to gain? He'd hardly likely to have offered Lothian to Óengus; it's too big a part of the kingdom. On the other hand he could well have offered Teudebur the
Cumbrian part of Galloway back.'

Eadbehrt's rage visibly diminished as he thought about what Ecgbert had said. 'You may be right, I suppose. We need to find out.'

His eyes narrowed as he looked thoughtfully at my father.

'How many horsemen have you got, Ulfric?'

'Twenty five in my gesith and thirty eight of my warband are mounted.'

'Sixty men should be sufficient. I want you to go and find out who these invaders are and in what strength they've crossed the

22

Kelvin. I don't want you to just report what you find; bring back captives who I can question myself. Understand?' 'Yes, Cyning,' my father replied stiffly.

The king couldn't have made his distrust any plainer. It was obvious why he had chosen us; if we all got killed he wouldn't shed any tears.

~~~

I sat beside my father on the ridge as the wind whipped around us and the rain hit us horizontally. It made seeing any distance difficult and, for all we knew, there could be thousands of our foes in the valley below us and we'd have been none the wiser.

'This is hopeless,' Uurad muttered. 'We can't see anything from up here and if we go down there, where they are likely to be, we'll run into them and get wiped out.'

'You're right. The best thing we can do is to seek shelter and hope for better conditions tomorrow,' my father muttered with a curse or two thrown in.

We were travelling light and so we were unencumbered by such luxuries as tents or cooking pots. Lighting a fire in such conditions was out of the question in any case. I was starving but all I had to eat was a lump of stale bread with mould growing on it and a lump of cheese that was nearly as hard as the bread. I'd be lucky if I had any unbroken teeth left by the end of the week.

That night I tried to sleep wrapped in my sodden cloak but without much success. I was actually glad when my turn to stand watch came round. I was surprised at how stiff I was until I'd moved about a little. I took over from another warrior who disabused me of the notion that at least I could now exercise my stiff limbs.

'Stand against this tree,' he instructed me in a soft whisper, 'and don't move a muscle. Keep awake and keep your eyes peeled. If you move any enemy out there will know where you are and you'll end up with your throat cut.'

For the first hour I was too petrified to move but I began to feel sleepy and thought that if I moved about quietly that should be alright. Besides I needed to take a piss. I was just about to edge away from the tree when I thought I saw something move.

It wasn't the first time I thought that. Staring out into the darkness with the rain pattering on the leaves had convinced me several times that I was about to be attacked but it was just my imagination. This time it wasn't. I could just make out a figure in the gloom and then I definitely heard a twig snap.

I didn't know what to do. No-one had actually told me what should happen if I suspected that we were about to be attacked. If I yelled out a warning the man a few yards away from me would probably attack me and, although I was trained, I had never actually fought anyone for real. The odds of me winning a fight were not good.

I had put my heavy shield against the tree with my spear and my sword and seax were in their scabbards. I tried to ease my seax out of its sheath as slowly and quietly as I could. The figure stopped for a moment and I thought that he'd spotted me. However, a few seconds later he continued to move, not towards me but to my left.

I held my breath and waited until he was two yards away and then I leaped out and thrust the point of my seax through his neck. I was rewarded by a metallic smell as hot blood sprayed over my face and byrnie. I remember cursing silently at the thought that now I'd have to clean it – a stupid reaction because I'd have to clean the rust off it anyway once the rain stopped.

The man gurgled and collapsed. The sound must have warned the others with him because they gave up all pretence at stealth and rushed towards the clearing where my father and his men were asleep.

'Wake up,' I yelled. 'We're under attack.'

I prayed my warning was in time. Everyone slept fully clothed and in their byrnies, if they had them - or leather jerkins if they didn't - with their weapons beside them so that they could lay their hands on them in the dark. Luckily most had enough time to get to their feet and arm themselves with spear and shield. The attackers must have thought that we were only a small scouting party because we later estimated that there was scarcely more than a dozen of them.

By the time I'd checked my opponent was truly dead and made it back to the clearing it was all over. Not only had we escaped with barely a scratch – two men had flesh wounds that were soon stitched up – but we had managed to capture two of our foes alive. One was a middle-aged man and the other was a boy a year or so younger than me. That was good news, but the even better news was that the boy was the other warrior's son.

'If the man won't tell us what we want to know, then torturing the boy should make him more talkative,' Uurad told me with a grin. 'You did well tonight, not only have you killed your first man but you saved us a few lives with your warning. Now go and find the body; anything valuable on it belongs to you.'

The threat to his son made the father only too willing to tell us what we wanted to know. They were indeed Britons from Strathclyde. We might not have seen anything from the ridge the previous afternoon, but they had seen the three of us sitting on our horses on the skyline and, thinking that we were just a few scouts, they had been sent to follow us and kill us. They had located us in the dark and the rain because they could hear the horses that we'd hobbled near our camp. Men could be very quiet but horses seldom are.

Of course, I was delighted by the praise my fellow warriors heaped upon me but Uurad brought me down to earth.

'You were lucky, boy. If that man you spotted had gutted you instead of the other way around we might have been killed in our sleep. Next time, slip away silently and wake me instead of trying to be a hero.'

~~~

The weather slowly improved over the next few days. The Briton had also told us that they were going to join up with Eardwine and his Irish mercenaries. By this time the Cumbrians and the men of Luncæstershire arrived and we set off for the junction of Ewes Water and the River Teviot where the Britons and the Irish were due to muster. It was a part of Lothian that was largely uninhabited.

It seemed to me to be a strange place to gather an army as the foraging parties would have a hard time finding enough for the army to eat, but my father pointed out that from there they would have an easy march along Teviotdale and the valley of the River Twaid to the east coast. He added that nearer to Hawic there would a lot more farms and settlements; we needed to intercept them as quickly as possible.

From Hexham we wound our way north up the valley of the North Tyne before crossing some hills before dropping down into Redesdale. It had taken us three days of hard marching but we knew we couldn't afford to slacken the pace. Hawic was still four days away and it was likely that Eardwine had reached there by now. The local ealdorman had sent a messenger to his family before we left Hexham so they and the local population should be safely hidden in the Cheviot Hills by now, but the settlement would have suffered.

That evening my father came back from a meeting of the war council grim faced.

'It seems we have another impossible mission,' he told us when his gesith and the leaders of the warband and the fyrd had gathered. 'This time I'm to take my horsemen and those of Eochaid and Æthelwold and try and delay the enemy until the king can catch up with us. I gather that my grandfather and Eochaid did something similar in the war against the Picts nearly twenty years ago.

'They held a pass and tricked the Picts into thinking that the whole Northumbrian army was on the reverse slope. That's not going to work a second time, especially as they are traversing a river valley.'

'So, what do we do, lord?' Uurad asked.

'They'll have to cross a small river at its confluence with the Teviot. There is a small settlement on the east bank called Gedwearde which has a hall with a palisade, so I'm told.'

'Can they not cross further down?'

'Not without considerable difficulty. The water at the confluence of the two rivers is quite treacherous and below Gedwearde the land either side of the river is marshy. There is one crossing place opposite the settlement and that is man-made. We need to get there first, remove the stones under the water and improve the defences on the east bank.

'Eochaid, is there anything you can add which might help us? I know the circumstances were different, but...'

My father's voice trailed away as Eochaid got to his feet.

'Yes, we rode double with an archer behind each horseman clinging on for dear life.' This was greeted by laughter but then everyone realised what a good idea it was. We could muster perhaps a hundred and fifty mounted men between the three shires, but the same number of archers could turn Gedwearde into a real stronghold.

~~~

It was a close run thing. Our men were still removing the stones from the ford when the enemy scouts appeared. Our archers killed a couple of them before the rest turned tail and fled, but it wouldn't be long before their main body arrived. Thankfully, it was less than two hours before sunset. They might try a quick assault before dark but the real test would come at dawn – or so we thought.

Nothing happened and we went to sleep wondering why we had been granted a reprieve. At the end of the night I spent two hours on guard, patrolling the parapet that ran around the palisade, but I neither heard nor saw anything. Everyone else was up and in position as a watery sun rose behind some thin clouds; still nothing happened. An hour later the three ealdormen met to confer.

'Right, we don't know why they haven't attacked us but we need to find out what's going on. Ealdorman Æthelwold is going to take a small party over the Teviot on the ferry near where it joins the Twaid. He will then ride back westwards to discover the enemy's whereabouts. As the enemy will be on this side they should be safe, but there's always the possibility that they have scouts across the Teviot.'

'Those who know the area have said that the ferry can only take two horses and their riders at a time so I'm only going to take three men with me. Volunteers?'

I was the first on my feet and, although my father glared at me, he could hardly forbid me to go. Uurad was one of the other two chosen, presumably to keep me out of trouble, together with one of Æthelwold's gesith - a man called Cynric.

It was a warm day for late spring as we covered the eight miles to the ferry in under an hour. The double trip across the river took an hour all told and then we were on our way again. As we neared Gedwearde across the river I half expected to see it under attack, but nothing had changed since we left. Then, ten minutes later we found out why.

I was riding point with Æthelwold and Cynric fifty yards behind me and Uurad bringing up the rear when we discovered where Eardwine's army was. Thankfully I heard them before we ran into each other. A horse neighed and I heard voices; both sounds were faint and so I judged that they were a little way ahead of me. I turned around and made my way quietly back to the others.

'It could just be a party of scouts,' Æthelwold said thoughtfully, 'but if the main body have managed to cross to this side of the river it would explain why they didn't attack Gedwearde. We need to find out. For now we need to get into the trees and let them pass us.'

Two minutes later half a dozen men on ponies road past us. We didn't have to worry about them spotting us; they were chatting amongst themselves in a language I didn't understand.

'Irish,' Uurad whispered.

We waited and a few minutes later another party of horsemen rode past us, this time they were better armed and mounted on horses, not ponies. I heard one of them address the man riding at the head of the small column as Cyning so it had to be Eardwine and his gesith. Behind them came warriors on foot. Those in the lead were wearing helmets and byrnies and carried shields, spears and swords, but the great mass following them wore just tunic and trousers and were poorly armed.

Behind the long line of baggage carts came a smaller group who looked like fierce fighters but, again, few wore anything to protect their bodies; indeed many were half naked.

After they had gone we conferred and came to the conclusion that those on foot ahead of the wagons were Britons from Strathclyde and those at the rear were Irish kerns. In all there were about two thousand of them. It was less than Eadbehrt had mustered but battles didn't always depend on raw numbers. The men we saw looked like fierce warriors in the main, whereas our fyrd hadn't been called upon to fight for decades.

Now we had the problem of warning my father and the rest that our foes were on the north bank.

'Where will they cross back again, lord?' Cynric asked Æthelwold.

'They've got two options now,' he replied grimly. 'If they do so they'll be heading for
Bebbanburg but, if they cross the Twaid where it meets the Teviot they'll be making for Berwic.'

Neither was good news for us because it meant that they would either be pillaging Æthelwold Moll's shire or my fathers'. Somehow we had to delay them.

~~~

When we reached the point on the north bank opposite Gedwearde again we waved frantically to attract the attention of the sentries but we needn't have bothered. They had evidently seen the enemy host going past and Eochaid and Ulric were already preparing to leave and head east.

When we got back to the ferry the two men who operated it had vanished.
Fortunately the ferry itself was on our side of the river so we rowed it across ourselves. It was overloaded with the two extra horses but we made it safely and left it on the south bank. Instead of waiting for the rest of our men, Æthelwold decided to press on with Cynric and shadow the enemy from this side of the Teviot. Uurad and I were sent back to tell the rest what he was doing and the conclusion he'd come to about the two alternative routes they could take.

'There is a bridge over the Teviot just south of where it meets the Twaid. I believe they'll cross there and head for Bebbanburg. If they can take the fortress quickly, Eardwine will be in a strong position. If he has to lay siege to it he risks being trapped between it and the rest of Eadbehrt's army,' Eochaid said dispassionately, trying to forget that our family was inside.

I couldn't help thinking that Renweard might have been safer with us after all. The threat to our family obviously worried father, though he hid it well and tried to concentrate all his attention on the task in hand.

'We need to get to the bridge first,' he said, looking at Eochaid for confirmation.

'Even with our few numbers we should be able to prevent them crossing.'

'I agree, let's get moving.'

The bridge was a simple timber affair which was just wide enough for a cart to cross one way at a time. That meant it could take perhaps three horsemen riding abreast or five men on foot. Those using the bridge had to pay a toll and the man who collected the payments lived in a hovel on the far side.

He was less than happy to be told we needed his hut but, when he heard about the pillaging horde coming towards us, he and his family loaded their possessions onto a small cart and disappeared into the hinterland, driving their few head of livestock before them, before we'd even finished dismantling his former home. We used the timbers and the wattle panels of which it was made to barricade the south end of the bridge and to make breastworks along the bank to protect the archers.

We didn't have long to wait after we'd finished our preparations. The priest with us was half way through celebrating mass when the scouts appeared. He hastily blessed everyone and we ran to our places.

The scouts debated amongst themselves for a few minutes then half turned tail and went back the way they'd come whilst the rest continued along the far bank. They sauntered past our position, calling out insults we didn't understand, until a few archers decided they'd had enough and sent half a dozen arrows their way.

Two of the six toppled to the ground wounded whilst a pony, struck in its rump by an arrow, bolted and unseated its rider. When he got to his feet two arrows struck his chest and he fell to the ground. The other three galloped out of range and then slowed to a canter.

'Seofon, take half a dozen men with you and shadow them. I'm fairly sure there is nowhere they can cross, but make sure.'

I thanked Eochaid for picking me and, nodding a farewell to my father, I went to find six of the warband who had trained with me. A few minutes later we were on our way, galloping until we saw the other riders again. They were studying the confluence of the Teviot and the Twaid. The weather had been fine for the last few days but the rain we had endured before that took time to come down from the hills to swell the rivers. Consequently the water was still quite deep and flowing fast; however, the level would be dropping all the time from now on.

The three scouts ignored us and eventually turned and headed upriver, following the Twaid. They were now heading back westwards.

'They won't find anywhere to cross the Twaid before they come to the junction with another river coming in from the west,' Edgar told us.

As he was the son of the local thegn he knew this part of the Twaid and the country around it well.

'Am I right in thinking that, if we can stop them crossing the Teviot for long enough, the king can bottle them up in this triangle of land between the Teviot and the Twaid?' Edgar shrugged. 'I suppose so, but we don't know where the rest of our army is.'

'Wherever they are, they'll be on the wrong bank of the Teviot,' another said.

'Not if we let them know the situation,' I pointed out excitedly. 'They can cross to the north bank of the Teviot where the Britons and the Irish did.'

'Come on, what are we waiting for? Let's go back and tell your father.'

~~~

We weren't the only ones to have archers. Some of the Irish and two hundred or so of the Strathclyde Britons had bows. For the first hour or so their attempt to capture the bridge was devoted to a war of attrition between our bowmen and theirs. Our archers were mainly members of the fyrd who owned the short bows used for hunting but they also had a few dozen men equipped with longer bows made from yew that had more range and greater ability to pierce chain mail.

Luckily our men had the protection of the wattle and daub panels taken from the toll collector's hut. After they had lost a few archers the enemy quickly provided each one the protection of a man with a shield. Whereas our shields were large and circular, theirs varied from the small circular type, called a targe, to the old-fashioned oblong Celtic shields like a fat figure eight which had been used by Britons since the time of the Romans.

Of course, the targes were of little use in protecting both holder and archer but the oblong shields gave their archers nearly as much protection as our breastworks. All the same, we managed to kill a few of their men but we lost a dozen or so too. It soon became apparent that they were intent on making us use up our arrows to no good purpose.

'Stop wasting arrows and retrieve as many of theirs as you can, provided you can do so safely,' Eochaid shouted. 'Wait for them to rush the bridge.'

We didn't have to wait for long. As soon as they realised that we were conserving our supply of arrows they surged across the bridge. The skilled warriors in chain mail were meant to lead but two score or so youths who weren't weighed down with byrnie and helmet overtook them and reached the bridge first.

For our archers it was like aiming at the side of an ealdorman's hall. They couldn't miss the tightly packed mass of bodies running across it. Those in front and on the outside were hit first but, as they fell wounded or dead, the men who had been in the middle started to take casualties. By the time the armoured warriors started to cross, the narrow bridge was full of the dead and the dying.

They were forced to pick their way over the obstacles and the momentum of their charge was broken. Several of them were also incapacitated by our archers. Chain mail may have protected their torsos in most cases, but not their legs or arms.

I was in the second row of defenders. The man in front of me stood hard up against the barricade with just his helmeted head exposed above his shield. He held his spear pointing downwards at the attackers' legs, whilst I rested my spear on his shoulder, aiming at their necks and faces.

Suddenly we were faced by men yelling and trying to kill us. A spear glanced off the helmet of the man in front of me and I had to move my head to one side to avoid the point. I was so petrified that I forgot to thrust back at his face but luckily someone else wounded him and he dropped out of sight with a cry.

He was immediately replaced by two men standing shoulder to shoulder with only their eyes showing between the rim of the helmets and the tops of the shields. I took careful aim and thrust my spear point into the eye of the man on the left. The man in front of me wounded another in the thigh at the same time. However, it gave another Irish mercenary the opportunity he needed. Whilst my companion was still extracting his spear he fell backwards into me with a sword in his mouth.

This had all come as something of a shock to me. Oh, I'd trained for two years but nothing prepares you for your first battle – the horror of it, the blood, the smell of piss and shit, and the noise. For a moment I was stunned but then I reacted, almost without thinking, and pulled my spear out of the dead man, stepped forward and raised my shield over my face to take the next blow by my opponent's sword.

We were too close for me to use my spear so I thrust it sideways into the neck of the mercenary attacking the man to my right and let go of it. I felt another hammer blow to my shield as I struggled to draw my sword in the confined space. Realising I didn't have enough room, I drew my seax instead and, lowering my shield, I thrust it into the surprised face of my adversary. The point hit the nasal bar of his helmet and was deflected into his cheek, which was sliced open as far as his ear. He yelled, as much in anger as in pain, and slashed at my head. I was slow in getting my shield up and I took the blow on my helmet.

The next thing I knew I was lying on the ground with a splitting headache and a raging thirst. At first I could recall nothing and then it all came flooding back to me like a wave crashing on the shore. I groaned and tried to lift my head but I seemed to have lost control of my body.

I felt someone lifting my throbbing head and pressing a drinking horn to my lips. I greedily tried to slurp the water it contained but my companion pulled it away before I'd taken no more than a couple of mouthfuls.

'Easy now, lord. Take it slowly or you'll be sick.'

I realised that the speaker was Seward – a Mercian boy who my father had given me as my body servant when I first became a warrior. He was reticent about his background but the rumour was that his parents had been very poor and had eight young children to feed, so they had sold Seward – the youngest boy – into slavery. He'd been seven at the time and had been a cook's boy up until the time that he was given to me at the age of twelve.

'What happened?' I asked trying to lift my head to look around me and failing.

I fell back and realised that Seward had my head cradled in his lap. I hadn't paid much attention to him up until now; our contact being confined to my giving him orders. However, I'd never beaten him for failing to understand what was required straight away or for not getting all the rust off my byrnie. I'd patiently explained where he'd gone wrong and I never had to tell him twice, so I suppose I was a kind master compared to many.

'You were knocked out and were passed back out of the line of defenders. I and another servant managed to get you loaded across your horse and I led you back to the baggage train. I went and fetched one of the monks who was tending the wounded and he bathed your wound and checked for damage before putting a bandage on it.'

I felt my face and realised that a strip of cloth had been wound over my head and under my chin to hold a wad of linen in place just above my ear.

'He said the blow had cut into your scalp but hadn't damaged the skull itself.'

Seward held my helmet up so I could see where the blade of his sword had dented and torn the metal. However, it had evidently taken most of the force out of the blow and the leather cap I wore under it must have helped too.

'He said he couldn't stitch a head wound but thought that you should be as right as rain in a few weeks. The hair might not grow back over the scar though.'

He said this as if he was fearful that I would blame him for it. I smiled and was about to reassure him when I suddenly felt extremely ill and vomited all over his right knee.

He didn't say anything but just wiped my face with a wet cloth before scrubbing the worst of it off his coarse woollen trousers.

'Sorry,' I mumbled.

His face registered surprise. Masters didn't apologise to slaves. He laughed.

'It's not the first time you've chucked up over me. I'll go for a swim in the river when this is all over.'

It was one of the things I'd noticed about him. Most slaves stank but he never did; well, not before today. Furthermore, he could swim; a skill few possessed. It crossed my mind that Seward was something of an enigma. Even his name, which meant guardian of the coast, was not something that a poor villein, or even a ceorl, would normally christen his son.

Later on I found out that his father had been a thegn but raiders had destroyed his vill and robbed him of nearly everything he'd possessed. He'd complained to his ealdorman but, as the raiders were led by his lord's cousin, nothing was done about it and he was reduced to the status of a ceorl, and a poor one at that. One of the features of our society was that a ceorl who amassed enough land to qualify as a vill could become a thegn, but movement down the social scale was possible as well.

'What's happening?' I asked, bringing my mind back to the battle.

'Oh, the enemy withdrew shortly after you got knocked out. Then they tried to wade across the river further down but several got washed away and our archers and spearmen stopped them climbing up the slippery mud onto the top of the bank. We lost a score of men but they must have lost ten times that.'

I thought he was exaggerating but I later learned that all told their casualties that day were over two hundred against our twenty five dead and forty wounded, including me. Still, we couldn't go on sustaining losses on that scale.

A little while later my father came to see how I was. To my surprise Acwulf and Bryce came with him.

'I see Seward is taking good care of you,' he said with a smile.

'Yes, he doesn't even seem to mind when I puke all over him.'

I tried to grin but stopped when I realised that any movement of my facial muscles made the pain worse.

'Well, there is one consolation, I suppose,' Bryce said with a smirk. 'You're so ugly that the scar won't make it any worse.'

'Might even make you slightly attractive to the ladies, God knows you need all the help you can get,' Acwulf added.

Their banter made me feel a little better. I tried to respond but suddenly I vomited again. This time I had regained some control over my neck muscles and, instead of Seward, my bile - for that's all I had left inside me – splashed over Acwulf's expensive leather shoes.

Both Bryce and my father roared with laughter and even Seward couldn't contain a chuckle. Acwulf looked as if he might hit me for a second, then he gave a rueful smile.

I don't remember any more and when I next woke up it was dark. I realised with a start that another, smaller, body was embracing me under the cloak which covered us both. Seward woke with a start and hastily scrambled to his feet.

'Forgive me, lord. You were shivering and ice cold to the touch. It was the only thing
I could think of to warm you up.'

The boy was shaking with fear. I shivered and realised that, for the time of year, it was much colder than usual. Perhaps the wind had shifted to the north and was blowing down from the snow covered mountains of Alba.

'Come back, Seward, I'm cold.'
The boy scrambled back under my cloak and I put my arms around him.

'Thank you,' I whispered in his ear. 'I couldn't have a more caring body servant, but you had better be up and about before dawn or people will get the wrong idea.'

He giggled and a few minutes later I heard him softly snoring before I drifted off again myself.

I felt better the next morning but my head still felt as if someone was trying to drive a nail into it. With Seward's help I managed to stand and go for a piss whilst he held me up. I wondered how I was going to defecate but he brought me a leather pail and a bench with a hole cut into it for me to sit on. How he managed to procure such an item I don't know and I didn't ask.

I could hear the noise of fighting from where I lay and I felt guilty that I was unable to join my fellow warriors in the shield wall. After an hour or so relative quiet returned; only the distant cries of the wounded and the ritual exchange of insults between the two sides disturbed the quiet. Then, about noon, the din of battle resumed.

'Go and find out what is happening,' I told Seward. 'I don't like to leave you, lord.'

'Put my sword in my hand and leave a tankard of water where I can reach and I'll be fine.'

He put my sword in one hand the leather tankard by the other before running off as fast as his legs could carry him. I smiled as I watched him go. He was in a growth spurt and his legs were disproportionately long for his body; so much so that he sometimes tripped over his own feet. He did so now, but he picked himself up and was off again so quickly that, had I blinked, I would have missed it.

I tentatively pushed myself into a kneeling position and tried to stand, something that Seward would never have allowed me to do on my own had he been with me. I made it onto my feet but I felt so dizzy I immediately fell down again. In doing so I banged my head and I passed out again.

When I awoke I found Seward fussing over me again. This time he was trying to get me to drink some broth.

'If you're determined to get back on your feet you need to get your strength back. This might make you puke all over me again but, if you can keep it down, it'll help.'

He propped me up so that I was sitting against a tree to keep me in position so that I could drink the broth. It smelt and tasted good

39

and, much to my relief, I manage to swallow some of it without being sick. It took a long time but eventually I'd consumed all that was in the wooden bowl. He lay me down again, covered me with my cloak and I went back to sleep. As I drifted off I remember thinking that I hadn't asked him about the fight at the bridge.

~~~

I felt a fraud lying in the back of a cart with other wounded men as it trundled back towards Bebbanburg. Seward was riding my horse alongside the cart looking as proud as a lord, so much so that I laughed out loud when I woke up and saw him. He looked hurt, but then he smiled.

'It's good to see you with some colour back in your cheeks, lord.'

'It's good to be going back home,'

'Yes, I suppose so,' he replied with a frown.

It was only then that I realised that he probably regretted the end to the intimacy that we had enjoyed after I was wounded. Once back at Bebbanburg, my mother and her servants would take care of me and Seward would be reduced to the status of a lowly slave, cleaning my armour, looking after my horses and emptying my piss bucket every morning.

His care of me when I was incapacitated had allowed him a degree of familiarity and we had become quite close. Now that was about to end. I was grateful to him but I failed to see it from his point of view. He was a slave, after all, and any form of relationship except that of master and servant was unthinkable. I put him out of my mind and found myself thinking about how the battle for the bridge had ended.

We had all but lost by the time that Eadbehrt eventually arrived. Over half our men were dead or wounded and, to my intense sorrow, both Acwulf and Bryce were amongst the fallen. They had died bravely, one in the shield wall holding the barricade on the bridge and the other driving back a party of Britons who had finally made it onto our side of the river - they had been able to wade across a shallower stretch a hundred yards south of the bridge once the depth of water had fallen sufficiently low.

Their deaths had broken Eochaid. He was an old man now but he had carried himself proudly up until then. He had doted on his sons and now he walked with a stoop, as if he was carrying a yoke weighed down at each end with pails full of iron.

Our men were losing heart when, just in time, Eadbehrt's scouts appeared and panicked Eardwine's men. They had lost several hundred in their futile attempt to cross the Teviot and now they were faced with a fresh army coming up in their rear which was probably nearly twice their number. Furthermore, they would be trapped in the triangle of land bounded by the Twaid and the Teviot. They did the only thing they could do. They surrendered.

Eadbehrt's terms seemed reasonable. Eardwine and the Irish leaders were to become captives, the latter pending ransom, and King Tuedeber of Strathclyde swore to recognise the Cumbrian enclave in Galloway as part of Northumbria. He too would be held as Eadbehrt's prisoner until his two sons were handed over, together with a chest of silver in exchange for his release.

It was plain that the Irish weren't happy about handing their leaders over but eventually Eardwine persuaded them that they'd be well treated until their ransom was paid. Once the enemy army had dispersed, Eadbehrt reneged on his promise and hanged the Irish leaders, together with Eardwine, from trees in a nearby copse.

Of course, I knew little of this at the time as I was still drifting in and out of consciousness. It was Seward who explained to me what had happened later, supplemented by what my father told me. I came to the obvious conclusion that the king's word was not to be trusted.

It was two weeks after my return home that I was strong enough to venture outside the hall on my own. My mother and her servants had smothered me with attention until I found it stifling. Of course, I also had to tell an envious Renweard every gory detail of my experiences over and over again until I was sick of it.

I breathed the salty air outside the hall with relish. It was now early summer and the hall was stiflingly hot, even in the chamber set aside for my use. Cooking fires were needed all year round and the heat and the smell of smoke permeated every nook and cranny of the building.

Slowly, and with many pauses to get my breath back, I climbed the steps up to the wooden walkway that ran just below the top of the palisade. I moved a little way along it and stared out to sea. The crests of the waves were white as the onshore wind whipped the spume away in streaks towards me. A mile away two knarrs, escorted by a birlinn, were making their way under reefed mainsails towards the new jetty my father had built in the relative shelter of Budle Bay just to the west of the fortress.

As I watched, enjoying the wind on my face, I was conscious of someone at my side.

Without looking I knew who it was.

'Come to lend me the support of your shoulder, Seward?'

'If you need it, lord, it's always here.'

'I know. I haven't thanked you properly for looking after me.' 'It was my pleasure, lord,' he replied quietly after a pause.

He seemed a little uncomfortable at being thanked and I was slightly surprised at myself for doing so.

'I think you probably mean that, you're not just saying it.' I glanced at him and he smiled shyly without replying.

'Come on; let's see if I can make it all the way round the palisade. If I stumble you can let me lean on your shoulder.'

42

He looked at me in alarm. It was the first time I'd been outside and even reaching the palisade had been a strain. I laughed at the expression on his face.

'Well, let's see if I can make it to the next ladder at any rate.'

I did but felt quite weak by the time we got back to the hall. My knees felt wobbly and I needed his help to climb the steps. Once back inside my chamber I lay down and he made to leave.

'No, don't go. Let me rest a while and then I'll teach you to play nine men's morris.'

The smile that lit up his face gave me a warm glow as I drifted off to sleep. When I awoke I found that he had set up the board and was waiting eagerly for me to explain the rules to him.

'It's a simple game of strategy,' I told him. 'The game begins with an empty board. The players determine who plays first, then take turns placing their men in turn on empty points. If a player is able to place three of his pieces on contiguous points in a straight line he has formed a mill and may remove one of his opponent's pieces from the board. Each player moves a man in turn to an adjacent point, continuing to form mills and remove the other's pieces. A player can break a mill by moving one of his pieces out of an existing mill, then moving it back to form the same mill a second time, each time removing one of his opponent's men. When one player has been reduced to two men, or can't move a piece when it's his turn, the other player has won. Do you understand?'

'I think so. Can we play and then I'm sure I'll pick it up.'

We did and, after a few games, he was winning more times than he lost. Far from being miffed, I was pleased to find out how bright he was. It was the beginning of a close relationship, albeit of master and servant, that would last until Seward died many decades later.

Chapter Two – Two Invasions and an Execution

750 AD

Five years later I was about to be married when another man tried to seize the throne from Eadbehrt. This time it was Otta, King Aldfrith's middle son. Both his brothers had been king but my father had told me that Otta was made in the same mould as his brother, King Osred the Wicked. Thankfully, the youngest brother, Osric, had been completely different. His reign was relatively peaceful and a time of prosperity for all. No one said that he was a good ruler though; he relied on others to manage the kingdom.

Otta had fled abroad after he had murdered King Cenred – the cousin who occupied the throne between Osred the Wicked and Osric the Good – and nothing much had been heard of him since then. It transpired that he had been earning a name, and a fortune, for himself on the Continent.

Now he was back, and with a warband of mercenaries numbering several hundred. He had landed at Beadnell Bay, midway between Bebbanburg and Alnwic. We felt safe within our fortress, but Eochaid's hall was vulnerable, especially since a few years ago Eadbehrt had passed a law limiting the number of armed retainers that his nobles could keep.

The king had never felt secure on his throne and, although he'd been unchallenged for many years, he had persuaded the Witan to approve a ruling limiting the number of armed warriors that a thegn could keep to six and an ealdorman to thirty. At the same time he increased the size of his own warband to three hundred. Furthermore, the fyrd could only be called out by royal decree. This meant that an internal revolt was unlikely to succeed, but it did make Northumbria extremely vulnerable to external invasion.

Although Eoforwīc was his capital, all kings had to travel the length and breadth of their kingdom if they wanted to keep it together. As luck would have it, Eadbehrt was at Caer Luel in Cumbria when Otta invaded. My father sent a messenger to warn him as soon as he heard about Otta, but it would take him at least three days to get there, so it would be the best part of a week before the warrant authorising the ealdormen of Bernicia and Lothian to call out the fyrd arrived.

Although Eadbehrt's distrust of our family seemed to have been assuaged by the stout defence of the bridge over the Teviot, my father daren't flout the law and call out the fyrd without the king's agreement. No doubt the other ealdormen felt the same. However, the gesiths of the three ealdormen of Lothian and those of the shires of Bernicia within a couple of days' march of us – namely Alnwic, Otterburn and Hexham – numbered perhaps two hundred and a fair number of those would be mounted.

As we feared, our scouts reported that Otta's small army had turned south and attacked Alnwic first. I was beside myself with anxiety. My betrothed was Hilda, the daughter of Alnwic's ealdorman, Eochaid. I paced the walkway around the palisade in a foul temper, watching for the other ealdormen to arrive, though I knew it was too soon.
Even Seward kept away from me and that wasn't like him.

I'd freed him two years ago when he reached fourteen but he'd remained my body servant. Over the years we had become close, something that was possible only because he never overstepped the mark.

My father was now fifty and recently he had allowed me to take a bigger part in ruling the shire. My brother Renweard had stayed at Bebbanburg for a while after he became a warrior, but a few years ago he'd been invited to join the king's warband. I was miserable when he left. I liked to think he was sad to leave me too but, if I was honest, I knew that I missed him more than he missed me.

A year ago I'd visited Eochaid with an invitation for him, my aunt Guthild and his daughter to spend the Christmas season with us. Eochaid had been sixty nine at the time and his wife sixty four. Both felt that they were getting too old to travel, especially in winter, but fifteen year old Hilda had been visibly disappointed.

She and I were immediately attracted to one another. Of course, it wasn't the first time I'd met her but the last time had been when she was a gawky child of eleven. The fact that I was ten years older than her didn't seem to matter and in the few days I spent at Alnwic I'd fallen in love with her and she with me.

Six months later we had been betrothed and would have married that autumn had not Guthild suddenly died in her sleep two weeks beforehand. After the funeral my father and Eochaid agreed to postpone the wedding until the following spring. We had waited impatiently through the winter and now it seemed that the wretched Otta would make another delay necessary.

However, that wasn't what worried me. Eochaid was now unable to ride and could only walk slowly with the aid of a stick. Hilda, assisted by the captain of his gesith, managed the shire for him and it had been agreed that I would take over that responsibility once I married her. However, if Otta attacked Alnwic the sensible thing would be for everyone to flee into the hills; defending it against an army of hundreds with twenty five warriors wasn't an option. Eochaid could only travel in a cart and that wouldn't be able to outrun mounted mercenaries. I knew Hilda wouldn't desert him and I had visions of her as a captive, or worse.

Then, instead of the ealdormen and their warriors, a messenger arrived with disastrous news. Óengus, the King of the Picts, was ill and his half-brother, Talorcan, had taken the opportunity to seize power and invade Lothian. I doubted whether it was just coincidence that it corresponded with Otta's sudden appearance on the scene. Whether that was so or just bad timing, it meant that no help would be coming from Lothian, nor from King Eadbehrt as he was rushing to confront the Picts.

~~~

A few days later the messenger we sent to the king returned with authority to call out the fyrd to deal with Otta. During that time we had sent out scouts to track the Picts. Having sacked Alnwic, Talorcan was heading south towards Durham. Whilst we mustered our fyrd and sent messengers to Otterburn and Hexham for them to do the same, I was permitted to take ten men and find out what had happened to Eochaid and Hilda. It wasn't much of an escort if I ran into trouble but it was all my father could spare from Bebbanburg's small garrison. Not for the first time he told me that Eadberht's paranoia about internal unrest put us all in danger.

Seward had loaded provisions for three days and a small leather tent for me to sleep in onto a packhorse, but I told him to leave the tent behind. If my men had to sleep wrapped in their cloaks, then so would I.

We rode out of Bebbanburg's main gates on a sunny morning in early May traversing the fields of the vill being weeded by bondsmen, villeins and their families. Some straightened up to wave a greeting or to watch us curiously but most carried on working industriously, knowing that all free men would soon have to report to the fortress with their weapons leaving only the slaves, the women and the children to look after the crops and the animals.

The road south went along the coast as far as Beadnell Bay and then headed inland but I knew that Otta would have left a guard there with his ships, and so we headed south west over the hills for a few miles before turning onto the road that ran from Berwic to Alnwic. Unsurprisingly we met no-one, other than a charcoal

47

burner with a wagon full of logs. No one in their right minds would journey into an area now controlled by foreign mercenaries, but charcoal burners were a strange breed.

We approached Alnwic cautiously but it was deserted. The place had been looted, but Otta had refrained from burning it. It was a sensible decision; if he succeeded in becoming king he would want the land to return to normal as soon as possible.

The hall was a mess. Evidently Otta's men had searched everywhere for Eochaid's hoard of gold and silver but I knew their search had been fruitless. It was lodged with my father at Bebbanburg for safekeeping.

Then I saw wagon tracks leading away from the hall. They were barely discernible after Otta's horsemen had milled about, but I spotted them because I knew what I was looking for. They led, not into the hills as I had supposed, but south east towards the coast.

Half an hour later we arrived at the mouth of the River Aln. The fishermen and their families who normally lived there had fled but we did discover an abandoned wagon. I came to the reasonable conclusion that Eochaid and Hilda had left in one of the fishing boats. If so, why hadn't they made for Bebbanburg? It was Seward who solved that mystery.

'If you recall, lord, the wind up until the last few days was from the north. It would have been difficult to sail up the coast and, of course, Ealdorman Eochaid wouldn't know whether Bebbanburg had been captured or not. The logical thing to do was to sail south, before the wind, to Jarrow at the mouth of the River Tyne.'

I breathed a sigh of relief; Hilda and her father were probably safe – for now. My desire was to go to Jarrow and make sure, but my duty was to help my father gather an army to defeat Otta. I therefore set off once more – this time into the Cheviots to find the men of Alnwic and call out the fyrd.

I was reasonably certain that Otta's men were long gone so I sent most of my men to the other vills in the shire of Alnwic to tell their freemen to muster at Bebbanburg.

I found the reeve and the inhabitants of Alnwic at the old hill fort near the source of the River Aln.

'Should we return, lord? Is it safe?' he asked after I'd told him what I knew.

'Our scouts say that they are headed for Durham. If he can take the fortress there he will be in a strong position, especially with Eadbehrt away in the north dealing with the Picts. Durham's a long way from here so it would be alright for you to return home except for the fact that Otta's fleet is at Beadnell Bay.'

'He can't have left too many men to guard it, can he? He'll need as many as possible with him.'

The reeve had a good point. If he had, say, five hundred men with him he would have needed perhaps twenty knarrs to transport them, their horses and baggage train. He'd have been a fool to take to sea without a few warships to protect him so he had probably brought a fleet of some twenty five ships. That probably meant well over a hundred sailors and ships' boys to crew them and perhaps another twenty warriors to protect the beached ships. Sailors and boys could fight but it wasn't something they were trained to do and they wouldn't be much opposition for my ten warriors, or even the fyrd, if it weren't for their numbers.

Alnwic was a sizeable settlement and was home to thirty five freemen, including their sons over sixteen. There were another ten boys who could use a sling or a hunting bow and so I wondered whether we would be enough to defeat the enemy at Beadnell Bay. If I could do so and burn Otta's fleet he would be trapped here if things went badly for him. I must admit that doing something as significant, if not downright heroic, as destroying his ships appealed to my ego and that decided me.

49

~~~

It turned out that my father had been ill with worry about me. The depth of his anger when he next saw me was dictated by the extent of his concern, of course, but I didn't realise that at the time. He had never berated me before like he did then and I reacted in kind.

'Did you not think that I might be concerned about you when you sent no word of where you were or about what had happened at Alnwic? You are a stupid, thoughtless brat. It wasn't until the fyrd of Alnwicshire started to drift in that I knew that at least you were still alive, but only because you sent messengers out to them.'

'I only had ten men,' I yelled back at him, something I'd never dared do before, but calling me, a grown man of twenty six, a stupid brat was not to be borne. 'What was more important, calling out the fyrd or reporting back to you? There was nothing you could have done to help me so I did what I thought was right. You should have trusted me.'

He glowered at me, the rage still burning inside him, not helped by my own anger.

'And then to try and defeat over twice the number of men you had with you in order to burn Otta's fleet - that was foolhardy in the extreme. You're nothing more than an immature seeker after glory. Did you not think that you might have led those men - and young boys too from what I've been told - to their deaths?'

He had a point. It was a little reckless but I felt that I had had a good plan and the prize was worth the risk and, when I thought about that night, I knew I'd been right.

My heart was pounding as Seward and I slithered forward on our bellies through the dunes until we could see the line of ships drawn up just above the high watermark. My estimate wasn't far out. There were nineteen knarrs of various sizes and four birlinns.

50

It was an hour before nightfall and the seamen and the warriors were gathered around a number of campfires on the beach eating and drinking.

Gradually the noise died away after dark until all that we could hear was the distant sound of snoring. They hadn't even bothered to set sentries and so there was little risk of being discovered until we'd executed the first part of the plan. We slid back down to where the rest of my men were waiting. I nodded to Seward and he led the ten boys off through the dunes to the north. The rest of us settled down to wait.

Slowly a glow began to appear towards the northern end of the beach. My expectation was that, having set two ships on fire, the sailors – or some of them - would rush to put them out. That would divide our foes into two parties and, hopefully, we would be able to overcome one half before the others entered the fray.

So much for careful planning. The snoring continued undiminished as the ships crackled and burnt three hundred yards away. As I crouched there, unsure what to do, one of the men on the beach got up and walked towards the sea in order to take a piss. Suddenly he became aware of the fire and yelled in alarm. Even that only wakened a few at first, but they started to run towards the fire and more and more woke up and ran towards the blazing ships.

As I had expected, the warriors didn't join them but armed themselves and looked around in case the other ships were attacked. As the craft were spread out over a distance of three hundred yards they couldn't make up their minds where to station themselves. In the end they moved off to stand in the middle of the beach. By now the sparks from one of the fires had set the furled mainsail of a third knarr alight. One of the sailors had the presence of mind to grab buckets from the unaffected ships and started to scoop up seawater to try and dowse the flames. Others followed suit.

It looked as if they'd be busy for some time so I quietly passed the order along for the boys and archers to launch their attack. Fortunately it was a moonlit night and the silver band of light that reflected off the dappled water lit up the waiting mercenaries in silhouette. The first volley caught them unawares, their shields hanging by their sides and five went down, wounded or dead.

That left a dozen. There had been slightly fewer of them than I had expected. The next volley of stones and arrows mostly struck their shields and only one lucky shot hit home, striking a man in the eye. I couldn't afford to wait any longer and gave the order to charge. We were eleven trained warriors, backed up by three times that number of the fyrd, against eleven hard-bitten killers.

However, they were still rattled and they couldn't tell warrior from weapon carrying farmer as we ran at them, illuminated by the moon in the sky behind them. No doubt it seemed to them as if we were a vastly superior force. We crashed into them, shield to shield, and forced them back by sheer weight of numbers. They fought for grip in the sand, and failed. First one and then more were pushed back and their shield wall broke. Then it was a free for all as we struggled to kill them all before the sailors saw what was happening.

I banged the boss of my shield into the fixed visor covering the top half of my adversary's face and he swore at me as he struggled to free his sword to stab me. I had opted for a seax, which was more manageable in close quarter fighting, and thrust it into his mouth, twisting it upwards so that the point entered his brain. He dropped away and I looked around for a new opponent, but it was all over. The boys and the fyrd were killing the few remaining wounded whilst we rested on our shields breathing heavily.

The sailors hadn't noticed the fight behind them and were still busy putting out the last of the flames. They needn't have bothered; the three knarrs at the end wouldn't be going out to sea again in a hurry. Those of us in chainmail trudged up the beach in line whilst the others ran ahead of us in a direction that would take them to the west of the sailors.

We were a mere fifty paces away when we were spotted, but at first they must have thought we were their warriors come to help. We soon disabused them of that notion when we started to cut them down. Then they yelled in alarm and desperately sought a weapon with which to defend themselves. Most had knives in their belts and some managed to pick up boathooks, pikes and oars from the other ships.

They had the advantage of greatly superior numbers and, despite their poor weapons and my helmet and chainmail byrnie, I found myself hard pressed until my other men hit them in the flank. The fyrd might not have armour or, for the most part, helmets, but they had spears, swords and shields. Hemmed in on two sides the sailors were being killed and wounded as if they were animals in a slaughter house.

Suddenly they broke and fled to the north. We managed to capture a few but perhaps fifty escaped.

'Let them go,' I shouted. 'We can round them up later.'

We'd captured seven sailors and four ship's boys. The rest were dead or badly wounded. My men went amongst the latter systematically slitting the throats of those who would die anyway. We set fire to most of the other ships but we kept three of the knarrs. We loaded the enemy wounded onto them and, with the unharmed prisoners as crew and the men of the fyrd to guard them, they set off the next morning to sail to Bebbanburg.

We had suffered some casualties, six dead and seven wounded – only one of the dead being a member of my father's warband, thankfully, and they went with the others on the knarrs. The enemy dead were left as a feast for the buzzards.

The wind was light and so we managed to keep pace on land with the small flotilla of knarrs out to sea and entered Bebbanburg first. I was full of pride at my achievement so my father's chastisement came as even more of a shock.

I glared at him when he'd finished his tirade. I was so full of righteous anger that it took all my will power not to hit him. He hadn't even congratulated me on destroying Otta's fleet and killing or taking prisoner their crews. I tried to control myself but failed, so I stormed off and re-mounted my horse. A few seconds later I rode out of
Bebbanburg blind to everything but the need to get away from my father. I had ridden for a good five miles before I calmed down a little and realised that I didn't know where I was going. Then I heard a rider behind me. It was Seward with the pack pony.

'Where are we going, lord?'

'To join my brother and King Eadbehrt,' I said without having really thought about it.

~~~

We spent that night at the hall of Æthelwold Moll in Berwic. He wasn't there of course; he'd taken his warband and the fyrd of Berwicshire to join the king. The reeve said that the muster point was Dùn Èideann on the south bank of the Firth of Forth so we headed there the next morning.

The weather had changed overnight and, although it wasn't raining yet, the sky was so dark it was almost black and a strong wind swept along the firth from the east. At least it was at our backs so when the rain did come it hit the shield on my back. Seward wasn't so lucky and his cloak was soon saturated.

In the early afternoon the rain stopped and the odd patch of blue sky appeared. Two hours later we were riding in sunshine. It took us over twelve hours to travel the sixty miles across country to Dùn Èideann. As darkness descended we saw the fortress on its rock outlined in black against an orange, purple and grey sky as the sun sank in the west.

There was no sign of an encampment so I rode on up to the gates of the stronghold. Unsurprisingly I was refused admittance until the morning and so Seward and I went to find somewhere to stay in the settlement at the base of the rock. It wasn't a big place and the only tavern was filthy. There were more rats in the taproom than there were drinkers. It was a fine night and so we eventually camped by the side of the firth a little way from the settlement.

The next day the reeve told me that the king had moved south-west into the Moorfoot Hills to confront the Picts. As that had been four days ago I reasoned that any battle would have taken place by now and, as if to confirm my logic, a messenger sent by the local ealdorman arrived to say that the king had fought a great battle and the Picts were in full retreat.

My concern now was for my brother and so we set off once more, this time accompanied by the messenger as he could guide us to the king's camp. We arrived there early in the afternoon and as I approached the large tent with Eadbehrt's banner flying outside it I saw Renweard being attended to by a monk. He'd taken a cut to his right biceps but it had been cleaned and stitched. The monk was merely checking it and changing the dressing. Otherwise he seemed fine.

We embraced as the monk protested at the interruption to his work and I waited for him to finish before asking my brother what had happened.

'Talorcan is a firebrand and launched an attack as soon as he saw us moving into position. As usual they came at us in no sort of formation and we managed to form a shield wall of sorts which held them off until the rest of the army could move into place. The archers started to fire at high trajectory into their packed ranks and then Eadbehrt led all the horsemen in a charge into the enemy's flank.

'I managed to kill three of them before the point of a spear raked my arm and I dropped my sword. Much to my frustration, there was little more of use that I could do at that point and so I came back to the baggage train to have it treated. I'd borrowed a spear and was about to ride back into the fray when I heard a great cheer go up and saw the Picts running as fast as their legs could carry them. I rode after them and speared a couple before someone blew three blasts on a horn to call off the pursuit.

'We harried them the next day all the way to the bridge over the River Forth and then came back here to our camp. Many escaped into the hills but they must have lost quite a few hundred, so I don't think they'll try that again soon. The word is that King Óengus is recovering and he's furious with his brother.'

Later that day I was called into the king's presence to tell him what I knew about Otta's invasion. He seemed delighted about the destruction of his fleet and clapped me on the back before presenting me with a silver arm ring. Such an honour was usually reserved for members of his warband who had rendered him a particular service, so I felt particularly pleased. It was in marked contrast to my father's reaction.

I wondered whether Renweard might be displeased as the king had yet to reward him, but he just seemed delighted for me. Two days later the army struck camp and started to move south towards Durham.

~~~

We never got that far. By the time we had travelled down Redesdale to Otterburn they had heard that Otta had been defeated by my father and the other ealdormen of Bernicia. He'd been trapped between the fortifications around the top of the hill that he'd been besieging and the advancing Northumbrian army. His

56

mercenaries had soon fled and were being hunted down, but Otta had escaped.

We later found out that he had returned to his ships and, finding them destroyed, had continued up the coast, avoiding Bebbanburg, to take sanctuary in the monastery church on Lindisfarne. Eadbehrt immediately left those on foot with instructions that they should continue until they linked up with my father and his army and then help track down the mercenaries. He himself set off along Coquetdale with all the horsemen, including me, to capture Otta.

From Alnwic we headed north and two days later we passed Bebbanburg on the road to Lindisfarne. As luck would have it, the tide was in when we got there and so Eadbehrt paced up and down the shore waiting for it to go out again.

'What do you think he'll do when we reach the monastery,' Renweard asked me as we sat in the shade of a tree, eating some hard cheese and stale bread, which was all that Seward had found for us to eat. He did well to do that; most of the rest hadn't eaten for a day or more.

'Ask Bishop Cynewulf to give Otta up, I imagine,' I replied with a shrug. 'You know the king better than I do.'

'Given the mood he's in now, I wouldn't put anything past him. Hopefully, Cynewulf will see sense and do as Eadbehrt asks.'

As soon as the sea had gone out far enough we remounted and splashed through the shallow water to the island. By the time we reached the other side the tide was well out and we covered the last mile on wet sand. It was soft going and, such was the pace set by the king, our mounts were blown by the time we rode up a slight slope and onto dry land.

Having more of a care for our horses than some, my brother and I were amongst the last to arrive at the gap in the thorn fence around the monastery that was designed to keep animals out. It wasn't intended as a defensive perimeter but to delineate the monastery boundary. However, it would be difficult to get through.

The entrance was a gap in the fence but this was blocked by the bishop and his monks who stood there impassively, the bishop holding his crook as if it was a weapon and the prior a crucifix on top of a pole like a banner.

'Stand aside, Cynewulf, or surrender Otta to me,' Eadbehrt demanded without preamble.

'Good afternoon, Cyning. It's been a long time since we've had the pleasure of a visit from you.'

'Don't fool with me; I haven't the time nor the patience. Now, bring him here to me or I'll come in and remove him by force.'

'You wouldn't dare! This is a sacred place, protected by Saint Aidan and Saint Cuthbert. If you commit sacrilege I'll excommunicate you, king or not.'

'Pah! What do I care for your threats, Cynewulf. Excommunicate me if you dare; you forget that one of my brothers is the Archbishop of Eoforwīc and your superior. He will lift it as soon as you impose it.'

'He answers to God, not to you, Eadberht.'

'You've been cloistered here, away from the real world, for too long, bishop. I appointed you and I hereby unappoint you. You are no longer the Bishop and Abbot of Lindisfarne. Oswulf and Oswin,' he said, turning to his two sons, 'arrest Cynewulf and take him to Bebbanburg with Seofon. He is to remain there in chains until I decide what to do with him.'

I reacted with a start when I heard my name. I couldn't believe what was happening. I watched as if in a daze as Eadbehrt's two sons dismounted and went to lay hands on Cynewulf. Not since King Ecgfrith had arrested Bishop Wilfrid seventy years ago had a senior churchman been held captive, and he hadn't been a bishop in Northumbria at the time.

One of the monks stepped forward and stood in the way, his arms folded across his chest.

'You can't do this, Eadbehrt. I don't care who your brother is; you know who I am and I forbid it.'

The king stared at the elderly monk for a moment and then a grim smile played across his lips briefly.

'Ceolwulf,' he said as he recognised his predecessor. 'You're not king any longer, I am. You are a lowly monk and you are defying me. Step aside or accompany Cynewulf to the filthiest hovel I can find to imprison you in.'

Oswin pushed Ceolwulf to one side and he and Oswulf grabbed the former bishop's arms. The two æthelings pulled him to where their horses stood and Oswin mounted before Oswulf helped the bishop, none to gently, to mount in front of his brother. They set off back towards the route across the sands and, with a despairing look at my brother, Seward and I followed them.

He told me later what had happened next. The king left most of his warband to keep a watch on the monks and the curious crowd of other inhabitants of Lindisfarne Island who had gathered whilst he rode through the monastery grounds to the little stone church where Saint Aidan and Saint Cuthbert were buried.

He sent two of his warriors inside it and two minutes later they dragged the Ætheling Otta from the dark interior. He was filthy and looked half starved.

'Kneel before me, wretch.'

Otta gave Eadbehrt a look full of hate and spat at him. The two men holding him twisted his arms so that he was forced to his knees. The king dismounted and took a battle axe from one of his warriors. He nodded at the two men holding Otta and they twisted his arms more and lifted them so that his neck and head were exposed.

'It was barbaric,' Renweard told me in a whisper, 'the man was the last surviving son of King Aldfrith for God's sake. The last of the House of Æthelfrith.'

I knew that many thought that Æthelwold Moll of Berwic was Otta's nephew, born to a nun raped by Otta's brother, Osred, when he was thirteen, but it was only a rumour.

'He beheaded him?' I asked quietly.

Renweard nodded. 'They threw his body and then the head into the sea.'

After a while he gestured to a slave to refill his goblet with mead. He drank it in two swallows, then sat morosely looking at the floor. He was in no mood to talk further and so I left him and went to see how Cynewulf was. Eadberht's sons had thrown him into a mean hovel which had been disused for a while. They forced the blacksmith to fit chains to his ankles and wrists and left instructions that he was to be fed only bread and water once a day.

I ignored them and, as soon as they had left, I asked Cynewulf for his oath that he wouldn't try and escape. He looked affronted then nodded, so I had the chains removed and took him from the hut with its leaking roof and rat infested floor to the guest chamber in my father's hall.

Two days later my father returned. At first he ignored me and asked Renweard to tell him what had happened on Lindisfarne, but my brother shook his head.

'No, father. I should have left to re-join the king before this. I must make haste now that I have seen you safe and well. Seofon knows as much as I do; he can tell you.'

My father glared at his younger son's retreating back before transferring his cold eyes to me. 'Well?'

'Can't we put this stupid animosity between us to one side, father? I, for one, regret that we fell out over something so trivial when either of us could have been killed these past few weeks.'

His shoulders slumped and he paced up and down for a minute or two before looking at me again.

'Very well. Apologise for not keeping me informed, as you should have done, not just because I'm your father, but also your ealdorman, and we'll forget it.'

'You are a stiff-backed idiot, father. You can ask Cynewulf to tell you about the atrocity that occurred on Lindisfarne. '

'Cynewulf? Where are you going? I haven't finished.'

'Well I have. I'm going with Renweard; you'll find Cynewulf in the guest chamber. By the way, he is meant to be kept a prisoner in chains until Eadbehrt decides what to do with him. I leave it to you to decide whether to do that or leave him where he is.'

Half an hour later I rode out of Bebbanburg accompanied by my brother, his body servant and Seward. I didn't look back but somehow I knew that my father was up in the lookout tower watching his two sons ride away.

Chapter Three – Strathclyde

750 to 756 AD

We took the road to Alnwic because I needed to find out where I stood with Eochaid. As far as I was concerned I was still going to marry Hilda, but my falling-out with my father might have made him change his mind. I prayed fervently that was not the case, but that particular worry was driven from my mind when I reached there. The reeve, who came out to greet us, said that Eochaid was gravely ill and not likely to last more than a day or so.

The servants had returned the hall to what it should be – more or less. The furs from the ealdorman's bed had been looted and Eochaid lay on a linen sheet laid over straw, covered in a horse blanket and a cloak. He smiled when he saw me but it was a weak one. Hilda got up from his bedside and came and took my hand. She gave me a chaste kiss on the side of my bearded face. In return, I put my hand on her shoulder and gave it a gentle squeeze.

'How is he?' I asked her.

'Still able to hear and speak,' Eochaid replied hoarsely.

'Don't tire yourself, father, you need to save your energy for getting better.'

'We both know that's not going to happen, daughter. I'm older now than anyone I know. I just want to last long enough to see you two man and wife.'

He stopped and for a moment his eyes closed. I realised what an effort speaking must be but he insisted on finishing.

'Fetch the priest; there's no time like now. I'm only sorry...' he paused for breath before continuing, 'that your father isn't here.'

I sensed Renweard giving me a startled glance but I ignored it.

'So am I, but it can't be helped.'

A few minutes later the priest bustled in and less than half an hour later we were man and wife. Eochaid sighed contentedly when the brief ceremony was over and went to sleep. He never woke up and died in the night with both of us keeping vigil beside him.

I sent word to my father and he came down for the funeral three days later but the brief conversation we had was stilted and uncomfortable. At least he congratulated me on my marriage and he was warm towards Hilda. At one point I thought he was about to try and mend fences between us, but he bit his lip and remained silent.

A week later we arrived at Eoforwīc only to find that the king was at Loidis. When we eventually caught up with him my brother re-joined his warband and I was left kicking my heels waiting for an audience. There was no room for a married couple in the king's hall and so Hilda and I had to stay in a tavern whilst I waited to be summoned.

I had expected to have to wait some time as there was much for the king to do after recent events but, to my surprise and delight, I was summoned to a private meeting the next day.

'I was sorry to hear about Ealdorman Eochaid; he was a good man who has served Northumbria well. Now I need to decide what to do about Alnwic. There are two options which I have discussed with the archbishop. He suggested combining the shires of Alnwic and Bebbanburg into one to improve our ability to defend that stretch of the coast, particularly in view of the number of invading fleets which have landed there over the years. However, I'm not so sure. It would place a lot of power in the hands of one ealdorman. What do you think?'

'It would be a large area, Cyning, covering much of the original kingdom of Bernicia. However, it is sparsely populated in comparison with the shires of what used to be Deira and Elmet. You would need a man who you could trust as its lord and my father is completely loyal.'

63

'Perhaps, but his brother usurped the throne and we've only just put down an uprising by your cousin. Some regard Ulfric as an ætheling, though his descent from Ida, and yours, is via a woman which makes it invalid.'

'I know that he has never thought of himself as a contender for the throne, Cyning; no more do I.'

'Hmmm. Well, I've decided to take a risk. I'm making you ealdorman of Alnwic on one condition.'

'Thank you, Cyning,' I said, delighted that Hilda and I could return and make the place where she grew up our new home.

'You haven't asked what the condition is.'

'No, but I'm sure it won't be a problem.'

'First you will go to Bebbanburg and make your peace with your father and get him to agree that you will co-operate closely to defend the coast. In due course you will no doubt succeed him and then I'll combine the shires into one.'

My father was quite a few years younger than Eadbehrt and I had serious doubts that this man would still be on the throne when that day came, but I wasn't about to point that out. No-one likes to be reminded of their own mortality, least of all a king.

~~~

I was full of apprehension as Hilda, Seward and I rode through the gates of Bebbanburg and up the murder trap to the open space where the Ealdorman's hall stood. The entrance was so called because a second gate could be lowered if attackers breached the first one. The space between the two was enclosed between two palisades. Once trapped in this area the attackers could be subjected to attack by rocks, arrows and spears. The story went that in one such attack over sixty years ago hundreds had been killed.

My father's hall was the only stone building in the fortress. There had been plans to build the warriors' hall in stone but it was prohibitively expensive compared to timber. The problem with the latter was that wood in contact with the ground eventually rotted. My father's solution was to build stone foundations with a timber structure on top. So far only the warriors' hall and the small church had been rebuilt in this manner.

Two steps led up to the door into the hall and my father stood on the top step with his arms folded as we dismounted. Hilda went to him first and embraced him. The frown on his face softened and he held her at arm's length looking into her eyes.

'Welcome to Bebbanburg,' he said with a smile.

'Father,' I said in the way of a greeting as my wife stepped aside and I stopped at the bottom of the steps, looking up at him. 'You've no idea how much I regret falling-out with you. I have never ceased to love you and I wish to put the past behind us.'

'Are you saying that just because Eadbehrt insists you make amends in order to become an ealdorman, or because you actually mean it?'

'I admit that the king forced me into this, but I am glad of the opportunity to become reconciled. I never wanted to become estranged from you but, at the time, I was angry that you berated me for not keeping you informed when I'd expected you to congratulate me. I was disappointed and hurt.'

I saw my father was bristling at what I'd said and Hilda was glaring at me so I hastily carried on.

'However, I'm sorry for causing you to worry about me needlessly. It was thoughtless of me.'

I watched with relief as the tense expression on my father's face softened. He nodded at me and smiled.

'I too was in the wrong. I should have praised you for how you handled the situation before telling you off. To be honest, it should never have come between us but you are so proud and obstinate that you won't admit it when you're wrong.'

I stiffened and was about to issue a stinging retort when his next words robbed me of my anger.

'The trouble is that we are too much alike. I can also be pig-headed.'

He held out his arms and I walked up the steps into them. We pounded each other on the back, both much relieved that we were friends again. That evening he and I got uproariously drunk in celebration whilst Hilda went off to sleep alone in disgust at us. I woke up lying on the timber floor under the bench I'd been sitting on with my face resting in a pile of vomit.

My head pounded as I lifted it up to look around. My father was still fast asleep in his chair with his head thrown back, snoring fit to wake the dead. I groaned as I got to my feet, with some difficulty, and made my unsteady way to the door. Once outside I felt a little better and I set out for the sea gate. At high tide the waves lapped at the base of the rock on which the citadel was built but the tide was now on its way out. I stripped off my stinking tunic and the rest of my clothes before walking into the sea.

Unlike most of our contemporaries, who had a healthy fear of the sea, Renweard and I had learned to swim at an early age and I now enjoyed making my way through the waves until I was a quarter of a mile or so offshore. I floated on my back and gazed at Bebbanburg. I was delighted to be the new Ealdorman of Alnwic but the place couldn't compare with my boyhood home.

Then I noticed two figures standing watching me on the beach: my wife and Seward. I sighed and swam back into shore. Seward silently handed me a cloth with which to dry myself and clean clothes to put on before picking up my soiled garments and trudging back to the sea gate. Hilda just glared at me.

'You left me to sleep alone last night,' she accused me.

'Believe me, wife, you wouldn't have wanted me in bed with you the state I was in.' 'Perhaps, but I felt neglected.'

I loved Hilda and our lovemaking ever since we wed had been tremendous; however, I hoped she wouldn't become clingy and demanding. I couldn't put up with that. Her next words reassured me and delighted me.

'I had something to tell you and I've been waiting to be alone with you ever since I found out. I think I might be pregnant.'

The last time we'd slept together had been in Eoforwīc. Since then we'd been travelling and staying at monasteries or taverns where men and women shared different rooms.

'That's tremendous news. When did you find out?'

'You wouldn't understand these things but my monthly cycle was late before we left Eoforwīc so I thought I might be, but I'm now really late and this morning I was sick – and not because I was drunk.'

This was said with a twinkle in her eye and I picked her up, gave her a hearty squeeze and kissed her – then put her down in horror.

'I'm sorry,' I stuttered. 'I didn't think.'

She laughed. 'It's alright. I won't break, and the baby is too tiny to be hurt at this stage, or so I've been told.'

If anything, I think my father was even more pleased than I was. I was going to get a wagon converted into a carriage for Hilda to travel in to Alnwic, but she told me it wasn't necessary. She was perfectly capable of riding, and would be for some months yet. I was beginning to learn that my wife was a strong character and had an independent mind.

She demonstrated just how resilient she was seven months later when our baby daughter was stillborn. I think I was more upset than she was. She shrugged it off, saying it was one of those things, but I knew that she was grieving inside. Her way of dealing with it was to insist that I got her pregnant again as soon as possible. Much to my surprise I succeeded and in December 762 my first son was born. As I had been named Seofon it seemed logical to call him Octa.

I hadn't been idle in the time we'd been back at Alnwic. I had built a new hall for my family and turned the old hall into one for my warriors. Eadbehrt had allowed me to recruit fifty men so that we could patrol the coast properly and so I needed more accommodation for them. I had replaced the old palisade with a new one around both halls which was eighteen feet tall. It wasn't a stronghold like Bebbanburg but it now had a much better chance of resisting attack, and it had room for the local population in time of need.

I'd also paid for two new knarrs to be built to increase my profits from trade. After all, I had to pay for the extra warriors and the building work somehow. Two years later my second son, Uuffa, was born. I felt that life was good and all I wished for was to be left in peace to enjoy my family and life as an ealdorman.

It could never last, of course. Eadbehrt came to Bebbanburg in April 756 and so we travelled up to join my father in hosting him and his retinue. Moments after he arrived we discovered that it wasn't a social visit. He was intent on war.

~~~

In early June I was camped outside Dùn Èideann with my father and an army three thousand strong. He and I watched as King Óengus mac Fergus and two thousand Picts set up their encampment a mile away. Rotri, the new King of Strathclyde who was supposedly Óengus' vassal, had been flexing his muscles ever since he had succeeded Tuedebur a few years previously. He had become increasingly bold and had raided into Dalriada, the area around Stirling and the Northumbrian enclave north of the Solway Firth, It was high time he was put in his place.

Unfortunately, Dalriada was in no position to deal with external aggression; it was too involved with an internal struggle for the throne. Óengus and Eadbehrt had therefore reached an agreement for a joint attack and, if necessary, to replace Rotri with someone who was less of a firebrand.

I had been less than happy to leave my wife and sons, but at least I got to see Renweard again. It had been three years since we had seen each other. He had visited my father and then Alnwic on his way back after escorting the newly restored Bishop Cynewulf back to Lindisfarne. Even Eadbehrt had to give in and release him in the face of increasing pressure from the Pope, the Archbishop of Cantwareburg, and latterly even his brother, the Archbishop of Eoforwīc.

We got drunk together that first night and I offered him the position of shire-reeve after the war was over. Reeves had been in existence for a long time and it was a general term for a managerial official. Every vill had a reeve to help the thegn and there had been a reeve at Bebbanburg for centuries. He assisted the lord on the administrative side whilst the captain of the garrison looked after its defence.

Shire-reeves were now becoming more popular. As the population within each shire grew, so did the complexities of maintaining law and order, collecting taxes and organising the fyrd. Many ealdormen now appointed shire-reeves to assist them and effectively they became their deputies.

Renweard had never married and, now that he was thirty one, I thought it was time he settled down. I loved Hilda and we discussed much more together than most married couples did, but I missed my little brother. It would be good to see more of him. He promised he'd think about it and let me know and with that I had to be satisfied.

'King Óengus and I have agreed that the only satisfactory outcome to this war is to get rid of Rotri. That means either killing him or deposing and exiling him. The problem is that his stronghold of Dùn Breatainn is as impregnable as that of Bebbanburg.'

His eyes flickered in my direction as he said this.

'We are both anxious to avoid having to starve him out so any suggestions would be welcome.'

I hesitated but no-one else seemed to be about to say anything so I put forward my idea.

'Cyning, as I understand it the fortress is built of timber and the buildings probably have straw roofs. Is that correct?'

Eadbehrt looked at Óengus, who stood beside him, and the other king nodded.

'What's your point, Seofon?'

'If the weather is dry we could tie rags soaked in oil or fat to the tips of arrows and fire them into the fortress. Of course, the disadvantage is that the whole citadel could burn to the ground, but it could force them out.'

For a moment both kings looked at me as if I was mad. It was not a tactic that anyone there had heard of and I'm not even sure that I knew from where I'd got the idea. I made a mental note to ensure that I installed troughs of water inside the palisade at Alnwic so that we could douse the roofs if someone else tried it. Bebbanburg was relatively immune as it stood so high above the surrounding land that few fire arrows would travel far enough to lodge in the roofs of the buildings inside.

'It's worth a try,' Óengus said thoughtfully.

Two days later the mighty host of over five thousand men set off westwards through Lothian towards the Picts' settlement of Glaschu on the River Clyde. To avoid possible friction, the two armies travelled separately and Northumbrian forage parties obtained food for both armies whilst we were still in Lothian. When we crossed into the Land of the Picts their men took over.

It worked surprisingly well, though there were minor incidents, of course. A small group of my men raided a farm as we approached Glaschu, raped the women and the girls, and stole their livestock. I hung the ringleader from an oak tree beside the road for all to see and deprived the rest of their status as freemen. When we returned home they would be sold as bondsmen, and their families with them. There was no more rapine and pillaging amongst my men or my father's.

'You acted wisely, Seofon,' was all he said but I felt gratified.

~~~

The two hills on which Dùn Breatainn was built loomed over the wide River Clyde and the land around it but it wasn't that which held my attention as I sat beside the two kings, the other ealdormen and the mormaers of the Picts. It was the army massed on the lower slopes of the Kilpatrick Hills to the north of us. Rotri must have gathered every able-bodied man and boy over the age of thirteen to have fielded so many. At a rough guess, I calculated that there must be over three thousand of them.

They banged their shields with their spears and yelled insults at us as we formed up facing them. Eadbehrt had a quick conversation with Óengus and called out to my father.

'Ulfric, gather as many housemen as you can and take them around the side of the hill where the Britons are formed up. Get behind them and charge into the back of them as soon as we engage them from the front.'

'That hillside is full of rocks, Cyning. It's not ground that horsemen can operate on. Can I suggest that I take some archers with us and weaken them first, then we can charge down on them on foot?'

71

Eadbehrt went red in the face at being contradicted, but Óengus grabbed his arm and said something to him. Whatever it was, he evidently changed his mind and nodded.

'Very well, but be quick about it.'

My father called for me to follow him and we rounded up as many mounted men as we could. Most were the gesiths of nobles and they were unwilling to release them until my father tensely asked them to go and explain to the king why they had refused his order. They didn't like it but they sent them with us.

It took a little time to organise everyone and for them to collect an archer to sit in front of them. Most were boys and young men, selected because they were lighter. In all we had gathered two hundred and sixty horsemen and about the same number of archers. It wasn't many to attack over six times our number but we would have the element of surprise and, hopefully, the main body would have engaged the front ranks of the Britons by then.

We went back the way we had come. If our foes guessed what we were up to, they made no move to counter it. We cantered for a few miles and then turned north-west up a re-entrant which took us behind the hill the Britons were defending.

We rode up the reverse slope of the hill as far as we could and then dismounted, leaving our horses with ten of the youngest archers. They were busy tying reins together so that they could manage the horses as we clambered up and around the side of the hill.

When we rounded a corner we could see the nearest Britons about a hundred yards below us. We traversed the slope as quietly as we could but inevitably the odd stone was dislodged, not that it mattered; the enemy were concentrating on the army advancing towards them.

The Picts were running into the attack in their usual disorganised way but Óengus had sensibly sent them to attack the enemy's flanks. The Northumbrians were advancing with a shield wall of warriors leading supported by seven or eight rows of the fyrd. As they closed the archers in the rear started to fire over their countrymen's heads into the mass of Britons.

We hurriedly scrambled into position and our archers started to let loose arrow after arrow into the Britons' rear ranks. It was a little while before they realised their danger but, when they did, at least a third of them turned to face us and started to vent their fury at us as they climbed up towards us.

The archers kept whittling down their numbers but it was evident that the warriors amongst us would be outnumbered by at least two to one when they reached us. I glanced at what was happening below us and was pleased to see that the Britons were giving way all along their line as the shield wall continued its relentless advance and the Picts were busy fighting hand to hand battles on the flanks. As they had many more numbers, it wouldn't be long before the Britons broke.

However, that was unlikely to help much. My father ordered us to form a shield wall and we formed a line three ranks deep, then we waited for the Britons to reach us. The archers stayed in front for as long as they dared to, bringing down several more of the enemy, before running along in front of our shield wall to form up on our flanks. From there they continued to send arrow after arrow into the mass struggling up the slope towards us.

The Britons must have been exhausted by this stage but adrenalin kept them going. We kept our shields low as our feet were the most vulnerable part of our body. I saw a Briton who can't have been much more than twelve try to pull the bottom of my shield to one side so that he could stick his only weapon, a dagger, into my legs. I was loathe to kill a child but if I hesitated I would be incapacitated or killed and so I thrust down with my spear, striking the boy's spine and breaking it. If he wasn't dead he would be paralysed for life.

I stepped on his neck and wrenched my spear free but I was too slow. A giant of a man with an axe chopped at the haft and cut it in two. The thing was useless so I threw the half I still held at him and he ducked. That gave me time to thrust my shield forward, smashing the boss into his face. I heard the cartilage in his nose snap and blood poured down his ruined face – not that he was much of a looker before.

I drew my seax and slashed it at his face just as he came at me with a roar of rage and an upraised battle-axe. His blind rush at me was his undoing. My blade connected with his neck just as he was about to split my helmet and my skull in two. I sprained my wrist with the force of the blow as I half severed his head from his body. He sank to his knees on top of the paralysed boy and toppled sideways.

My father was fighting beside me and I was suddenly conscious that he was in difficulties. A boy had crawled under his shield as he fought a man with a sword and a targe and the lad had stabbed him in the patellar ligament of his right knee. I bent down and thrust my seax into the boy's neck, but I was too late. My father's leg collapsed and he fell against the man on the other side of him. For a moment his guard was lowered and his opponent slashed downwards.

It was a wild stroke which connected with the chain mail protecting my father's shoulder. The sword must have been blunt because it didn't break any of the iron links, but it slid off the byrnie and connected with my father's forearm. Even above the noise of battle I heard the bone snap and his yell of pain.

I had to get him out of there before he was killed and so I pulled him along the ground until we reached the rear of our men. Others filled the gap in the shield wall, but
I needed to get back to the fight. Desperately I looked around and called over four of the archers. They bound up the wound to his knee to staunch the bleeding and made a splint for his arm from two arrows and a bowstring.

'Take him back to the horses. He can probably sit astride one with help. Lead him back to the baggage train and find Seward, my body servant. He'll know what to do.'

Of course my father had his own servant but Seward was more skilled at dealing with wounds. I watched the four men carry him gingerly over the rough terrain for a minute and then, satisfied that he was in good hands, I hurried back to the fight.

The Britons were losing heart. The battle below us was all but over with more and more of the enemy fleeing for their lives and those facing us were now looking nervously over their shoulders, rather than pressing home their attack. A few at the rear turned and ran and that started the rout. By the time I regained my place in the front rank it was all over.

I was tempted to rush after my father but I was now the leader of this small army. Many were wounded and quite a few were dead. I went through them congratulating them and making sure that the wounded were tended to as best we could on the barren hillside. I sent someone back to bring some of the horses forward. If we took it slowly they could carry the bodies and those too badly hurt to walk back down the hillside.

It was only then that someone pointed out that I had a cut to my upper arm and another to my calf. I hadn't noticed them at the time but, now that the inevitable reaction to the battle had set in, they stung like hell. The cuts weren't deep and someone bound them with strips of cloth torn from a dead Briton's tunic before I made my way after the others. I glanced back at the heap of bodies and marvelled at how many we'd killed. At a rough guess I'd say that there were five hundred of them. All were dead. My men had cut the throats of the injured.

~~~

I gazed up at the fortress of Dùn Breatainn and thought that it going to be as difficult to capture as Bebbanburg would be. It sat on top of two tall outcrops of rock linked by a saddle near the summit of each. The lower hill to the east was protected on three sides by tall cliffs whilst the western hill, which stood some 250 feet or so above the River Clyde, was similarly protected to three sides, except the cliffs to the south-west were shorter with a steep slope running from their base down to the mouth of the River Leven where it joined the Clyde.

The only practical route to the top lay up a steep defile between the two hills. This was protected by a tall gate between two towers with a palisade running from it up the slope to the west until it abutted the cliff face. A much shorter length of palisade linked the eastern side of the gatehouse to the cliffs on that side.

The obvious thing to do would be to burn the gatehouse down but someone had obviously thought of that and it was now built of stone. The stone was uncut and badly laid and the mortar looked as it had been applied by a child but, however badly constructed it was, it wouldn't burn, but there was room in front of it to use a battering ram and there were plenty of trees nearby.

'It doesn't look as if your idea of burning them out is going to work,' Eadbehrt said to me when I reported back what I'd seen.

I tried to ignore the fact that he seemed almost pleased about it.

'No, Cyning, but we can attack the gate with a ram.'

'Even if we take the gatehouse, there is a second palisade around the top of the two hills.'

'Yes,' I explained patiently, 'but then we can get close enough to use fire arrows.' 'What do you think?' he asked Óengus.

He shrugged. 'It's the only sensible proposal I've heard so far.'

'Right, Seofon, get your ram built but be as quick as you can. The fyrd are already asking about getting back to their fields.'

I didn't have the knowledge to design and make a battering ram so I went to see my father. Our main camp was five hundred yards away and stretched between the Rivers Clyde and Leven. My father was recovering in his tent, his knee wound sewn up and his right forearm in a splint. He had been told to rest by the monk looking after him; an instruction he complained about constantly. His enforced inactivity hadn't put him in the best of moods.

'What do you want Seofon,' he greeted me with a surly frown.

'Come to make sure I'm doing as I'm told.'

'No, but I'm pleased to see that you are. The more you rest, the quicker you'll be back on your feet. No, I came to ask if you knew how to build a battering ram.'

His whole attitude changed immediately. Now he had something to occupy his mind he didn't seem to object to being immobile. He gave me a rough idea what was required and sent his body servant to find a man called Godric, a carpenter in the Bebbanburg fyrd.

Five days later the ram was ready. I have to say that I was impressed. A heavy tree trunk with the thick end chopped into a point and covered in iron plates, was suspended from a stout frame by chains. The frame was mounted on four axles with eight wheels made by a wheelwright who was serving with our fyrd. It was covered by a sloping roof to which the skins from cattle had been nailed.

It stank because the latter hadn't been treated and it weighed a lot; so much so that it took a hundred men to get it moving. However, once it was moving, it took half that number to keep it going, pushing at handles attached to the frame. Other men walked alongside it with shields raised to protect the ones doing all the work from arrows and stones launched by the defenders.

'Well done, Seofon,' Eadbehrt said, albeit a trifle grudgingly I thought, whilst Óengus clapped me on the back and added his congratulations.

I was a little uncomfortable at all this praise. I had merely told my men to follow the instructions of Godric and the wheelwright;

besides, it hadn't reached the gates yet, let alone battered them down. I had visions of an axle breaking under the weight and the whole thing coming to an embarrassing halt.

It didn't. It reached the gates and the men manning the bars sticking out of the massive tree trunk at right angles pulled it back and let go. It struck the gates with a crash and the wood trembled, but the gates held. No doubt the enemy had braced horizontal timbers against them to strengthen them. However, I thought I saw a little mortar drop down from the archway above the gates.

This was something I hadn't considered. I knew the stonework was poorly constructed; suppose the archway collapsed? It would fall on top of the ram and kill quite a few men. I voiced my concerns to the king, but he just laughed.

'If it does, then we'll just have to climb up the rubble and get in that way.'

'But what about the men manning the ram?'

'What about them? You can't fight a war without casualties.'

That was a statement of the obvious, of course, but it was his callous attitude that shocked me. I thought back to the execution of Otta outside the church on Lindisfarne.

Perhaps it helped you become a successful king if you didn't have a conscience.

Although the thump of the ram against the gates brought down more mortar dust and even the odd stone, the keystone and the rest of the bottom row of the arch held. The problem now was the rocks that the defenders were dropping onto the ram from above the arch. It was stoutly built but the roof couldn't stand that sort of battering for long.

Without waiting to consult either king, I sent a group of archers forward to keep the defenders' heads down. Each took a warrior with a shield to protect him from the enemy archers. The hail of rocks stopped. The roof of the ram had been damaged but not the frame. It continued to batter at the gates.

Suddenly there was a tremendous crack and the left hand gate split down the middle. Two more blows from the ram and it collapsed; the left side hanging drunkenly from just the bottom hinge and the right hand part falling backwards onto the ground.

I ran forward yelling for my men to haul the ram out of the way and for the archers to dissuade the defenders from congregating beyond the entrance to oppose us. I needn't have bothered. The Picts were the first through the shattered gate and found no opposition. The defenders were scrambling up the path towards the palisade on top of the two hills as fast as they could go.

The Picts chased after them but to no avail. The single gate at the higher level was slammed shut well before they got there. A hail of arrows, spears and stones shot by boys with slings greeted them and, leaving a few dead and wounded behind, they retreated out of range.

Breaching the bottom gate had taken most of the day and we settled down to wait for the dawn. When the sun rose we couldn't see it through the thick blanket of dark grey cloud. The past three weeks had been dry and, even if not sunny all the time, there had been no rain. All that changed overnight. The weather got worse as the rain swept in from the west.

In such conditions the archers kept their bowstrings dry in greased leather bags and, even if we could get fire arrows into the citadel, the thatch on the roof was now too wet to burn well.

To say that King Eadbehrt was displeased would be an understatement. He blamed me for not getting the ram ready earlier and dismissed me curtly. If I had expected him to congratulate me on capturing the gatehouse then I was in for a disappointment.

The one good piece of news was that many of those fleeing the battle had sought refuge in the fortress and so King Rotri would have a lot of mouths to feed. With any luck we could starve him out quite quickly.

The next day we discovered that Rotri had come to the same conclusion. The gate opened and a stream of women, children and wounded men filed down the hill and out of the shattered gates at the bottom. Now whatever rations he had in there would last twice as long.

Rotri must have known the fate that awaited those he'd ejected. They were rounded up and kept under guard until a stockade to keep them in could be built. They would be shipped off to the slave markets in the Land of the Picts and in Northumbria. There were some three hundred of them, probably five per cent of the total population of Strathclyde.

The rain didn't stop for three days. Sometimes it poured down and at others it was reduced to a fine drizzle. Then, on the fourth day the clouds parted and the sun came out.

'Well, what are you waiting for?' Eadbehrt asked me impatiently. 'The roofs need to dry out, Cyning. Wet straw won't burn.'

'I'm beginning to think that conditions will never be right for this scheme of yours. I'll give you one more day and then we'll try a direct assault.'

My heart sank. The palisade was fifteen feet high – too tall to lift people up and over and the steep ground on which the palisade stood meant that we couldn't use ladders – at least not in the quantity we'd need for any chance of success. My already low opinion of Eadbehrt as a war leader dropped further.

The sun continued to shine for most of that day and so I gathered the archers and briefed them the following morning. By midday the sun was at its zenith and clouds were approaching from the west. Furthermore Eadbehrt was getting impatient again.

We sent several volleys of fire arrows arcing up into the blue sky to fall beyond the palisade. From below we had no idea where they had landed and what damage, if any, they had done. I was beginning to think my idea hadn't worked when a column of black smoke began to curl upwards from inside the palisade on the east side. Soon it was followed by a few more and then we could see bright red and yellow flames leaping up into the sky.

No smoke appeared from the hill to the west and we later found out that, apart from a watchtower and a few huts, there was nothing there. All the flat ground was on the eastern hill. I could see a curtain of rain out to sea and I was fearful that it might put out the flames but, as the dark clouds approached, so the wind picked up, fanning the flames. I ordered the archers to send three more volleys into the east side and then we waited.

The wind from the west was now blowing quite strongly and the conflagration had spread so that all of the eastern summit seemed to be ablaze. As the rain started the gate opened and smoke blackened men stumbled out. We got ready to charge into them, but then I realised that the enemy were throwing down their weapons as they emerged. We had won.

~~~

Eadbehrt was delighted at the easy victory, for which he claimed credit, of course, but he did eventually remember to thank me for my help, albeit begrudgingly, which I suppose was something. The fire was dying down, dowsed by the heavy rain, but we the Picts were destroying what was left of the fortress as we prepared to depart at dawn the next day.

Óengus hung the unfortunate Rotri and announced that henceforth Strathclyde was no longer a subordinate kingdom; it would become part of Pictland. A man called Dumnaguel was appointed as its mormaer and Eadbehrt received three things as his share of the spoils: some land which abutted Lothian and had been part of Strathclyde, two chests of silver and a treaty of friendship between him and Óengus. In particular the latter included recognition that the Cumbrian enclave in Galloway was part of Northumbria.

However, the mood of celebration was somewhat spoiled when a messenger arrived from the king's brother. Æthelbald of Mercia had invaded and had burned much of Eoforwīc to the ground. Archbishop Eanbald had been forced to flee to Loidis, which was now under siege.

Chapter Four – The Battle of Newanberig

756 – 757 AD

I learned later that King Cuthred of Wessex had died and was succeeded by his distant kinsman, Sigeberht. His election as king wasn't universally popular and his position on the throne was precarious. Instability within Mercia's long standing rival for leadership of Southern England left Æthelbald free to attack Northumbria. The fact that Eadbehrt and his army was in the far north must have made the temptation irresistible.

I sent a few men to accompany my father and the other wounded men from Bebbanburg back home whilst I headed south with a hundred mounted men. My task was to find out the whereabouts and the strength of the Mercian army. Although I felt flattered to have been chosen, it was a mission fraught with danger and difficulty. Noone seemed to know where the Mercians had gone after Eoforwīc and, although a hundred men sounds a strong force, it isn't if you are seeking a foe numbering several thousand.

I decided to ride to Loidis first and talk to Archbishop Ecgbert. However, when we got near we encountered a stream of refugees heading north away from the place. From what I could glean from their often contradictory accounts, the Mercians were besieging the town and not only the archbishop, but also the king's daughter, Osgifu, and her husband Alchred, were inside.

Alchred was a man who was recognised by most as an ætheling. As Ida was reputed to have sired twelve sons, more and more nobles had emerged recently who claimed that they were descended from one or other of these sons. In Alchred's case he traced his descent from Eadric, the fourth of Ida's sons. Not everyone accepted his lineage as true, but evidently Eadbehrt thought him enough of a rival to buy his loyalty with the hand of his only daughter.

We set up camp near a settlement on the River Wharfe called Otley, some ten miles north-west of Loidis. From there I sent out patrols, not to find the main body of the Mercians - I knew by now that they were encamped to the north of the town – but to find a foraging party. I wanted prisoners who I could interrogate. I needed to find out the reason for the Mercians' invasion and their exact strength.

I struck lucky on the second day. Scouts came back to say that there was a party of thirty of the enemy at Guisley, which was barely two miles away. Thirty of my men were still out on patrol but I had enough to deal with this group. Whilst I led thirty men on the northern approach I sent the other forty across country at a canter to reach the track that led from Guisley to Loidis. I reasoned that the foragers would retreat as soon as they were attacked. It was a reasonable assumption but I prayed that my logic was sound.

I was correct, but only partly so. The Mercians had killed the men of the vill and rounded up the women and children to sell them into slavery. They were also encumbered by livestock and plunder. They were largely on foot whereas we were mounted. A few did flee but the majority elected to stay and fight for their ill-gotten gains.

Some of my men were trained to fight from horseback, but for most of them their steeds were no more than a means of transport. We therefore dismounted and formed a shield wall to face the enemy. I had, foolishly as it turned out, sent the few archers I had with the cut-off group. And so we were at something of a disadvantage as five of our enemy had bows with them.

It wasn't so much that they could seriously damage us, but advancing quickly with your shield held just below your helmet brim restricts your vision, slows you down and leaves your lower legs and feet vulnerable. An arrow pinged off my helmet and I felt another strike my shield just before we reached the enemy line. I pushed my shield at the man opposite me and, as expected, he pushed back.

I held my sword ready above my shield and now thrust it forwards, aiming at his eyes, but he ducked down and it struck his helmet. He responded by doing the same but then he surprised me by letting go of his shield so that he could use his left hand to pull my shield down. His sword snaked towards my neck and I only managed to deflect it at the last moment by batting it to one side with my own sword.

He was left exposed with no shield to protect him and he was slow to bring his sword back into action. In that fraction of a second I thrust the point of my sword into his mouth and out through his neck. He exhaled sharply and the sharp tang of urine and faeces struck my nostrils. A moment later his body collapsed to the ground.

I placed one foot on the corpse to move forward and confront my next opponent. He was a boy, no more than thirteen or fourteen, but he was dangerous. He had screamed when he saw my first opponent fall and his face was contorted with rage. I assumed, correctly as it turned out, that he was related to the dead warrior.

He forgot all about what he had been taught and tried to skewer me with his spear held in both hands, his shield hanging by his side. I brought my sword across and chopped the end off, then batted what remained away with my shield. The boy stood there open-mouthed, staring at the useless lump of wood in his hands as I stepped forward and brought my sword up to strike at his helmet. The stupid boy hadn't fastened the leather strap properly and it went flying. I brought the pommel of my sword down on his head, knocking him unconscious.

85

Another warrior swung an axe at me and I lifted my shield to intercept it. The axe stuck fast in the lime wood and I brought my sword over hand to shove the point into his face, but he was too quick for me. He ducked, let go of the axe and drew his seax from its sheath in one fluid movement. He mistimed his cut though and the seax scraped off my byrnie doing no more damage than breaking a couple of links.

Suddenly my adversary arched his back and fell down, a spear embedded in his back. My other forty men had arrived on the scene. It didn't take long after that to finish off the rest. Twice I called upon them to surrender but they refused. I cursed when it was all over because I needed a captive to question. Then I remembered the boy.

He wasn't the only survivor. There were two servants who'd been left to look after the horses – a man and a youth. The man had foolishly tried to fight off forty armed men and had died for his stupidity but the youth couldn't talk fast enough. He was a slave - a Northumbrian who had been captured during the sack of Eoforwīc so I trusted what he told us.

Unfortunately, he knew nothing of Æthelbald's plans, not even rumours, but he told us that the man I'd killed was a Mercian ealdorman. The warriors had been his gesith and the boy with him was his one and only son whose name was Higbald.

Higbald had recovered consciousness by then. He had a lump the size of a duck's egg on his forehead and had been violently sick. He was lucky. If my blow had been two inches to the right I would have hit his temple and he'd be dead. As it was he was feeling very sorry for himself.

'What were you doing here?' I began with a simple question.

The boy glared at me but said nothing so one of my men cuffed him hard about the head.

'Ow! My father got bored with the siege so he thought he'd amuse himself by plundering these hovels,' he said before spitting out some blood. Evidently he'd bitten his tongue when he'd fallen.

'How many men does Æthelbald have? How many warriors and how many in his fyrd?'

'No idea.'

He looked at the ground instead of continuing to glare at me so I knew he was lying.

'Oh dear, it looks as if we're going to have to do this the hard way. Let's get a fire going and find some lengths of wood to make a tripod.'

A look of panic crossed the boy's face as several of my men went to do as I'd ordered. 'What are you going to do?' he asked in a whisper.

'Hang you above a fire and burn your feet. If that doesn't work we'll lower you bit by bit and burn your legs and then your crotch.'

His face turned ashen and he vomited again, though there was only bile left in his stomach.

'You can't do that! I'm an ealdorman's son!'

'A dead ealdorman's son,' I reminded him. 'Either you're the ealdorman now or Æthelbald will appoint someone else and you'll be homeless.'

He thought about this for a moment or two, then his shoulders sagged.

'I'll tell you what you want to know,' he said listlessly, all his antagonism and defiance had vanished like last winter's snow.

I felt sorry for the lad but I had a job to do and so I forced myself to remain stern and threatening. I'd never have tortured him and I wasn't quite sure what I'd have done if he'd called my bluff about roasting him alive.

'What did your father tell you about your king's plans?'

'King Æthelbald isn't popular, to put it mildly. From what I've been told he's seduced too many nobles' daughters, and even the odd wife, for him to keep their loyalty. He wanted to invade Wessex again as it's in turmoil, but he only made peace with their previous king a year ago and my father said that the Witan was in no mood to allow him to break the treaty.'

He paused and sobbed for a while, no doubt upset at the thought that his father was now dead.

'He needed to unite his nobles somehow and so he decided that Northumbria was a ripe plum for the picking – or that's how my father put it. He and his fellow ealdormen thought, that with your king away in the far north, they could raid Eoforwīc and this place Loidis and then withdraw back into Mercia before Eadbehrt could do anything about it.'

'So he thought to unite his nobles by bribing them with Northumbrian gold, silver and slaves? Did he not think that there'd be a price to pay once Eadbehrt returned?'

'I've no idea. I can only tell you what my father said to me.'

'And you picked up nothing else that's useful in the camp? What morale is like, for example?'

Higbald shrugged. 'The men are happy now. They've all got plunder from Eoforwīc and a goodly number of women and girls they've captured to warm their beds at night. Some are getting fed up with the siege and are apprehensive about the arrival of the Northumbrian army the longer we stay there, but most don't seem too worried about it, but I don't know why. I agree; we're strong enough to beat Eadbehrt if he tries to come to Loidis' relief.'

Some of the boy's former cockiness had returned as he spoke.

'What's Æthelbald really after?' I asked.

It was a rhetorical question. I was puzzled by the Mercian king's motives. He'd given his men their reward and no doubt restored his standing amongst most of his nobles, at least for now. Why not just head for home and dare Eadbehrt to venture into Mercia? Instead he was risking being trapped between Loidis and the Northumbrian army.

The only thing I could think of was that he intended to lure Eadbehrt south into a trap. A major victory like that would make his position unassailable. If my reasoning was accurate Higbald must have heard rumours. Nothing stays secret for long in a camp.

'How close is Æthelbald to capturing Loidis?'

'Not very. He doesn't seem to be in much of a hurry. There's been no assault so far.'

'Are they building a battering ram?'

'No, I don't think so; at least, I've seen no sign of it, or of siege ladders even.'

The boy said it as if he was genuinely puzzled. Perhaps it hadn't occurred to him to wonder why before this.

'How many men do the Mercians have?'

I had asked him the question before but this time Higbald answered.

'There are a dozen ealdormen and their gesiths and warbands – perhaps eight hundred trained warriors in all. I'm not sure how many there are in the fyrd, perhaps a couple of thousand but some have deserted and gone home since we've been at Loidis; and then another thousand or so camp followers – servants, slaves, carters, women and so on.'

'Thank you Higbald, you've been very helpful.'

'What are you going to do with me?'

'Well, I could kill you, or I could return you to Æthelbald, but he'd execute you once he found out how helpful you've been.'

I paused as I watched the fear in Higbald's eyes. For all his bravado initially, the boy was a coward at heart.

'Or I could keep you as a slave.'

I watched as he bridled at the suggestion. He still had some pride then. To descend from noble to bondsman was unthinkable to someone of his breeding. 'Never,' he hissed. 'Kill me and have done with it!' Not a coward after all, just weak.

'Or you could become a
monk on Lindisfarne.' He
thought about that idea and
slowly nodded.

'Give me your oath that you won't try and escape and I'll take
you there when this is over.'

'Couldn't I return to Lichfield?   I was being educated there
before my father decided that accompanying him on this campaign
would be a more useful lesson than learning the scriptures.'

I shook my head. 'You could but you'd still be at Æthelbald's
mercy. Lindisfarne is safe.'

Little did I know then how close Higbald would come to a violent
end at the monastery, albeit nearly forty years later.

~~~

'Cyning, I'm certain that the siege of Loidis is a ploy. As soon as
you approach then Æthelbald will retreat into Mercia and hope that
you will pursue him. If you do he'll ambush you on ground he
knows and we don't.'

I nearly added 'like the Picts did to King Ecgfrith seventy years
ago' but thought better of it.

'So you advocate letting the Mercians burn my capital and then
return home unmolested, do you?' Eadbehrt sneered.

'No, Cyning. But I think it would be prudent to cut off their line
of retreat and force them to fight on land we know.'

'Thank you for the information you managed to glean from the
Mercian, Higbald, but
I'll decide what to do about it. You may go.'

I started to leave the tent but evidently the king had thought of
something else.

'One moment. Send the boy to me. I'd like to question him
myself.'

'Of course, if you wish it; but I'm certain he's told us everything he knows.'

'Perhaps, but my methods might not be as gentle as yours.'

'I've given him my word that I'll send him to Lindisfarne to become a novice. What do you intend to do to him?'

Eadbehrt grew red in the face.

'That's none of your business. Are you questioning my order?'

'If it's a matter of my honour, then yes. I am.'

'Sentry!'

A nervous looking member of the king's gesith poked his head inside the flap of the tent.

'Yes, Cyning.'

'Come in, don't stand there gawping. Arrest this man.'

The sentry looked shocked, as well he might do; after all, he was my brother. In his rage it appeared the king hadn't made the connection.

'Er, yes, Cyning. What shall I do with him?'

'Take him to your tent and set a guard on him.'

As Renweard came to take me out of the tent the king barked at him again.

'Disarm him first, you fool.'

'Oh, yes. Of course, Cyning.'

Once outside Renweard hissed at me 'What do we do?'

'Give me back my weapons and get a message to the other ealdormen about what's happened. I promise I won't abscond.'

An hour later a dozen ealdormen approached the king's tent and asked to see him.

'Why have you come to see me?'

I came with the others but kept out of sight at the back.

'We want to know why you have arrested one of our number. From what we hear he gave you good advice and you over-reacted.'

The speaker was Ealdorman Fenton of Luncæstershire. After my father he was the senior noble present.

'Don't you dare speak to me like that! I'm your king.'

'Elected by the Witan; in other words by us. We made you king Eadbehrt and you wouldn't be the first king to be forced to abdicate.'

Eadbehrt recoiled in shock at being spoken too so bluntly. He was furious but he wasn't so much of a fool that he didn't realise that he was now treading on dangerous ground.

'Very well. I will listen to what you have to say but Seofon defied me. I told him to produce the Mercian boy he captured so I could wring the truth out of him and he refused. That's treason.'

'But you were aware that Higbald was his prisoner and he'd promised the boy that he could become a monk on Lindisfarne in exchange for information?'

That wasn't exactly what had happened but I wasn't about to argue with that version.

'Well, yes. I suppose so.'

'So you were asking one of your nobles, and a highly successful military commander at that, to perjure himself?'

'No, that's wrong. He had sworn no binding oath to the boy, just made him a promise.'

'You may be in the habit of breaking promises, Cyning, but most of us don't,' another ealdorman interjected. 'One of Seofon's virtues is that he takes matters of honour very seriously.'

'This is getting blown out of all proportion. I had the wretched man arrested to give him time to think about his decision to defy me. I was confident that he'd turn the Mercian brat over to me for questioning if he thought about it for long enough.'

'If that's true why did you send your men to forcefully take Higbald from my custody as soon as you had me arrested?' I broke in.

'You! I ordered your arrest.'

'Yes, by my own brother. You've been discovered to be a liar and a man without honour, Eadbehrt. I for one renounce my oath of allegiance to you as king.'

Several others joined me in denouncing the king but then the Ealdorman of Catterick spoke up.

'We are we bickering like dogs over a bitch in heat? The Mercians are besieging Loidis a few miles from where we are and we're tearing ourselves apart. This is madness.'

Several men nodded their heads or expressed their agreement with him. Only I, Fenton and the Lothian ealdormen remained visibly angry with the king.

'Let us put this squabble behind us, at least until we have vanquished the Mercians' he went on. 'If the king will forgive Seofon, then I'm sure we can all agree to unite behind his leadership for the coming battle.'

That made sense to most but those of us who knew Eadbehrt better than the others were well aware that tonight's challenge to his authority would not be forgotten or forgiven. Both Fenton and I were marked men. More than likely my father would also suffer through association too. I was foolish to point out that the warrior who had released me had been Renweard. He too was now in grave danger.

That night there was a commotion in the camp as Eadbehrt's gesith sought my brother but, thankfully, by then he was on the road north towards Bebbanburg and sanctuary, taking Higbald with him.

~~~

I sighed in frustration. As I had warned the king, Æthelbald had broken off the siege as soon as we came near Loidis. He had crossed back into Mercia and, like a lemming, Eadbehrt had followed him. I had tried to warn him again of the folly of this but, now confident that he was back in command again, he had told me to shut up and not to speak in council again unless he asked for my opinion which, he sneered, was most unlikely. The ealdormen who supported me earlier looked uncomfortable but no-one said anything.

Eadbehrt asked me to stay behind after the meeting and I had a bad feeling about this.

'You may have fooled that idiot Fenton and your friends in the North, but you don't fool me, Seofon. You're a traitor who seeks my throne. Your great uncle usurped the crown and his son tried to unseat me. Your family is a nest of vipers and I'll make sure that you don't survive the coming battle. I'll deal with your father and your brother once I've defeated Æthelbald; it's just a pity you won't still be alive to see that. Now get out.'

'Æthelbald is my cousin, did you know that? Admittedly a distant one but a cousin none the less. You are walking into his trap, Cyning, so I doubt if I'll be the only one to die.'

A week later we reached the River Dove well inside Mercia. Æthelbald had stripped the land bare of people, livestock and crops so our army was starving by this stage. I wasn't the only one urging the king to turn back, but he remained obstinate. The Mercian army was drawn up on the low hills to the south of the river, near a place called Newanberig. There was a crossing over the river but it was a series of stepping stones, each about a square yard in size. It must have taken them a long time for the whole army to cross. The horses could have swum over, but I had no idea how the baggage train had crossed.

Much to my surprise, the king gave me command of all the horsemen except for his own gesith and told me to find another crossing point. He would wait until I attacked the enemy from the rear and then he would lead the assault across the river. I was dubious about his plan. The river was too deep for men on foot to wade across and so it would mean fighting their way across the stepping stones. By the time they had done that my men and I would have been overwhelmed. Perhaps that was his intention.

I eventually found a ford five miles upstream and hastened to cross the river before heading inland to the low hills that bordered Lower Dovedale. When I calculated that we were near to where the two armies faced each other across the river I halted and waited for the scouts moving ahead of the column to report back.

'Their baggage train is in a hollow behind the first line of hills, lord,' the chief scout said. 'The funny thing is that there are only a dozen or so carts. There should be far more for an army two or three thousand strong.'

I thanked him and led my men in an attack on the baggage carts – anything to put off the time when we rode to our deaths against the main Mercian army: except it wasn't.

It took very little time to kill or drive off the men guarding the wagons and, as my men looted them and then set them alight, I rode forward to reconnoitre the main body. From the other side of the river the opposite bank looked full of men lined up to oppose our crossing; from the ridge behind them I could see that there was less than a thousand men in all and most of them were members of the fyrd. Only the front rank were warriors.

As I watched I saw men begin to stream over the line of hills behind our army. As I had feared, Æthelbald had lured Eadbehrt into a trap. Our army was now confined between the river and the main Mercian host; even worse, the most inexperienced members of our fyrd were at the rear and it was these men who would have to turn and face the trained killers at the forefront of the advancing enemy.

I watched with dismay but then I realised that there was something I could do.

'Form wedge and follow me,' I yelled and with one of my gesith beside me and my banner bearer behind me proudly holding aloft the wolf banner of my family we charged down the slope into the rear of the deception force holding the crossing.

As I changed from a canter to the gallop twenty yards before reaching the enemy I had an impression of horrified faces turning to stare at us, too stunned to move. Then, almost as one, they ran, jostling each other and pushing men over, to get out of our way.

My vision was limited by the eyeholes in the metal guard which was riveted to my helmet to protect my face above my mouth, so I could only see straight ahead without turning my head. Suddenly I saw a spearman stop when I was almost on top of him and shove the point towards my body. He was on my right side – the side unprotected by my shield – so I aimed my own spear at him.

Unfortunately his had a longer reach so all I could do was to knock the point away. As I rode past him he thrust his spear into the rump of my horse. The spearman died a second later as one of my men in the third row of the wedge lopped off his head with an axe, but the damage was done.

My stallion squealed in pain and reared up, throwing me over its hind quarters to land with a thump on the ground. For a few seconds I was winded and couldn't move as the rest of the wedge galloped around and past me. After the last row had passed I lay there astonished. I'd fully expected to be crushed to death by the hooves of the following horses but, apart from two glancing blows to my shield and a kick to my helmet, which did no more damage than put a dent in it, I was unscathed. It was a miracle and I thanked the Lord more fervently than ever I had done before that I'd been spared; not even wounded, apart from a bruised left arm and a headache.

I scrambled to my feet and realised that I wasn't out of danger yet. Our charge had scattered the Mercian fyrd and many of them were in full flight, but at least two hundred of them and the eighty or so warriors in their front rank had stayed and a full scale melee against my horsemen was in progress. I quickly realised that a stationary horseman surrounded by armed men on foot was very vulnerable. For a moment I stood there watching helplessly as my men were pulled from their saddles and killed.

Then I spotted a horn that one of the Mercians must have discarded as he fled.

I blew three blasts as hard as I could, then kept repeating the signal. It meant withdraw and reform. Now my men laid about them with renewed vigour trying to break free from the press of the enemy. One hundred and fifty men had been in that charge and some seventy mounted men and fifteen on foot made it back to me. However, they had given a good account of themselves and the ground was strewn with Mercian dead as well.

What I couldn't see was the river. Eadbehrt had taken one look at the Mercians streaming down the hillside to the north and had led his gesith into the river. It was too deep for men to cross safely. Although the water would come no higher than their chests, the strength of the flow would sweep them off their feet and carry them away to drown. It was a different matter for horses. They could swim, which most men couldn't, and the king and his gesith emerged from the river a couple of hundred yards downstream.

At the same time warriors on foot were crossing via the stepping stones as quickly as they could. Of course, they were fleeing the approaching Mercians, but they encountered the very much smaller force remaining on the south side of the river when they got there. As they started to fight them I grabbed a horse off one of my men and led a second charge.

The combined attack on two fronts was too much for the two hundred or so Mercians who had remained and they were quickly routed. My only contribution was to chop down a fleeing warrior in a chain mail byrnie. Once I was satisfied that we had secured the south bank, I sounded the recall with my borrowed horn and looked around to see what was happening elsewhere.

I had expected to find the king trying to rally his men but he was nowhere to be seen. I later found out that he and his gesith had fled to the ford I'd used to cross the river and had then headed north as fast as he could go, leaving his men to fend for themselves.

A quick count showed me that I now had about three hundred men on my side of the river with others crossing all the time. Someone had obviously taken charge on the north bank after the king's flight and they were holding off the Mercians to allow as many as possible to make it to safety on the south bank.

I watched impotently as the Mercians gained the upper hand. By the time the sun dipped below the horizon and darkness descended just over fifteen hundred men had reached me, but the rest of our once proud army had died on the north bank. Only four ealdormen, including Fenton of Luncæstershire and Æthelwold Moll of Berwic, had survived. It had been a complete and utter disaster.

Chapter Five – Aftermath

757 – 758 AD

I had been elected as the hereræswa of the army by the four remaining ealdormen and I led our defeated army back over the Dove further upstream and then north until we eventually reached Northumbria again. The Mercians had also suffered heavy casualties and, apart from the odd minor skirmish, we arrived back at Loidis without further trouble.

Eadbehrt had taken over the town as his temporary capital as it would take a long time to re-build Eoforwīc. Of the eighteen ealdormen in Northumbria, less than half had survived. Beorhtmund had remained in Lothian just in case there was further trouble on the border and his counterpart in Cumbria stayed in the North for the same reason. Apart from me, there were a few other nobles who survived the Battle of Newanberig. They included my father, who was slowly recuperating, and Alchred of Elmet. A significant number of thegns had also been killed.

We remained at Loidis for the winter as Eadbehrt anticipated a further invasion by the Mercians. It never came and then at the start of 757 he heard that Æthelbald had been murdered by his own gesith. The story I heard was that the Mercian king had got very drunk at the feast held to celebrate his victory and had then raped the wife of the captain of his gesith. Whatever the truth of the matter, Mercia was suddenly thrown into chaos and the captain, a man called Beornred, had seized the throne.

For all his philandering, Æthelbald had never sired a child – not one that was acknowledged as his at any rate. His nearest relative was his nephew Offa, the King of Man at the time, and my father's second cousin. As soon as he heard about his uncle's murder, Offa started to muster allies to depose Beornred and get himself acknowledged as king by Mercia's Witan.

News of all this filtered through to us very slowly and was accompanied by wild rumours. Eventually we heard that Offa had defeated his rival in battle and Beornred had fled into exile – some said to Ireland and others to Wessex. Whatever the exact truth, by the spring of 757 it seemed that Offa was the undisputed King of Mercia.

I had avoided contact with Eadbehrt throughout the winter and, thankfully, he had never summoned me. The Witan had met in February to discuss the vacant posts for ealdormen and to agree that the fyrd could be dispersed. Some of the new ealdormen were the sons of the dead, but many had been killed with their fathers. Others were too young to take over their father's shires. In some cases guardians were appointed and in others the widows found themselves married to new husbands, who took over as the ealdorman. Inevitably this meant that the previous ealdormen's children were dispossessed. It was the king's decision, with the Witan's advice, but I was certain that it would store up trouble for the future.

I had kept quiet at the meeting, except to acknowledge the thanks of the Witan for my part in saving the rest of the army. As the meeting drew to a close I was astonished when Eadbehrt got to his feet and added his own words of gratitude to me for my outstanding conduct at the battle – his words. He then confirmed me in the post of hereræswa. I was truly astounded and it took me a moment or two before I could stammer my thanks.

Of course, the words were politically motivated. It must have stuck in his craw to have had to make such a statement and to accept me as his army commander. It occurred to me that, whoever had forced him into this, had done me no favours. If the king had wanted me dead before the battle, he must want that more than ever now.

The summons came just as we were all preparing to travel home, now that the danger of invasion by Mercia seemed to have faded. I tramped through the muddy streets of Loidis, wishing that I had ridden the short distance to the king's hall. The town was little more than an overgrown settlement, apart from the palisade around it and the small stone-built church. Stone was still an uncommon building material – there weren't enough skilled masons in England, nor enough wealth, to construct more, although the raw material was abundant enough.

The hall itself was built in timber and, as it was originally that of the Kings of Elmet, it was old and beginning to need remedial work. The bottom of the frame and the timber lining were rotting where they met the ground, the walls themselves needed recaulking with mud and straw or wool to make them windproof, and the roof leaked in places.

The interior was dark by comparison to the daylight outside, despite the fact that it was a gloomy day with rain in the offing. It took my eyes a minute or two to adjust then I spotted the king deep in conversation with his brother, the archbishop. I waited patiently and finally he glanced my way and an expression of distaste crossed his face before it was replaced by an insincere smile which quickly faded. If he was about to greet me civilly, he had apparently changed his mind.

'Seofon, I don't like you and I don't trust you,' Eadbehrt said, 'but I need a couple of envoys to go and see King Offa to negotiate a formal treaty between us. I have chosen
you, as the hereræswa, and my brother,
Archbishop Egbert.' The latter gave me a
nod and a half smile.

'He has all the details and he'll brief you. This mission is vitally important so don't screw it up. You depart in the morning. That's all; you may leave.'

I found his curt dismissal infuriating. Obviously what he had said in the meeting of the Witan was pure lip service. It crossed my mind that I could be walking into a trap, but the company of the Archbishop of Eoforwīc was a comfort. Surely he wouldn't endanger his own brother? Especially as he was such a powerful ally.

When I went to see Egbert in his own, smaller, hall beside the church that evening I was somewhat reassured. The mission was genuine. Eadbehrt wanted to renew the lasting peace that had existed with Mercia for several decades before Æthelbald had broken it. He was prepared to pay for it, but not in gold. We were to offer part of Luncæstershire as the price. I gathered that the king wasn't specific about the size of the concession, but he did at least want it kept as small as possible. I was horrified at the idea, however small it was.

'He can't do that,' I almost shouted. 'It's been part of Northumbria ever since Oswiu became King of Rheged over a hundred years ago. Besides it'll increase the vulnerability of Elmet and the rest of Deira if it has Mercian territory to the west as well as to the south of it.'

'Not if we secure a lasting peace, Seofon,' the archbishop replied calmly.

'No peace treaty lasts for ever. Eventually it gets broken by one side or the other.'

I knew why Eadbehrt had come up with this mad idea: he wanted to punish Ealdorman Fenton for defying him. Egbert sighed.

'Our role is not to question the king's orders, but to obey them and secure as good a deal as we can get. Better to lose a small part of our south-westernmost shire than to suffer another invasion. Offa has already shown himself to be ambitious. He covets Kent and East Anglia from what I hear.'

Evidently the senior clerics had a grapevine of their own.

'Well, if he's going to be fully occupied conquering East Anglia and Kent, that will keep him occupied for quite a while, not to mention the fact that such ambitions will bring him into conflict with Wessex again. He'll be too busy to concern himself about us.'

'That's the point,' Egbert said calmly. 'He'll be eager to conclude a treaty with us so that he can concentrate on making himself Bretwalda of the South.'

'If he succeeds in doing that, he'll be powerful enough to conquer Northumbria as well.'

'That's where the Welsh come in.'

'The Welsh?'

'They would love to take back the land to the east of the River Severn that Mercia pushed them out of long ago. We are to call and see the King of Gwynedd on our return home.'

~~~

It had taken us months to track down Offa as he traversed his new kingdom, binding its nobles to his side.   By the time we found him he was in Lundenwic and it was nearly the end of the summer. I had expected the old Roman city to be occupied, as was the case at Eoforwīc, but a new town had been built near it. The old city was deserted, which seemed strange to me. It seemed a waste of the once strong defensive walls and the stone built buildings inside them. However, it was reputed to be haunted by the ghosts of the past and the local people never went inside it.

The town which had sprung up to the west of it had expanded over the years and was now much larger than anywhere I'd seen before; perhaps twice the size of Eoforwīc. Sited as it was on the River Tamyse, it had become a major trading port. Originally part of the Kingdom of Essex, it had been captured by the Mercians ninety years ago.

As it lay in the extreme south-eastern corner of Mercia it was too vulnerable and too isolated to be its capital, but it was by far the most important settlement in the kingdom.

It sprawled along the Tamyse and along the River Fleet which ran into the Tamyse from the north. The merchant's warehouses lay along the larger river whilst it's tributary provided a sheltered harbour for the fishing fleet.

I thought that Loidis stank, but it was nothing compared to Lundenwic. The archbishop wanted to pay his respects to the local bishop and so we headed for his church, a stone building near the old Roman walls, and the adjacent monastery. Presumably it had been sited there so that the masons could utilise the stone from the old city. Unfortunately, as we found out when we got there, the king's hall lay at the other end of the settlement and so we had to make our way right through Lundenwic along the muddy streets that ran parallel to the river.

They were narrow, choked with people and littered with the rotting carcases of vermin, dogs and other animals. The inhabitants evidently just threw out the contents of the pails they used at night rather take them down to the river to dispose of. There were a number of communal latrines, but not enough, and many needed filling in, to judge by the smell that emanated from them. I was at a loss to understand how people could live there, but I supposed that they got used to it.

However, the stench got far worse when we reached the street of the butchers. Fly blown meat hung from hooks outside their huts and the bones and intestines that they couldn't use were discarded in the street. The next street housed the fishmongers and, if anything, discarded heads, tails and fish that had rotted stank even worse. It was a relief to leave that part of the town behind as we carried on around a curve in the river and saw better quality huts, houses and even the odd hall on either side of the street. A couple of hundred yards further on we saw a palisade which ran up a gentle slope. A gate with a wooden tower beside it lay in the middle of the line of fortifications and another tower marked each end of the palisade before it turned and ran parallel to the river.

Piles of stone lay nearby so presumably Offa planned to replace the gateway in stone soon. As we approached the gate our two banners were unfurled – mine displaying a black wolf's head on a yellow background and the archbishop's rather more elaborate one. The banner had been made by nuns and consisted of a crimson cloth fringed in gold bullion with two crossed keys – symbolising St. Peter's keys to the gates of Heaven – embroidered on it in silver wire.

The gates had been open but, seeing a group of well-armed riders approaching, the sentries quickly slammed them shut.

'Who are you? What do you want?' a voice called down from the tower.

'Archbishop Egbert of Eoforwīc and Ealdorman Seofon of Alnwicshire, Hereræswa of Northumbria, are here as representatives of King Eadbehrt to see King Offa,' Egbert's chaplain called back a trifle pompously.

'Wait here.'

It was over half an hour before one of the double gates opened sufficiently for two riders to emerge. One was dressed in a blue tunic of good quality and the other was a cleric of some sort, though I didn't recognise the cream habit he wore as being that of a priest or a monk.

'I'm Ealdorman Godric and this is King's Offa's princeps domus.'

The latter was a term I was unfamiliar with, apart from knowing it was Latin, and I looked at Egbert for clarification.

'It means head of the household, I assume.'

'That's correct, archbishop. He will show you and Seofon to your chamber. I fear that you'll have to share. Your men will have to camp down there by the river.'

I turned to look at the marshy area between us and the river and shook my head. 'No, that's not a suitable place for them to set up their encampment.' He shrugged his shoulders.

'Well, they'll have to find somewhere else then. The compound is full to overflowing.'

'They can camp outside the palisade here then,' I replied. 'Can you at least provide them with water and food?'

'I can loan a cart and a couple of barrels for them to fetch water in, as we have to.

There is no well inside the palisade,' the princeps domus replied.

I thought that it was pointless erecting a palisade for defence if there was no source of water inside it. All an enemy had to do was to wait for the garrison to die of thirst, but I didn't comment.

It wasn't until noon the next day that Egbert and I were sent for. Offa sat on an ornately carved throne at one end of his hall. Oddly enough it wasn't raised off the floor and, as we were standing and he was sitting we ended up looking down at him.

'It's customary to kneel in the king's presence,' the princeps domus, who was standing on one side of the throne, said reprovingly.

'May I remind you, whatever you name is, that I am an archbishop? I don't even kneel to the King of Northumbria. I'm afraid a nod of the head will have to suffice.' I thought I detected a ghost of a smile flit across Offa's face.

'Harrumph, that excuse doesn't apply to a mere ealdorman,' he said looking pointedly at me.

'Do you require me to kneel in your presence, cousin?'

'Cousin?' Offa's piercing eyes switched to me. 'How are we related?'

'My great grandfather was your grandmother's brother.'

'Rather distantly related then, but my grandmother was the daughter of the

106

Ealdorman of Bebbanburg, not Alnwic, I think?'

'Yes, Cyning; and my father is the current Ealdorman of Bebbanburg. I'm his eldest son and I will become Ealdorman of both shires in due course.'

'Your grandfather, Swefred, was a good friend to my Uncle Heartbehrt, from what I've been told.'

'And I believe that your father gave Swefred and his family sanctuary and land when he fell out of favour with King Osred.'

'So it seems that our houses were bound together by more than ties of blood, although that was a long time in the past now.'

'Our ancestors were allies then, yes, and I hope that we can at least be friends again, rather than foes.'

'It wasn't me that invaded Deira and sacked Eoforwīc, it was my fool of an uncle,' he replied sharply.

'May I assume from that that you disassociate yourself from King Æthelbald's actions?' Egbert interrupted smoothly.

'To some extent,' he replied warily. 'Your brother invaded Mercia and he must be held to account for that. Æthelbald has already paid the price for his folly.'

It wasn't the same thing, of course. Æthelbald had been killed in retaliation for raping the wife of the captain of his gesith, not for invading Northumbria, but I held my tongue.

'And what price did you have in mind, Cyning, bearing mind we shall have to pay for the rebuilding of most of Eoforwīc, including my church and monastery?'

'I thought it might be sensible to move the eastern part of our common border north from the Mersey to the River Ribble, archbishop.'

'But that would give you two thirds of Luncæstershire and make the whole of Elmet defenceless against you,' I said, aghast.

'That wouldn't matter if I signed a fifty year treaty with Northumbria.'

I knew full well that no treaty would last anything like as long as that, especially as thrones seemed to change hands so quickly these days.

'May we consider your terms, Cyning, and come back again soon?'

'Take as long as you like. For the moment I have my hands full with my quarrel with Essex and Kent. Once I have resolved that to my satisfaction, I still have Wessex to deal with, not to mention the Welsh. Eventually though, I shall turn my attention to my northern border and, one way or the other, I'm determined to secure that. Good day to you, cousin; you too archbishop.'

~~~

We had gone back to see Offa two days after our first meeting merely to say that we would convey his terms to King Eadbehrt but that we didn't think that they would be acceptable.

'Those are my terms for a treaty. Without one your southern border will never be safe,' he replied and with that we departed.

Our meeting with Cadwaladr had been more productive. He had readily agreed that if Mercia tried to take the southern part of Luncæstershire by force he would raid Mercia. In return he wanted our help to take Caerlleon back from Mercia. It was a promise that was easy to give. The old Roman town lay next to the border between Gwynedd and Mercia and a few miles south of the Mersey, which formed our current border with Offa's kingdom. In the hands of allies Caerlleon would help strengthen Luncæstershire's defences.

After my return from Gwynedd I had returned to Alnwic in time for Christmas and then travelled north in February, once the snow had started to thaw, to see my father. Hilda had insisted on coming with me; she complained that she had seen nothing of me for a long time and she wasn't about to let me out of her sight again. The boys came too, as did my brother Renweard, who was now the shire-reeve of Alnwic. To be honest I was away so much that the routine management of the shire fell almost completely onto his shoulders.

My sons were now six and nearly five and, as the journey wasn't an arduous one, I allowed them to ride their own ponies. They rode alongside Hilda and me looking as proud as anything. Of course, they became tired after a while, but both were determined not to show it.

My father had made a good recovery and was delighted to see us. We had invited him to spend the Christmas period with us but the snow was too deep for travel. It seemed to me that the winters were getting worse. Most of the snow had melted in a sudden thaw the previous week so the roads were muddy. In places the road was like a quagmire and we had to make a detour to avoid it.

We stayed at Bebbanburg for a week and I took the opportunity of taking my sons to visit Lindisfarne. One of first monks we saw was Higbald, the captured Mercian boy who I had saved from torture at the hands of Eadbehrt. He was with a group of other novices repairing a hut whose roof had collapsed under the weight of snow.

He had coming running up with a look of delight on his face as soon as he saw me, but stopped as soon as the Master of the Novices, who was supervising the work yelled at him. I dismounted and went and introduced myself to the latter and explained my connection with the boy. The monk smiled and, after admonishing him for stopping work without permission, allowed Higbald to come and talk to me.

We walked through the monastery to the church as I wanted to show Octa and Uuffa where Aidan and Cuthbert were buried beside the altar. Northumbria had many saints, including two previous kings, Oswald and Oswiu. However the two most important were Aidan, who founded Lindisfarne and brought Christianity to Northumbria, and the most celebrated and revered of all - Cuthbert.

Higbald told me how well he was settling in. At first the fact that he was a Mercian had caused him a little difficulty, especially with his fellow novices, but his engaging personality had soon won them over. As we left the church it started to sleet and I prayed fervently that this wasn't the precursor of more snow.

'You had better make haste, lord,' one of the monks told me as we remounted. 'The tide is coming in fast.'

It was still sixty yards out when we started across the sands but it came in at an alarming rate. By the time we were halfway across it had nearly reached the hooves of our cantering steeds. The boys were laughing as they whipped their ponies into a gallop, exhilarated by the danger and the excitement. Their ponies little legs were splashing through water a foot deep by the time we made the other side and were exhausted, their sides heaving with the effort they had made. I jumped off my equally shattered horse and ran to scoop my sons into my arms and hugged them to me.

'You're squeezing us to death, father,' Uuffa complained.

I set them down, realising for the first time how truly precious they were to me. Hilda and I had hoped for another baby, and we had certainly tried hard enough, but so far there was no sign of her getting pregnant again.

We returned to Alnwic after my father had promised to visit us later in the year. In the event it was sooner than we had expected. The Witan had been summoned to meet at Ripon in April to hear the outcome of our negotiations with Offa of Mercia.

~~~

I entered the church at Ripon Monastery beside my father, wondering what would happen at today's meeting. We had travelled down together and I realised for the first time that my father was getting old. He was forty six and, though he tried to hide it, he evidently found riding long distances each day very tiring.

All eighteen ealdormen were present, along with all but one of the senior churchmen. The Abbot of Jarrow was too ill to travel. Hwaetberht, the Abbot of Ripon, took the chair as our host and called us to order. The chatter slowly died away and Archbishop Egbert got to his feet to explain the outcome of our negotiations with Offa. Before he was finished there was uproar in the church and no amount of shouting by Hwaetberh could restore order. He looked at the king for help but Eadbehrt just sat there stony faced. When we had reported back to him he had merely nodded and muttered that was what he'd expected Offa to say.

Eventually the tumult died down but the Ealdorman of Luncæstershire remained on his feet.

'This is an outrage, Cyning. You cannot seriously consider giving away two thirds of my shire? Quite apart from the dishonour and loss of revenue, it would leave the rest of my shire and the whole of Elmet at Offa's mercy.'

'What do you suggest then? Another war with Mercia?'

Once again everyone began to talk at once. This was getting us nowhere. As the king was obviously not going to do anything, I walked up to the table behind which the ineffectual Hwaetberh sat and, drawing my dagger – the only weapon we were permitted to bring into a meeting of the Witan – I thumped the pommel on the table until order had been restored.

'With your permission, abbot, this is getting us nowhere. We need to discuss this calmly and rationally. Now, let Abbot Hwaetberh decide who speaks. Unless he calls upon you to do so, I suggest you remain silent. Archbishop, I think you had the floor.'

'Thank you Seofon,' he said, turning to address the Witan. 'The hereræswa and I both think that Offa is testing our resolve. If we give way to his demands he will know that we are weak. Besides he is engaged in a struggle with Essex and Kent, both of which he wants to add to his domain, and he still has problems with Wessex and the

111

Welsh. It will be a long time, if ever, before he can worry
about Northumbria.' That statement was greeted warmly
but then the king spoke.

'I disagree. That is not what we decided, brother. Mercia is
getting stronger all the time and everything I've heard about him
convinces me that Offa would be a formidable foe. He is offering us
a fifty yearlong peace; we should accept his offer.'

This statement was greeted by a stunned silence initially.
Pandemonium threatened to break out again but Beorhtmund of
Dùn Barra leaped to his feet and gestured for quiet.

'You may disagree, Eadbehrt, but no-one else in the Witan
supports you. You led us into the disastrous invasion of Mercia.
Had we stopped at the border we could have demanded
compensation from Offa for his uncle's actions. By pursuing the
Mercians, against our advice, you gave Offa a legitimate complaint
against us. I say you are no longer fit to be our king.'

Everyone was stunned; everyone except Æthelwold Moll
that is. Obviously the Ealdorman of Berwic had colluded with
his neighbour to the north to challenge Eadbehrt.

'I second Beorhtmund's proposal to force Eadbehrt to abdicate.
No-one who is prepared to cede part of Northumbria to a potential
foe is fit to lead us.'

Gradually several of the other ealdormen got to their feet to
support the motion. Then Bishop Cynewulf of Lindisfarne added
his voice to those calling for the king to resign. It was hardly
surprising, given the fact that Eadbehrt had once imprisoned him
and had dragged Otta out of sanctuary on Lindisfarne to kill him.
The archbishop glared at him but Cynewulf ignored him.

Ecgbert got to his feet and fixed everyone with his eyes before
he spoke.

'How dare you challenge the king? He is your anointed and
consecrated ruler, blessed by Almighty God to lead you. You
commit sacrilege as well as treason to challenge his authority.'

'You are biased, Ecgbert. He is your brother.' This time it was the Bishop of Hexham who spoke. 'I seldom agree with Cynewulf but he is correct. Eadbehrt is no longer fit to be king.'

Hwaetberh looked perplexed, not knowing what to do at this unexpected turn of events, so I leaned over and whispered in his ear.

'Harrumph, well; it seems that a motion had been put to the Witan, proposed by Beorhtmund and seconded by Æthelwold Moll, that King Eadbehrt be um, er....' 'Forced to abdicate and become a monk,' I whispered.

'Invited to abdicate and become a monk, perhaps at his brother's monastery? Yes, well, all those in favour stand, those against remain seated.'

Only Ecgbert and the Bishop of Whithorn in Cumbrian controlled Galloway stayed sitting.

Eadbehrt got up to stalk out of the church muttering that he would see them all damned in hell before he would abdicate, but I indicated to the sentries on the door to keep it closed.

'You don't leave here until you have signed the deed of abdication and sworn on holy relics not to seek the throne again,' I told him. 'You will also be tonsured and take the vows of a monk.'

He stood there fuming for some time but then his shoulders slumped and he nodded.

'Very well, but on one condition. My son, Oswulf, succeeds me.'

I had a very low opinion of his son. He was weak and loved flattery. His gesith was composed of cronies and hangers-on who were, in the main, dissolute young men. They were useless as warriors and their only conquests were in bed. I caught Æthelwold Moll looking at me. He came over and whispered in my ear.

'Agree. I'll make sure he isn't king for very long.'

'What? Oh, I see,' I said, realising that he meant he would dispose of Oswulf, and quickly before he could do any damage. 'Who do you have in mind to succeed him?'

'Have you forgotten that my father, Osred, was of the House of Æthelfrith?'

Chapter Six – Regicide

758 – 759 AD

Life at Alnwic returned to normal after the meeting of the Witan. Oswulf had dithered over what response to send to Offa of Mercia and in the end no reply was sent. I thought it was significant that Offa didn't send anyone to enquire further about the proposed peace treaty, but no doubt he was occupied with events in Essex. Its king, Swaefred, had died and there had been a struggle for the succession. Offa had sided with Sigeric, son of a previous king, and in return Sigeric recognised Offa as his overlord. Essex had now become a vassal of Mercia, so Offa's power was growing - not a comfortable thought.

Hilda and I got used to each other again, not that there had been friction after I returned, but we weren't as easy in each other's company as we had been; we'd both changed. Gradually we relaxed into our old loving relationship though. We joked and poked fun at each other and we could cuddle and kiss without always having to have sex, though we did a lot of that too. It was an idyllic existence, especially as my brother Renweard lived in a hut in the compound and took on some of the routine tasks that are an ealdorman's lot. I enjoyed his company too, of course, and we often hunted together.

He hadn't married and showed no inclination to do so. This puzzled me, of course, but it was his business, not mine.

Summer changed into autumn and the harvest was gathered in by the beginning of October. I had taken to riding up to Bebbanburg with my sons to visit my father once a month.

Renweard didn't always accompany us. Not only did he have his duties as shirereeve but Eadbehrt's edict about the size of nobles' warbands had lapsed, in practice if not in statute. He was therefore busy raising and training more warriors. I had decided to dispense with a separate gesith and intended to replace it by a mounted force of fifty men with another thirty spearmen and archers to garrison my new fortress on the banks of the River Aln. Some of the mounted contingent could act as my escort when necessary, but their main duty was to patrol the coast, with warriors from Bebbanburg, and to escort Renweard and his clerks when they collected taxes.

In late October the weather was beginning to deteriorate. As we rode north it began to rain and the wind picked up. By the time the fortress on its crag hove into view the rain was coming at us horizontally off the sea and we were all soaked. I sent the four mounted warriors who had accompanied us to get dry whilst stable boys took care of our horses.

The boys and I made for my father's hall, together with our two servants – my body servant, Seward, and a Welsh boy I had bought as a slave to serve my sons.

He was eleven and had been captured by the Mercians during a raid across the River Severn by the troublesome Welsh. He'd been sold in Caerlleon and bought by an agent of the Ealdorman of Luncæstershire. He'd sent the boy to me as a gift in return for my support at the Witan. It was a small price for him to pay in return for saving the greater part of his shire, but he didn't have to do it, so it was appreciated.

The boy was called Bleddyn and had been the son of someone in the raiding party, a leader of some sort – perhaps a minor chieftain. He'd been knocked out when the raiders had been defeated and that had saved his life. When he woke up he found himself a captive whereas everyone else in the raiding party was dead.

When he'd arrived escorted by two warriors he'd been filthy, dressed in rags and spat at everyone. He'd been made to walk behind the escort's horses and his feet were raw and bloody. Instead of beating him, I ordered him bathed and had his feet treated. A certain amount of force was needed for the former and he was told that he wouldn't be fed until he behaved. He spoke no English but he understood that. After he was clean he was given new clothes but shoes would have to wait until his feet healed.

Food was taken to the hut where he was kept and, if he spat or tried to kick his jailer, the meal was taken away again. After four days he got the message and grudgingly accepted the food without any bad behaviour. He was taken down to the river every so often and encouraged to wash. His clothes were laundered regularly and he began to learn a few words of English. He seemed grateful but I didn't trust him yet.

After a month he was introduced to my sons and I explained to him that he was to be their servant. If he behaved he would be treated well, but if he didn't he would be imprisoned in the hut again. He was never to hit either of my sons, nor were they allowed to beat him. If they did they would be punished. If he did he would be whipped.

From then on he conducted himself properly and even began to smile and play with the boys. I came to the conclusion that my patience with Bleddyn and care of his poor feet had been rewarded. He became a faithful and loyal servant to Octa and Uuffa and they, in turn, looked after him, even sneaking choice pieces of meat from the table during meals for him.

We walked into the hall to find that my father already had other visitors - Æthelwold Moll and Beorhtmund. After greeting my father I gave Seward my sopping wet cloak and sent the boys off with Bleddyn to get dry and changed whilst I went over to the central hearth to get warm. Soon the wet was steaming out of my clothes and I began to feel more comfortable. Once I had a goblet of mead in my hand I went over to join the others, who were huddled together evidently discussing something important.

It was unusual for the ealdormen who controlled the whole of the east coast from the Firth of Forth to the River Tyne to gather together in one place but I soon learned what was causing them consternation.

'That fool Oswulf would do anything to avoid war.' Æthelwold explained once we were alone in my father's chamber after the evening meal. 'He's ceded the land his father won in Strathclyde to King Óengus. Now the Picts control all the land north of the Clyde and the Firth. Only Dalriada in the west stands between Óengus and domination of all of Alba.'

'All except the coastal strip in the south of Galloway that's part of Cumbria,' my father added.

'You may be certain that Óengus has his eye on that too.' Beorhtmund muttered.

'Why on earth did Oswulf give it up without a fight?' I asked.

'Because Óengus asked him to as an expression of his good intentions. Some rubbish about renewing the treaty he'd agreed with Eadbehrt if he did.' Æthelwold explained.
'The question is, what are we going to do about it? The man is spineless.'

'It's not just that,' my father added. 'Two ealdormen died this autumn leaving no adult sons to inherit so Oswulf has given the shires of Catterick and Leyburn to two of his toadies. He is obviously building up a powerbase. The lesson of what happened to his father has hit home.'

'He has to go and go before too long,' Beorhtmund said. 'He plans to marry soon, from what I hear, though no bride has yet been mentioned. Once he has a son it will be more difficult.'

'What about his brother, Oswine. Won't he be the obvious candidate to succeed him?' I asked.

'He's even more of a fool than Oswulf. No, we need a proven warrior,' Beorhtmund said. 'There is only one man who should be considered: the last direct descendant of Æthelfrith, the first King of Northumbria - Æthelwold.'

'I think we are agreed on that,' my father said, looking at me. I nodded. 'How do we achieve our aim though?'

'Oswulf has to die,' I said, speaking for the first time, 'but we can't be implicated.'

'I agree. He would remain a threat if he was allowed to retire to a monastery. Death is final,' Æthelwold said. 'With any luck Oswine will then challenge me for the throne and we can dispose of him too.'

When I went to bed that night I realised that I had just become a member of a conspiracy to commit regicide, and so had my father. I just hoped that we had backed the right side in the coming struggle for power.

~~~

The next morning I caught Bleddyn giving me funny looks and I realised that he wanted to speak to me, presumably in private. I went for a walk along the parapet and stopped to look out over the grey German Ocean. Thankfully the rain had stopped but the wind now came from the north east and chilled my face and hands. I felt invigorated.

The boy sidled up to me and stood a foot away looking at the restless sea and the spume that the wind whipped from the crests of the waves.

'I'd like to learn to swim,' he said wistfully.

It wasn't what I'd expected him to say and I reflected that perhaps it was time my sons learned too. My grandfather had drowned in a storm and both my father and I had learned to swim after that.

'I'll arrange for you to learn with Octa and Uuffa when we return to Alnwic, if you like.'

'Would you, lord? Thank you.'

His English had more of a pronounced Welsh accent when he was excited.

'Perhaps I could do you a favour in return?'

'Favour? What kind of favour?'

My voice must have conveyed my displeasure that a slave should presume to offer to do his master a good turn. Slaves did what was expected of them. What additional service could he mean?

'You want someone to kill the king,' he said 'I have very sharp ears and I heard what you were discussing when I came to put your sons' clothes to dry in front of the fire.'

I was dismayed. If the boy had overheard us he would have to die. We couldn't afford to let word of what we intended leak out. Before I could think further he continued.

'I could do it. I've killed before, for my father, so it holds no horrors for me despite my youth.'

'You? How?'

'Send me as a present to the king as an expression of your loyalty. I'll find the right opportunity, but it may take time. I need to be accepted and to be part of the background, then no one will suspect me. Not only do I want to get out of there alive but, as a gift from you everyone would know of your connection to the murder if I was caught.'

'Even if you could manage it, they would know it was you as soon as you disappeared.'

'Ah, but I wouldn't. I'd wait until a new king was elected. The household would be transferred to King Æthelwold and he would pick who he wanted and who he didn't. He could send me back to you.'

'You've thought this out, haven't you? I'll have to discuss it with my fellow ealdormen but what do you want out of it? Your freedom so you can return to Wales?'

'No, there's nothing there for me now my father is dead. His brother will have taken his place and he'd likely as not kill me as a potential rival. I'd like to stay and serve your sons, we get on well and I enjoy life here, but I want to be free.'

'If the others agree, then you have a deal.'

'I hope they do. I'm not such a fool as to think that you'd let me live if they don't.'

~~~

It took a great deal of persuasion on my part but eventually they did agree and Bleddyn was sent off to Loidis, this time on a horse, with two men to escort him. Eoforwīc was still being rebuilt but this time Oswulf was building the church and his hall in stone using masons from Frankia and Italy. No expense was being spared and we were paying for it. Oswulf had levied a special tax on all landowners, which hadn't added to his popularity.

We heard nothing for a while and then news filtered through about the king's progress through his kingdom. He had visited the building work at Eoforwīc and expressed himself dissatisfied with the progress of the work before heading for Beverley. I gather that the plan was to visit the monasteries at Whitby, Jarrow and Wearmouth before travelling on to Alnwic, Bebbanburg, Lindisfarne and Berwic. He never got that far.

It wasn't until much later that I heard the full story from Bleddyn; all I heard at the time was contained in a somewhat terse letter from Archbishop Ecgbert, saying that Oswulf had been assassinated on the night of the twenty fourth of July whilst he was staying with a thegn at Wicstun, on the site of the old Roman camp of Delgovicia. He asked me, as hereræswa, to join him at Loidis so that we could rule the kingdom jointly until the Witan could be summoned to appoint Oswine as the new king.

I smiled grimly at that. I knew that Oswine was currently in Wessex arranging his marriage to a daughter of King Cuthred. What I didn't know then was that Cuthred had died just before

Oswulf was murdered and his successor, a distant cousin called Sigebehrt, had been elected to succeed him against significant opposition. Sigebehrt was destined to rule for less than a year, not that it mattered to Oswine. He had set out to return by sea immediately after Cuthred's death. Marriage was now the least of his priorities, particularly to the daughter of a dead king.

Although I wasn't aware of this at the time, I was determined to get Æthelwold Moll elected and crowned as soon as possible. The longer we delayed the more time we allowed other candidates to canvas support, especially Ecgbert on behalf of Oswine. There was also Oswulf's son, Ælfwald, although he was still a young boy.

Accordingly I sent out messengers calling the Witan to meet at Durham on the seventh of August, just two weeks after Oswulf's death, and wrote to Ecgbert informing him of what I had done and to the Ealdorman of Durham asking him to host and preside. I was acting well outside my powers as hereræswa but speed was of the essence. The next day I set out for Loidis to comply with Ecgbert's summons, expecting a difficult meeting.

To say that Ecgbert was furious with me would be an understatement. Obviously he'd wanted to hold the meeting at Loidis, chaired by him, after Oswine had returned. He yelled and swore at me, calling me a traitor and worse.

'When you have quite finished, archbishop, I think you should calm down and listen to what I have to say,' I told him when he stopped his tirade for a moment to draw breath.

'How can you explain what you've done,' he sneered. 'You have deliberately undermined my authority and evidently want to prevent Oswine taking the throne that is rightfully his.'

'There is no right about it,' I replied sharply. 'Oswine is merely one ætheling amongst others. His claim stems from his descent from Ida, who was King of Bernicia, not Northumbria. The only true æthelings are those of the House of Æthelfrith, and there is only one of those left alive - Æthelwold Moll.'

'That's merely a rumour,' he scoffed. 'There is no proof that King Osred was his father.'

I didn't reply but handed him a scroll.

'What's this?' he asked suspiciously.

'Read it, Ecgbert, and then tell me it's a rumour.'

He gave me a long hard look, then unfurled the document and scanned it. His expression at first was dismissive, then he frowned and read it more carefully, his face paling as he did so.

'I see. And the veracity of this statement was sworn on holy relics?'

'His mother came to Bebbanburg to swear it on the arm of Saint Oswald, witnessed, as you can see, by my grandfather and by Eadfrith, the then Bishop of Lindisfarne. However, they agreed to keep the document secret unless it became necessary to reveal it. All involved were anxious to preserve the good name of Æthelwold's mother if at all possible.'

'I assume that she's now dead?'

'Unfortunately; she died the year after signing the document.'

The archbishop peered at the two seals hanging from ribbons attached to the piece of vellum. One seal was the wolf's head used by my family and the other the Celtic cross symbol used by the Bishops of Lindisfarne since the time of Saint Aidan.

'Then I agree that Æthelwold Moll is entitled to be considered alongside Oswine.'

'Set aside your family interests, Ecgbert. You and I know that Æthelwold will make a far better king than that callow youth, Oswine. He's a proven warrior and an experienced ealdorman as well as being something of a scholar in his own right. Oswine likes to get drunk and bed women. Even his brother didn't deem him fit to become an ealdorman when vacancies arose. Instead he appointed his cronies.' 'He is still the son of King Eadbehrt,' he stubbornly maintained.

'Who was deposed for incompetence, hardly much of a recommendation is it?'

'Very well, but the Witan must be postponed until Oswine can be present.'

'That will hardly please all those who have already set out for Durham,' I pointed out. 'Surely, as his uncle, you can stand as proxy for Oswine and present his case?'

Ecgbert scowled, then nodded, all signs of his previous fury having dissipated. He waved a hand in dismissal and I left him to his thoughts.

Chapter Seven - Æthelwold Moll

759 to 764 AD

I had never been to Durham before. It consisted of a relatively small settlement perched on top of a steep hill above the River Wear. The whole place was surrounded by one palisade with another inside the first to defend the ealdorman's hall. Beside it lay a timber church surrounded by huts within a thorn fence. This was the monastery of Durham, which was part of the diocese of Lindisfarne.

Although not as impregnable as Bebbanburg, it would certainly be difficult to attack. My first task was to talk to the ealdorman and the abbot and, hopefully, enlist them to support Æthelwold. My initial conversation with Ingwald, the ealdorman, was not promising.

'What the devil do you mean by calling the Witan to meet here without consulting me first?' he asked me, eyes blazing, as soon as I rode in through the gates of the compound surrounding his hall.

'Didn't you get my message?' I replied coolly, sitting on my horse and looking down at him.

'The message telling me that I was hosting the Witan? Who do you think you are, the king?'

'No, the message before that asking you if you would mind hosting the Witan here. I asked you to let me know if you weren't prepared to do it.'

'No, there was no message,' Ingwald replied, clearly puzzled.

I was lying of course; there hadn't been time for that sort of nicety. However, it put him on the back foot and took the heat out of the situation.

'Then I can only apologise. I am concerned about what happened to the messenger though. Well, we're here now and the rest of the ealdormen, the bishops and the abbots will be on their way so it's too late to change the venue.'

I dismounted and, still grumbling under his breath, my unwilling host led me inside his hall.

The rest drifted in the following day and the morning after that the Witan met. Ecgbert had asked our host to delay the meeting but, as Ingwald was having to pay for the food and drink we were consuming, he firmly refused the archbishop's request.

Ingwald called the meeting to order and asked those who wished to be considered as candidates for the vacant throne to stand. Æthelwold Moll went to rise but Alchred beat him to it. Ecgbert also got to his feet and said that he was representing Oswine who was still on his way to Durham and also Ælfwold, the son of the late King Oswulf.

'But Ælfwold is still an infant. You're surely not suggesting that he could take the throne?' Bishop Cynewulf asked.

'That is for the Witan to decide. He is the son of the last king and should at least be considered,' Ecgbert replied somewhat frostily.

There was no love lost between them. Lindisfarne had been the seat of the bishops of Northumbria since Saint Aidan's time and we in the north resented the primacy of Eoforwīc dating from when the original single diocese was divided into three. Now, of course, there were four sees with the addition of Whithorn on the north coast of the Solway Firth.

'Very well, it seems we have four candidates. Archbishop, perhaps you would start by outlining the cases for Oswine and Ælfwold?'

'Very well, Oswine is the brother of our late lamented King Oswulf,' he began.

'Not lamented by me,' one of the ealdormen called out.

That brought a smile to several faces and a murmur of agreement. Ecgbert glared at the man who had interrupted before continuing.

'It is customary not to comment when candidates are stating their case. It is not only bad manners but it is unfair.' He paused before continuing. 'He is a man of excellent character and would make an exceptional king. As to Ælfwold, I agree that, at two years of age, he wouldn't be able to rule on his own for at least twelve more years. However, I would be more than happy to act as regent and bring him up to be a true Christian king.'

'Thank you, archbishop. Ealdorman Alchred, would you state your case please?'

'I'm not only married to the daughter of King Eadbehrt but I'm an ætheling in my own right, being descended from King Ida via his son Eadric. I am young, not something that Æthelwold Moll can claim, so you can look forward to a long and prosperous period with me as king. However, I'm not so young that I'm inexperienced. I have ruled my shire for several years and I'm a proficient warrior. In that regard, I have a distinct advantage over Oswine who, at twenty, has scarcely managed to grow any hair, except on his head.'

That raised a chuckle. Most men remained clean shaven or grew a moustache in adulthood - few grew beards - but Oswine was notorious for only having a few wisps of hair in his armpits as yet. His gesith had presented him with a shaving knife as a jest on his eighteenth birthday and he'd flown into a rage.

When he sat down to some muted applause, Æthelwold got to his feet.

'You all know me. I'm no callow youth, as Alchred so kindly pointed out, but neither am I yet in my dotage. Yes, I'm in my late forties as is Ealdorman Ulfric of Bebbanburg, but no one would regard him as old; neither am I. The other æthelings are descended from Ida but he was King of Bernicia, not of Northumbria. I'm not proud of my father - in fact I've always detested him. King Osred was not a man a son could regard with any respect. However, he was descended from Æthelfrith, the first King of a united Northumbria. I therefore hold that, despite being born a bastard, I have a better claim than any descended from other branches of Ida's family.

'Alchred had been an ealdorman but a short time and his only experience of warfare, as far as I'm aware, was being shut in Loidis whilst the Mercians besieged it. He is therefore something of an unknown quantity as far as being a ruler and a military leader is concerned. As for Oswine and Ælfwold, I don't think I need to repeat what Alchred has already said. In any case, they are not here to speak for themselves and to answer any questions you might have so I suggest that they should be eliminated by default. If you choose me I promise I will rule Northumbria justly and fairly and, if necessary, defend it by diplomacy and by force when needed.'

The applause that greeted this speech left the result in little doubt but the Witan was invited to question the candidates. The only question came from the new Ealdorman of Catterick, one of Oswine's toadies.

'You say you are the son of Osred, son of Aldfrith, son of Oswiu, son of Æthelfrith, but what proof do we have that this is true?'

'Perhaps I can help with that,' my father said, getting to his feet. 'I was on
Lindisfarne when my father, Swefred, told Æthelwold of his parentage. I wasn't actually present when my father told him, but he was very upset to learn how he was conceived. He was my foster brother and we were very close, so it was natural for him to confide in me.'

'But how do we know that what Swefred told him was true?' the man who had queried Æthelwold's claim persisted.

Cynewulf sighed as he stood and beckoned one of his monks who had been standing at the back of the hall. The man gave him a leather pouch and then withdrew again.

'I was hoping to avoid this but it seems that, as Ulfric's word is being questioned, I have little option. This is the written statement from the Abbess of Coldingham concerning the deathbed confession of Æthelwold's mother. She very nearly carried her secret to the grave but decided to confide in the abbess at the last moment. She in turn wrote down what she was told and entrusted it to my care the month before she herself died.

'I don't propose to read the statement as that would break the seal of the confessional, but I will tell you the essence of what it says. King Osred raped a novice whilst he was staying at Whitby and she became pregnant.

'I am told that subsequently the novice was sent to Bebbanburg to give birth and the child was fostered by Ealdorman Swefred and his wife Kendra, who had given birth to Ulfric at around the same time. The novice entered Coldingham monastery and stayed there as a nun for the rest of her life. Her son was baptised Æthelwold, later being given the nickname Moll.'

He sat down to stunned silence. Everyone avoided looking at Æthelwold. There was no shame in bastardy - King Aldfrith, Oswiu's eldest son, had been a bastard – but being conceived through rape was a different matter.

'I hope that the Ealdorman of Catterick is now satisfied, having caused my good name to be dragged through the mire,' Æthelwold said bitterly, fixing the man with a venomous stare. 'What you have been told is true, but it must never be repeated outside this hall. If I am elected as your king I shall require all of you to swear an oath to that effect.'

'It shouldn't have been necessary to make my brother bishop reveal the circumstances of Æthelwold's birth,' the archbishop said in the silence that had descended on the hall. 'Ealdorman Ulfric's word should have been sufficient. I accept
Moll as a member of the House of Æthelfrith.'

The result was a foregone conclusion after that and Æthelwold was crowned as king. Crowning was a new ceremony as far as Northumbria was concerned. Previously kings had been anointed by a bishop, but the placing of a gold circlet on his head was something practiced on the Continent that had been adopted in Wessex and Mercia some time ago. Now it had reached Northumbria too.

I didn't fancy the Ealdorman of Catterick's chances of keeping his shire for long but, as it turned out, the king didn't have to do anything. The man fled to Ireland with his family a few days after his return from Durham.

~~~

One of the first things the new king did was to return Bleddyn to me. As I'd promised I freed him and he returned to his duties serving Octa and Uuffa. They were delighted to see him back as his temporary replacement, a miserable old man from Frisia, had refused to play with them or do anything other than the duties required of a slave.

'Well, what happened?'

'Happened, lord?' he replied, looking at me with his innocent brown eyes and a mischievous grin playing on his lips.

I had sent for him as soon as the boys were in bed the first night after his return. Both Hilda and I were eager to know how he had managed to kill Oswulf without being detected.

'Yes, don't play games with me Bleddyn. You know what I'm talking about.'

'No, lord. I apologise,' he said, not looking the least bit sorry for teasing us. 'Well, it took time but in the end it was easier than I thought. As you know, I became a slave in the king's household. Because I had been the body servant to your sons, I was given to the reeve of the king's hall to serve his ten year old son, a vindictive pint-size brat called Godric. He looked for any small excuse to beat me. I nearly ruined my mission by killing the little bastard, but I bided my time and eventually I was moved to serve the captain of the king's gesith.

'His body servant had died suddenly and, as it was just before Oswulf's tour of his Deiran shires, he needed someone in a hurry. I was therefore loaned to him despite Godric's protests that he couldn't do without me. I went out of my way to please my new master and my efforts were rewarded. After a while he gave me my own horse so I could ride behind him instead of travelling in the baggage carts.

'However, I couldn't get near the king, not until we reached Wicstun. There was nowhere else nearby to stay so the king had to make do with the thegn's hovel of a hall. It was poorly constructed: the wind howled through the gaps in the wall planking and the roof leaked. In consequence the beaten earth floor developed mud patches under the strewn straw covering it.

'It had rained heavily during the day and I was given my master's clothing and cloak to dry by the fire. There were others trying to get near the central hearth but the king's body servant took priority and he invited me to share the space with him. I think he rather fancied me,' Bleddyn added coyly.

That startled me. Of course, I'd heard tales of monks seeking solace with each other and one had even been executed at Lindisfarne for raping a novice many years ago, but the idea still shocked me.

'Anyway, when the clothes were dry I offered to take the king's clothes back to him. Of course, he had a spare set which he had changed into and there was no-one in the thegn's chamber, which the king had taken over. I laid the clothes on his travelling coffer and was about to leave when the king came in and looked at me suspiciously. I explained who I was and what I was doing there and he muttered about his servant being a lazy sod, then told me to take his boots off. Whilst I did so he took off his jewel encrusted belt and threw it on top of his clean clothes on the coffer.

'He lay down on the bed and went to sleep, snoring softly. Of course, it was the chance I was waiting for so I put down the boots and quietly drew his dagger from its sheath. I put my hand over his mouth and drew the sharp blade across his neck, severing both carotid arteries. I stepped back to avoid the spurt of blood but it stopped almost instantly as he died. I was tempted to steal the jewelled belt but its possession would have identified me as the murderer. Only the body servant knew I could have killed the king so I went and found him and suggested we went for a chat in the stables.

'His eyes lit up at what he thought I was suggesting and I killed him with my eating knife as soon as we got there. I hid his body in the straw and left unseen. Fortunately most of the king's entourage was camped outside the hall compound and so there was constant coming and going through the empty gate. I walked out of there with my master's dry clothes and went to find him in the gesith's camp. After that I behaved normally. When the king was discovered and the body servant couldn't be found, suspicion fell on him. It wasn't until we'd left that his body was found.

'Back at Eoforwīc I resumed my duties serving the brat until King Æthelwold arrived and told the reeve that he was making a present of me to you. Of course, Godric kicked up a fuss and was given a clip round the ear for his pains. The morning I left I put a powerful emetic in his breakfast. Hopefully he's still sitting on the latrine with crippling pains in his stomach; that is unless it's killed him, of course.'

'Well done, Bleddyn. It seems to me that you're wasted as a servant. I'll have to see if I can't make more use of your obvious talents.'

The boy said nothing in reply but his handsome features lit up with a wolfish grin.

~~~

I hadn't expected Oswine to accept Æthelwold's coronation with good grace but he seemed to have disappeared off the face of the earth. Then two years later, in the spring of 761 rumours started to circulate that he was mustering an army in the Eildon Hills to challenge the king.

It seemed a strange choice to me at first. The hills were south of the monastery at Melrose in Lothian, which could be counted on above all to support Æthelwold. From time immemorial the Lothian ealdormen had stuck together, back as far as when the area was known as Goddodin after the tribe of Britons who were the original inhabitants.

We soon found out that Oswine had been busy in Ireland ever since he'd failed to secure the throne. He'd landed in Cumbria with a small army of Irish mercenaries eager for plunder and had been backed by its ealdorman.

Then came disastrous news. Óengus had died and been succeeded by his brother Bridei as the third King of the Picts of that name. Óengus had ever been an honourable man, aside from taking advantage of that fool Oswulf, and had kept the peace throughout his long reign, even enlisting our support to conquer Strathclyde. Now his hot headed younger brother ruled all of Alba except for Dalriada, and we couldn't expect help from that quarter.

As we assembled the fyrd and the ealdormen of Deira, Bernicia and Lothian marched to the rendezvous at Yeavering in the Cheviot Hills we heard that Bridei had joined Oswine. Now we had the armies of Pictland and Strathclyde to contend with in addition to that of Cumbria and the Irish mercenaries. I wondered how Cumbria and Strathclyde could be allies when they were in dispute over the coast of Galloway. Perhaps they had put aside their differences somehow? I needed to find out if that was indeed the case and, if so, why? It was a task for someone with both cunning and the ability to pass unnoticed. I knew of just the boy.

On instructions from Æthelwold, the ealdormen of Luncæstershire, Elmet and Eoforwīcshire had remained at home just in case Offa was tempted to take advantage of the situation. The remaining fourteen shires had managed to raise a force some three thousand strong, six hundred of whom were thegns or members of permanent warbands. Of these some two hundred were mounted. It was a sizeable army but we didn't know how many men Oswine had.

When Bleddyn arrived I sent him off with a party of scouts under the command of Uurad and I waited impatiently for him to return.

'It all went according to plan, lord,' Uurad told Æthelwold and me as soon as he returned. 'We chased the boy into the enemy encampment and then raced away as soon as they sent men to intercept us. It was a bit of a race but we managed to get away without any losses.'

'How many men did they have?' the king asked, more interested in Oswine's strength than the fate of a servant.

'We studied their camp for a while before the pretend chase and I counted a hundred and forty ponies and fifty horses, but that would have included some pack animals. The camp itself was divided into three sections, the largest one being that of the Picts and Strathclyde Britons. I would think there were something like two thousand of them.

The Cumbrians were perhaps six or seven hundred strong and the section around

Oswine's tent contained about three hundred men.'

'So it seems that we are evenly matched,' Æthelwold mused. 'I had hoped to have the advantage.'

'You may still have, plus the element of surprise, if Bleddyn does what I asked him to.'

'You put a lot of faith in an eleven year old boy, Seofon,' he replied sceptically.

134

'He gained you your throne, Cyning,' I reminded him. 'And he's twelve now; he had a birthday last month.'

'Eleven, twelve – he's still a young boy. He may be able to slit a throat but getting to see the Ealdorman of Cumbria, let alone bribe him successfully, is a tall order.'

'Well, if he fails all I've lost is a body servant to my sons.'

The boys would never forgive me, of course, I thought gloomily as I lay on the hard ground in my tent that night. The other problem was that I would never know if Bleddyn had managed to do what I'd asked until battle was joined.

~~~

I rode forward to examine the enemy position. Oswine had occupied the crest of a steep sided hill. In the small valley below it a stream ran through boggy ground. It was a good position and, to make matters worse for us, heavy rain was falling. This would make the hillside slippery and our archers would be of very limited use. Once bow strings got wet they stretched, even if treated with beeswax, and consequently lost power.

Æthelwold rode up to join me.

'We'd lose too many men if we tried a frontal assault,' he concluded gloomily.

'Perhaps the other side of the hill might be an easier climb?' I suggested. 'If we line the army up here to distract them, I'll go and have a look.'

He nodded and, taking six of my mounted warband with me, I rode through the hills and around the enemy position out of sight. I was conscious that Oswine might have scouts out and we went cautiously. There was no hurry; we weren't going to attack that day and, hopefully, the rain would stop by tomorrow so that we could use our numerical advantage in terms of archers.

The going wasn't easy and visibility in the heavy rain was poor but eventually we emerged onto a shallow saddle between two hills from where we could just make out the reverse slope of the hill which our foes occupied. A narrow river ran through the valley at the bottom of the hill and I could see their baggage train on the far bank. The slope itself was nearly as steep as it was on the other side, but a broad ridge linked their hilltop to the next one. If we could occupy the second hill, we could advance along the ridge and would only have a shallow ascent to cover during our attack. Admittedly this would be on a relatively narrow front but the topography would be the same for them.

We circled the hill out of sight so that I could examine the other side of the enemy's hill but that too was steep sided. A plan began to form in my mind and we carried on to complete the circle and ride back to join the king.

That night we left a small party of boys and old men to tend the camp fires on top of our hill whilst the main body set off for a night march. This is not something that is easily achieved with a large body of men, especially if they need to move quietly. To reduce the risk of whole sections getting lost I took three groups of guides in turn and showed them the route that afternoon. When we set off we did so in groups of two hundred.

Thankfully we made it to the rendezvous having lost no more than a handful and without making any noise that might have alerted our foes. The rain had petered out during the previous evening and, although their clothing was still wet, at least the men could get some sleep before we attacked at dawn.

We were halfway across the ridge before the enemy realised what was happening. This was no terrain for horses to charge over – too restricted and too many boulders – and so Æthelwold led the attack on foot. I wasn't with him. I went to attack and secure the enemy baggage train first and then waited for Oswine to try and escape.

I couldn't see what was happening on top of the hill – the convex slope hid the battle from me – so I rode up to the top of the next hill. I could see that our men were pushing the enemy shield wall back whilst our archers sent volley after volley into their rear. More importantly a large group of the enemy were gathered at the back of the hill and were taking no part in the fighting. This had to be the Cumbrians. It looked as if Bleddyn's mission had been successful.

Suddenly a rider broke away from the rear of the enemy formation and, accompanied by a few other horsemen, he rode up to the Cumbrians and what looked like a heated exchange broke out between the leaders of the two forces. One of them, either Oswine or one of his commanders I suspected, drew his sword but one of the Cumbrians standing beside their leader thrust his spear at the swordsman.

It was a poorly aimed blow and the swordsman deflected the spear with his shield. Unfortunately for him, the point ended up piercing the rump of his horse and the animal reared up in pain, depositing its rider on the ground.

The other riders tried to go to their leader's aid but they were few and the Cumbrians were many. It was all over in a minute or two; the riders were all killed and their winded leader was hauled to his feet. As I watched he was forced to kneel and an axeman stepped forward to chop his head from his body. The head was fixed atop a spear and waved up and down. From where I watched I could make out faint cheering over the din of battle. I assumed, correctly as it turned out, that the head was that of Oswine.

Although only a few men owed fealty to Oswine personally, and many of them were now dead, he was the paymaster of the mercenaries and the ally of the Picts and Britons. Without him the only thing they were fighting for was their survival. It wasn't long before the rout started and men fled for their lives. I watched carefully for the banner of Bridei, King of the Picts, and when I saw it amongst a group of riders, mostly on mountain ponies, heading north-west towards the crossing over the River Forth, I set off to intercept them.

I estimated that Bridei's escort numbered no more than fifty, easily outnumbered by the hundred men I had with me. The problem was the terrain. Boulders and smaller rocks littered the ground, which the ponies were nimbler at negotiating, and we fell behind. However, once we were out of the hills and onto open pasture we began to gain on them. Bridei must have realised that we would catch him long before he could reach the bridge below Stirling and changed course, heading for a large area of woodland.

There was no road through the wood and so he would be forced to follow animal trails. I sent twenty men after him to keep up the pretence of pursuit whilst I headed around the trees, making for where I thought that the Picts would emerge.

I was a little out in my calculations and they appeared a little to the north of where I was waiting. However, we were only a few hundred yards apart now and ten minutes later we started to overhaul the back markers, spearing them and chopping them from their ponies as we went.

Suddenly the Picts turned to make a stand. They were outnumbered two to one but they put up a tough fight. Many of my men weren't adept at fighting on horseback - they used them to travel quickly and then fought on foot – but I had trained some to charge and break a shield wall. Fighting against another mounted warrior was a different matter though. Fortunately the Picts were even more unused to mounted combat than we were.

My first opponent made a clumsy attempt to stab me with his spear and overbalanced when I moved my horse to the right to avoid it. He fell off to be trampled underfoot by those following. The next man was more careful. He held his spear across his body, aiming to knock me off my horse with the haft. I tried to bash it out of the way with my shield but it rode up and hit my helmet. For a moment I felt dizzy and lost concentration. Fortunately my galloping horse took me past my assailant and I had a moment to recover before the next man appeared in front of me. This time I threw my spear, not at him, but at his steed. It was only when the animal sank to its knees with my spear in its chest that I realised that it was a horse, not a pony. This Pict was a noble.

He leapt from his dying horse and, having dropped his spear, drew his sword. He deflected my own sword when I cut down at his head but I pulled on the reins so that my horse barged into him causing him to lose his balance. He sat down heavily and, by the time he'd regained his feet, I'd dismounted.

He'd also lost his shield so it should have been an unequal contest. By this time the rest of my men had galloped past in pursuit of the remaining Picts and the two of us were alone. He charged me and, making a succession of quick cuts and thrusts, he forced me back. If it hadn't been for my shield I've have been killed, but the effort had tired him and his blows slowed.

Now it was my turn to press home the attack. I banged his sword aside with my shield and sword alternately, whilst making quick stabs at him when the opportunity presented itself. He got in one lucky blow to my shoulder and I felt the chainmail rings part. Thankfully the thick leather jerkin I wore under my byrnie prevented anything worse than a bad bruise.

I saw an opening and thrust the point of my sword at his left eye. He moved his head just in time but the blade knocked the ornate helmet from his head. Now I could see the face of the man I was fighting and realised with a shock that it was Bridei. I had only seen him once standing at the side of his brother Óengus, but his features and shock of red hair were unmistakeable.

With a snarl he leaped towards me, sword uplifted to strike down at my shoulder again. This time the leather wouldn't stop the blow and he'd probably cut through and break the bone, or even give me a fatal wound.

It would take too long to get my shield across and my sword was out of position to block the cut in time so I did the only thing I could; I dropped to one knee so that his sword struck my back, where it harmlessly bounced off the chainmail. I drove my shoulder forwards and upwards, winding him, before dropping my sword and pulling out my seax. As he doubled over I thrust the point of the seax up behind his jaw through his mouth and into his brain. He was dead before he hit the dirt.

I was exhausted and, as the adrenalin drained from me, reaction set in and I experienced melancholia instead of the euphoria I had expected. By the time that my men returned, having killed the rest of the Picts, I had recovered sufficiently to join in their sense of triumph.

I returned with Bridei's body draped over a pony to find Æthelwold; I couldn't bring myself to order his head chopped off to join that of Oswine on the tip of a spear, the man had been a king after all. That night there was a feast, mainly consisting of roasted dead horse, to celebrate the victory so it was the next day before I could locate Bleddyn and find out what had happened.

'No one challenged me when I walked into their camp,' he told me as he sat inside my tent eating yet more horsemeat. 'And I was lucky enough to get close to the big tent in the middle. I think it belonged to the King of the Picts; anyway two men were talking inside it and, with my ear pressed to the back of the tent I could hear what they were saying.

'One man was protesting at some agreement the other had made with the Ealdorman of Cumbria. It appeared that he had agreed that he would formally cede the coastal strip in Galloway, which the Cumbrians had conquered some time ago, in return for their help to put Oswine on the throne.

'The other man maintained that it belonged to Strathclyde. 'And so it does.' the other voice had said. 'I agreed that Cumbria could keep it only to enlist their support. However, Oswine has promised that he will surrender all of Cumbria to me in return for my help once he is on the throne.'

'That seemed to satisfy the other man and they went on to talk of other things. Of course, I realised that the Cumbrians had been betrayed, but I didn't know at first how to get the information to their ealdorman.'

'How did you manage that?'

'I made my way over to the Cumbrians' camp but there was a guard on the tent which I assumed was the ealdorman's as it had a banner outside it. I waited until the middle of the night and then cut a slit in the back of the tent. There were two men asleep inside, one on the floor – presumably his body servant – and one on a palliasse.

'The latter was snoring heavily and so I made my way over to the servant. I pricked his neck with the point of my dagger just enough to draw blood and I clamped my hand over his mouth. He woke and looked at me terrified. I told him to lie still as I gagged and bound him using his own clothes.'

He stopped for a moment as he chewed on a piece of particularly tough meat whilst I waited impatiently for him to continue.

'I woke the ealdorman in the same way and told him what I'd overheard. I said I'd kill him if he moved or cried out, then removed my hand. He asked why he should believe a common little tyke like me, especially one who came like an assassin in the night, so I asked him why I'd risk my life to get the message to him. I explained that I worked for you and asked him why else the Picts and Britons of Strathclyde would support Oswine. What did they have to gain?'

'Did that convince him?'

'Not at first but the more I prodded him to explain why they were helping Oswine when they wanted the Galloway strip back, not ceded to Cumbria, the more I think he was convinced. Anyway, I'd done all that I could, so I made him promise not to sound the alarm and left by the same way I'd entered the tent.

'I'd slipped into the encampment during the chaos of setting up, but now they had perimeter guards in place, so I went and slept under one of the baggage carts and waited for the battle to start so I could make my escape. The rest you know.'

~~~

There was one thing that continued to worry the Witan after the defeat and death of Oswine. Æthelwold Moll had been married years ago but his wife had died giving birth, along with the child. That meant that he had no heir. He was unwilling to marry again but eventually he gave in and became betrothed to Æthelfryth, daughter of the Ealdorman of Catterick, a young girl of fifteen. I could only imagine what she must have felt when she was told she was to marry a man of nearly fifty. I wondered if being queen was compensation enough. It might be to some girls, I supposed.

My father and I travelled down to Catterick, where the wedding was to take place, on a chilly day in March 762. Hilda came with us, of course, as did the two boys. Octa was now ten and Uuffa nearly eight, so each rode their own steeds. Octa's was a small mare and Uuffa's one of the mountain ponies I'd brought back from the Battle of the Eildon Hills. Octa used to tease his brother about the pony until they had a race up in the Cheviot Hills over broken terrain, which the more agile pony had won.

Now they rode side by side chatting about whatever boys their age talk about. Both were big lads, not a family trait. My father and I were short of stature but broad of shoulder. The boys took after their mother in that they were taller and slimmer than either I or Renweard had been as boys. Their colouring was lighter too. I was swarthy with black hair whereas my sons had skin that tanned to a more golden colour in summer and their hair was brown. If their faces hadn't closely resembled mine I might have been suspicious about their parentage!

I had invited Renweard to come with us but he'd fallen in love at long last. As he was now thirty two he'd left it overlong. His betrothed was the widow of one of my thegns. She was twenty five and had a nine year old son and a six year old daughter. Hilda and I joked that he would find the sudden change from bachelorhood, where he could please himself, to being husband and father a rather greater transition that he imagined.

I had agreed to him becoming the thegn but, as the vill was adjacent to Alnwic, he would stay on as my shire-reeve. He was busy preparing for his own wedding and getting to know the people in his new vill and so I wasn't too surprised when he declined the invitation.

The settlement of Catterick lay beside a small stream known as the Beck. It was surrounded by rolling countryside consisting of good pastureland, open moorland and a number of large woods. The settlement itself was dominated by a large timber church built on stone foundations.

We continued through the assortment of huts, barns and animal shelters towards the ealdorman's hall on top of a gentle rise. Unlike the settlement, it was surrounded by a stout square palisade some twenty foot high with towers at each corner and as well as at either side of the main gate. This obviated the need for a platform over the gate itself. I was impressed. With no natural defensive features to utilise, whoever had built this fortress had nevertheless made it difficult to attack.

With the king and his party to accommodate it came as no surprise when the reeve told us, with feigned regret, that the hall was full. He called a name and a boy came running. He was well dressed for a servant, which probably indicated how wealthy his master was. He led us to an area of level ground beside the Beck about two hundred yards from the hall compound. We had the place to ourselves for a while and managed to get the tents up, put out the stakes and ropes for the horse lines and generally settle in before the next group arrived.

When Æthelwold had become king, he had appointed a new ealdorman for Berwicshire. My father had met him but I hadn't. When he came across to greet my father and to meet Hilda and me, he brought a pretty young wife and small boy of three with him. He was only young himself – in his early twenties I guessed – and was clean shaven; unusual when the fashion was for men to grow a moustache with ends as long as they could manage.

His name was Beadurof, which meant bold in war. I thought it a somewhat pretentious name for his parents to have given their son, but that was none of his doing. He was the younger brother of the Ealdorman of Hawick, although I recalled that some time ago my father had told me that they didn't get on.

Our servants had prepared a meal and so we invited Beadurof and his wife, Botilda, to join us. Bleddyn gave me an annoyed look and I smiled to myself. The two extra mouths to feed probably meant that the portion that he and Seward had intended for themselves would now have to be given to our guests.

I found him pleasant company and Hilda chatted away happily to Botilda. I was pleased. I would have made myself agreeable to the new lord of Berwic whether I liked him or not - one can never have too many allies – but making a friend of him was a bonus, especially as I didn't much care for his elder brother.

The weather had been unseasonably warm for our journey down but it changed overnight. I awoke to the sound of rain pattering onto the oiled leather of the tent I shared with Hilda, the boys, Seward and Bleddyn. When I went outside to visit the latrines with my cloak wrapped around me I was surprised that it was cold as well as wet: so cold that I wouldn't be surprised if the rain turned to sleet or even snow. It was not the weather that the king would have been hoping for.

The street that ran through the settlement had turned from hard baked earth to thick, cloying mud overnight and I was glad that we had decided to ride to the church. Of course, every other noble and their family had done likewise and there were two score of horses outside the entrance to the church. Thankfully the reeve arrived at that moment to try and restore some sort of order. He had brought every groom and stable boy he could find with him and soon the horses were being led away whilst we made our way carefully through the glutinous mud to the church door.

The fifteen year old son of the Ealdorman of Beverley slipped and fell into the stuff, quite ruining the scarlet trousers and blue cloak he was wearing. Octa and Uuffa started to laugh until I cuffed them both around the head.

'Never laugh at the misfortune of others. It can make you an enemy for life, quite apart from the fact that it's bad manners,' I told them quietly.

We made the interior of the church without further incident and stood waiting patiently as it filled up. The floor was made of timber planks suspended across the gap between the stone foundation walls with supports, presumably also stone, at intervals. Not that you'd know it due to the amount of mud deposited on it from shoes and boots. Nevertheless it was superior to the usual floors of beaten earth.

My musings were interrupted by Æthelwold's arrival. Unlike many of his brightly coloured nobles, he was dressed in a full length green woollen robe trimmed at collar and cuff with the fur from a brown bear. As these were becoming rare in Northumbria, and even in Scotland where they had been more plentiful, especially in the north, it must have been expensive. He wore the plain gold circlet with which he'd been crowned on his head.

We scarcely had to wait more than a couple of minutes before his bride came to stand by the king's side. She wore a light blue surcoat over a dark blue under skirt. She had apparently arrived in a carriage with her husband-to-be and the delay had been so that she could be carried to the doorway to prevent the mud splattering the bottom of her skirt. She needn't have bothered; by the time she reached the altar the mud on the floor of the church had stained the hem brown.

The service and the feast that followed were unremarkable except for something that Beadurof said to me whilst we sat drinking into the small hours.

'Rumours are beginning to circulate that you and Æthelwold were involved in Oswulf's murder,' he murmured into his tankard of ale.

My heart went cold and I sobered up immediately. Had Bleddyn been bragging? It didn't seem likely. He had a reputation for being taciturn and, even if he had been drinking, he was unlikely to have got so drunk that he became indiscreet. It just wasn't like him. Nevertheless the rumours must have come from somewhere. 'Why do you say that?' I asked. 'Has someone been telling lies?' 'Lies? No.'

His voice was slurred and he wasn't making much sense. What he said next sent a chill down my spine.

'From what I heard, your son's servant, Bleddyn, was seen carrying some clothes into Oswulf's bed chamber. Oswulf's servant was later found dead in the stables. I suppose someone has just put the two things together and drawn the obvious conclusion.'

His voice was still slurred but what he'd just said made perfect sense, of course.

'Why has it taken so long for this story to start circulating I wonder? Where did you hear it?'

'I suspect that the girl who saw Bleddyn may have been sweet on him and kept quiet. However, she recently got married and told her husband. I gather he's the one who's been spreading the tale.'

I had a difficult decision to make. If someone got hold of Bleddyn and questioned him he might talk, especially if he was tortured. He wouldn't want to betray me but most people will talk if they are in enough pain. It was a risk I couldn't afford to take. He would have to die or disappear.

'I'm sure it's just coincidence,' I said much more calmly that I was feeling. 'I'll have a word with the boy. Who is this girl's husband, by the way?'

Beadurof shrugged. 'No idea.'

I changed the subject and after a while we both left the feast; Beadurof for his bed and I to find Bleddyn.

'Who is this girl? Do you know?' I asked him after telling him what I'd been told.

He blushed furiously.

'Perhaps it's Roswitha. She made it pretty clear that she liked me.'

'Liked you? You were eleven. How old was she?'

'Thirteen. We didn't do anything, well not much. I was too young, but we did kiss and fondle each other. She said she would wait until I was older. She never said anything to me about the king's death afterwards, not even when I said goodbye to her when I came back to you, though she was very upset.'

'Well, she continued to carry a torch for you I suppose, at least for the past two years or so; but now the cat is out of the bag.'

'I thought I could move unnoticed. I'm sorry, lord.'

'I don't suppose you could do anything without her eyes being on you if she was in love. It's not your fault.'

'What are you going to do?'

'You have to vanish before someone thinks of questioning you. You'd be safe inside Bebbanburg but it would look suspicious if my father failed to hand you over when asked.'

'Are you going to kill me?'

'To be honest with you, the thought had crossed my mind, but you've served me too well for your death to be on my conscience.

No, you can change your name and join one of my father's knarrs as a ship's boy.' He smiled with relief.

'I think I might enjoy that. Would you like me to kill Roswitha's husband before I go?
He's a member of the king's escort.'

'How would that help? That would just give credence to the story.'

'I suppose so. When do I leave?'

'You can depart with us and then travel on to Bebbanburg, but separately from my father. If anyone asks for you I'll say that you ran away. Does anyone in Lord Ulric's household know you?'

'No, I keep myself to myself.'

'Good, what new name will you choose?'

'I don't know. I rather like Bleddyn. Ah, well; perhaps Acwel.'

He grinned at me to let me know he was jesting. It meant killer in English.

'Sorry. I shouldn't be flippant.'

'No, you bloody well shouldn't. By all that's Holy, Bleddyn, your situation is serious, and my good name and the king's would be in jeopardy if this story was ever given credence.'

'I know. I apologise, lord. Perhaps Anarawd?

'What does it mean?'

I knew Bleddyn meant son of the wolf, but my knowledge of the Brythonic languages was limited.

'Free of shame,' he replied with a cheeky grin.

I laughed. 'It suits you, but a more inappropriate name for an assassin would be hard to find.'

When I said goodbye to my father I saw Bleddyn out of the corner of my eye as he slipped away into the trees. He had the horse I'd given him and a few coins together with some rough homespun clothes to change into. A few days later he would appear at the jetty near Bebbanburg on foot with a letter from my father to one of his sea captains. No doubt his horse would find its way home to Alnwic, if it wasn't stolen en route. He would have to burn the clothes he was wearing now. Henceforth he was Anarawd the ship's boy.

I would miss him and my sons would do so even more so. They didn't believe me when I said that he'd run away until I explained that he was wanted for theft. What I didn't ever tell them was that the thing he'd stolen was the previous king's life.

~~~

Two years later Æthelwold had a son and heir. It should have been the cause for celebration but instead the king was heartbroken. His wife, Æthelthryth, had died from loss of blood shortly after her son was safely delivered. He mourned her for six months then he sent out a summons for the Witan to meet at Bebbanburg.

When I arrived there to help my father and his reeve to prepare to host the gathering I was greeted by devastating news. My father had died in his sleep the previous night. My son Octa had come with me as he was due to travel on to Lindisfarne to start his education there now that he was twelve. Hilda and Uuffa had stayed at Alnwic, as had my brother, so it fell to Octa to comfort me and to help me to cope. Apart from the meeting of the Witan, there was now a funeral to arrange.

I'm not sure how I got through the next two weeks. It all seems like a blur now. Octa was magnificent. He might have only been twelve but he got on with things. He would come to me for decisions and then get whatever I decided carried out. I think he grew from boyhood to manhood over those two weeks and I was immensely proud of him.

The funeral was held on the first day of October. It was a sunny day with barely a cloud in the sky, but the wind off the sea was bitterly cold. I had intended to ask for him to be buried on

Lindisfarne but he had left instructions that he was to be laid to rest in the graveyard below the fortress beside my mother. At least the bulk of the rock on which the stronghold stood shielded us from the worst of the wind.

Once we had sent my father off with all due ceremony, Octa and I turned our attention to the meeting of the Witan the following week. One of my ancestors had built a separate hall to accommodate the king and his family on his infrequent visits so at least Octa and I wouldn't have to vacate the lord's hall. The warriors' hall would be full to overflowing though with the men who'd come with me, the Bebbanburg warband and the king's escort.

The rest of the Witan – the ealdormen, the bishops and the abbots, plus their various entourages – would have to camp outside the walls. The problem, as ever, would be water. There was a well inside the stronghold and another in the settlement, but that could only cope with the inhabitants' requirements. Extra barrels of water would have be carted up to the fortress to cope with the extra numbers living there as it was and then there were the hundreds camping outside.

There was no river near Bebbanburg, not even a stream, so the visitors' encampment would have to be sited several miles away on the far side of Budle Bay, upstream of where the Belford Burn ran into the sea. Either that or my men would have to cart water in barrels from there to wherever the encampment was sited.

Octa suggested that that was just too much extra trouble and I agreed with him. The nobles and the churchmen wouldn't be happy making a five mile journey to and from the fortress every day, but they would just have to make the best of it. With any luck, they might dislike the arrangements enough that this would be the last time that the Witan met at Bebbanburg.

To add to everyone's discomfort the day of the meeting dawned with the sun hidden behind clouds and the sea the colour of iron.

Rain was in the air, but it was so cold that when it inevitably arrived it turned out to be a mixture of sleet alternating with short bouts of hail. This did not make for a comfortable ride from the camp the far side of Budle Bay and everyone arrived in a foul mood.

Archbishop Ecgbert entered my hall first and I greeted him with Octa at my side. Benches had been arranged in rows in the body of the hall with three chairs on the low dais at the far end. The other sixteen ealdormen, three bishops and a dozen abbots followed him and joined him at the central heath, where they tried to restore some feeling to their cold limbs. I took my seat on the dais with Octa sitting on my left.

I had no idea what the king's plans for Bebbanburg and Alnwic were but I had assumed that I would inherit the former and my son was there to represent the latter. Æthelwold Moll entered grim faced and everyone stood in silence until he'd seated himself on my right. Ever since the death of his wife he'd worn nothing but a black robe but today he had chosen to put on the same green one he'd worn for his wedding. The circlet of gold on his head glinted, reflecting the dancing flames of the fire.

'This is a sad day,' he began. 'Seofon, I'm sorry that I couldn't be here for the funeral of my foster-brother but I feel his death keenly. I shall miss him and I mourn for him.'

I think that most of those present had either forgotten, or were too young, to know that he and my father had been brought up together as boys. I felt proud of the association and was grateful for his kind words.

'Thank you, Cyning. His demise was untimely and I know that Northumbria will be all the poorer for it.'

'Which brings me to the matter of his replacement. I am well aware that King Eadbehrt had intended to combine the shires of Alnwic and Bebbanburg to better defend the east coast of Bernicia and to make you the ealdorman after Ulfric was gone. I see no reason not to proceed with that plan, provided the Witan have no objection.'

He looked around the hall, fixing every man there with his eyes, before nodded his satisfaction.

'So be it. Congratulations Seofon. I suggest that the combined shire should be named Islandshire as it includes Lindisfarne and the other offshore isles.'

'Thank you, Cyning. I am most grateful.'

My head was full of what this now meant for my family and I also wondered what to do about the hall at Alnwic. However, there would be time for that later. I was meant to be presiding, but I had no idea why Æthelwold had called the meeting. His next words dumbfounded me and everyone else present. The only people who knew, it seemed, were Ecgbert and Cynewulf of Lindisfarne.

'The death of my foster brother, who was the same age as me, has emphasised that the time that we have on this earth is all too short. I have decided that the burden of kingship is too heavy for me and I therefore propose to abdicate. I want to devote however many months or years I have left to preparation for the new life. I will therefore retire to Lindisfarne to live out my days as a simple monk.

'I give the care of my son, Ethelred, to my foster-brother's son, Seofon. You now need to decide who should replace me. I will travel with you when you return to Lindisfarne, Bishop Cynewulf, if I may.'

'Of course, Cyning.'

'No, not Cyning,' he said taking of his gold circlet and handing it to me. 'Just Brother Æthelwold from now on. I shall sign the deed of abdication today.' With that he strode out of the hall.

The stunned silence was broken by excited chatter as soon as the door closed behind him. I had trouble restoring order and banged the pommel of my dagger on the table for some time before the babble of conversation died away.

'Thank you. Æthelwold's abdication came as much of a surprise to me as it evidently did to most of you.'

I looked at Ecgbert as I said this and a smile played at the corner of his mouth.

'It now falls to us to elect a new king. As this has come to all of us as something of a shock, I believe that those who are eligible to be considered should have a little time to prepare what they wish to say. I shall represent the interests of the Ætheling Ethelred. Although still a baby he could still be selected as king with a council of regency to rule until he is fourteen. I therefore cannot continue to preside over the Witan. Bishop Cynewulf, will you please take over when we reconvene in, shall we say, an hour's time?' He nodded and I retired to my private chamber at the back of the hall with Octa.

'You didn't know?' he asked me as soon as we were alone.

'No, of course not. Æthelwold is being foolish. He is so depressed over the death of his wife and now his best friend that he has forgotten his obligations to the kingdom. I'm told that he can't even bear to look upon his son because he blames him for Æthelthryth's death. Now he has saddled your mother and me with his upbringing.'

'Is that such an arduous responsibility?'

'Not in itself, but he will be a strong contender for the throne as he grows up and that will make us enemies. The next king may well decide to eliminate him and, because I am now his guardian, my family is vulnerable too. This is a mess.'

'You don't think the Witan will elect him with you as regent then?'

'No, I do not. No-one can prove that I was involved in Oswulf's assassination now that Bleddyn has disappeared but, as you are well aware, the rumours still circulate. I am therefore tainted. I'll be surprised if I remain as hereræswa under the new king.'

The Witan eventually chose Alchred, Ealdorman of Loidis, to succeed Æthelwold. He claimed to be an ætheling in that he was descended from Eadric, Ida's fourth son. His cause was supported by the archbishop, mainly because the man was married to his niece, Osgifu, brother of King Oswulf.

I had spoken eloquently in favour of the baby Ethelred as the last descendent of King Æthelfrith, the first King of a united Northumbria, but few wanted a child on the throne after what happened when his grandfather, Osred, was a boy king.

There were other contenders but all the churchmen followed the archbishop's lead, even Cynewulf. It helped that Alchred was a devout Christian and had even talked about sending missionaries across to pagan Germania. I watched gloomily as the gold circlet was placed upon his head by Ecgbert and then we all lined up to swear him fealty.

When it came to my turn he gave me an icy stare and bent forward to whisper in my ear.

'You and I need to talk about the murder of my wife's brother. I know you sent the boy Bleddyn to him and he is rumoured to have entered Oswulf's chamber just before he was killed. Then Æthelwold sent him back to you. This stinks worse than fish left out in the sun. You will come to see me at Eoforwīc next month where we can discuss this matter properly.'

I nodded, my heart in my boots. Once Alchred questioned Roswitha he would have all the proof he needed to convict me of complicity in Regicide.

Chapter Eight – The Court of Charlemagne

764 to 770 AD

The wind in my hair and the salt spray in my face as the birlinn crashed through wave after wave did much to lift my spirits. I felt the brooding menace posed by Alchred's accession to the throne lifting to be replaced by a sense of freedom as Bebbanburg dropped below the horizon behind us.

I grinned at Bleddyn – or Anarawd as he was now called – and he grinned back. The young boy had changed; now he was a brawny lad of seventeen and one of the sailors who formed the permanent crew. The rowers were found from amongst the warriors of my warband.

Late autumn was not the time to venture across the German Ocean but I had little choice. Just when I had inherited Bebbanburg and been given Islandshire to govern I had to abandon both and flee the kingdom. I was under no illusion that Alchred would find me guilty and execute me and I also feared for the safety of my family and little Ethelred. Alchred might have a reputation as a devoutly religious man but he was also known for his vindictiveness.

Consequently, at the age of forty I had gone into exile. I took my family, my brother and his wife, the servants and those warriors who wanted to come with me and we set sail in three birlinns and two knarrs for Frankia. I was gratified that most of my men decided to accompany us, even Cerdic, the captain of the warband, and many other married men came with their families. I already had a warehouse in Paris, which was my trading base on the Continent, and that is where I intended to settle. I could earn a comfortable living as a merchant. It was not what I was used to, or what I wanted to do, but there was little other option unless I wanted to become either a pirate or a mercenary captain.

With a sigh I left the prow and went aft to check on my family. The boys were fine but Hilda was a poor sailor and had been violently sick as soon as we hit the choppy motion of the open sea. Thankfully she was sleeping and I left her to the care of her slaves. Beckoning the boys to follow me, I emerged from the awning that had been erected to give my family some shelter and privacy.

My sons were now ten and twelve and, whilst their mother wasn't there to panic about their safety, I thought it was a good opportunity to teach them how to climb the rigging. I had been taught as a boy but now, at the age of forty I was happy to leave such antics to younger men. After a quick word to the captain I called Anarawd across to teach the boys the technique. The mast was supported by eight stays, one each fore and aft, three each side attached to the gunwale. Two of the latter formed a double brace, spaced a foot apart with ropes tied horizontally every six inches to act as a ladder.

This was how the lookout climbed to the junction of the spar - from which the sail was suspended - and the mast. It was also how the sail was reefed. The sailors and ship's boys climbed up to the lookout's position and edged out along the spar with their feet gripping a slack rope behind the sail between the end of the spar and the mast. They were then able to haul the sail up and tie the reefing points whilst the ship was hove to. It was a skill that took time to master. The rope could swing to and fro quite alarmingly in a pitching sea and many a boy had fallen to his death: either being crushed when they landed inside the boat, or drowning if he landed in the sea as precious few could swim.

However, the object of today's game was to race up either side of the rope ladder and touch the bare feet of the lookout. It took Octa a little longer than the smaller Uuffa to get the hang of climbing, but when he felt that both boys were ready Anarawd glanced my way. I nodded and he yelled 'go.'

At first Uuffa took the lead but then Octa's greater strength and stamina allowed him to catch up. I was delighted when both my sons slapped the feet of the amused lookout at the same time.

'It's a tie,' I called up at the two grinning boys, their eyes alight with excitement.

Then I was brought down to earth by a scream behind me. I turned around to see that Hilda had woken and was standing behind me, her face a picture of horror.

'Get down here right now!' she screamed at them.

'Stay right where you are.' I called before turning to confront my wife.

'Are you mad? Do you want to kill them?' I asked her. 'If they came down at speed in response to the urgency your cry demanded one or both would be in danger of falling.
Going up at speed, now that they have been taught how to do it, is relatively easy.
Coming down is not and needs to be done calmly and slowly.'

'They should never have been up there in the first place,' she shouted at me, her face almost purple with rage. 'What were you thinking of?'

'Preparing them to be men,' I told her curtly. 'I did it when I was a boy and so did Renweard, and my father before us. I took in a reef in a strong blow when I was thirteen. Their boyhood is fast becoming a thing of the past, Hilda. If the ship's boys can do it, they need to be able to as well, if they want to earn respect.'

Hilda said nothing for a moment but the angry glare spoke volumes. She glanced at the sailors and the grinning warriors.

'We'll continue this conversation later when we're alone. Now get my sons down from there.'

She retreated to the awning and I told the boys to come down slowly.

Hilda said nothing to me for the rest of the voyage but I heard an angry exchange between her and our sons. I went to intervene but I stopped myself just in time. I was on their side and I decided that I would only make matters worse.

Aix-la-Chapelle was the capital of the King of the Franks, Pipin the Short, the first Carolingian monarch. He controlled Neustria, Frisia and Austrasia whilst his elder brother, Carloman, ruled Swabia and Burgundy. However, Paris was still the major centre for commerce and the king or his elder son visited there from time to time to hold court in the old palace on an island in the centre of the River Seine.

When I arrived in December 764 Pipin had just turned fifty and his elder son, Charles, who was twenty two, assisted him to run the kingdom. Matters were complicated because the original kingdom had been divided between Pipin and his brother when their father died. I gathered that it was quite usual on the Continent for a father's kingdom to be divided amongst all his sons under something called Salic Law. Charles had a thirteen year old brother and on Pipin's death the kingdom would be further divided. It was an idiotic arrangement that was destined to make brothers bitter rivals and it weakened the kingdom overall.

I was required to present myself at court if I wanted to settle in Frankia as an exiled noble. Thankfully I was saved the journey to Aix-la-Chapelle as Charles was on one of his infrequent visits to Paris. I had taken Renweard, Octa and Uuffa with me as well as Cerdic and two of my warriors to clear a path through the crowded streets. Hilda still wasn't speaking to me so she stayed at the place I'd rented pro tem. As we rode I couldn't help but draw a favourable comparison between Paris and the streets of Eoforwīc, Lundenwic and Loidis.

Here all the important buildings, the homes of the nobles and rich merchants were built of stone and the main church – that of the

Monastery of Saint-Germain-des-Prés – had been in existence for over two hundred years, long before Lindisfarne Monastery was founded. The church was both larger and more magnificent than any which existed anywhere in England.

Of course, there were the usual wattle and daub and timber hovels of the poor and somewhat better built huts occupied by the artisans, like any other town or settlement. As usual the streets were muddy and strewn with filth but, as we crossed the timber bridge onto the Île de la Cité, we found the streets on the far side were paved with small stones like a Roman road. There was rubbish and other detritus in the gutters but the main thoroughfare was clear.

Our horses' hooves sounded loud in my ears as the noise of them striking the stones reverberated off the buildings that lined the street from the bridge to the gateway that led into the palace. We were challenged as we reached the entrance and had to surrender all our weapons before we were allowed to proceed. Boys came running to take our horses as we reached the doorway into the king's hall. We dismounted and, leaving Cerdic and his men to make sure our horses were properly cared for, we climbed the stone steps up to the magnificent doorway.

The construction was all in stone, but not rough cut as in our few stone buildings. The masons had faced each exposed surface so that it was perfectly flat; the chisel marks showed how painstaking this work must have been.

We were met just inside the hall by a man who introduced himself in Latin as the princeps domus, a term I had last heard at the Mercian court. No doubt Offa had got the idea from the Continent. I had learnt quite soon after arriving that there were dozens of different languages and dialects spoken in Frankia. Each region seemed to have several.

Thankfully nobles and the clergy spoke Latin as a matter of course.

The man told us to proceed through the door in front of us and wait to be summoned forward to the throne. Unlike every other hall I'd been in, where the entrance door led directly into the main hall, here there was a room between the entrance and the hall. I thought it a good idea as it kept the cold wind, rain and snow from blowing into the hall every time someone entered. It was an idea I intended to copy if I was ever allowed to return to Bebbanburg.

The hall was big, it was packed and it was cold. There was no central hearth, just a brazier in each corner which made little difference, except to produce smoke, not all of which made it through the holes in the sloping ceiling above. Even for early January it was cold and the stone walls and floor seemed to suck the heat out of you. It may have been my imagination, but I thought it was colder inside than outside. But the hall was undoubtedly impressive.

Prince Charles sat on a raised dais at the far end of the hall. A servant would come and find someone in the crowd and take him, or them, to stand at the foot of the stone steps leading up to the throne where they would wait their turn to go up and have a brief word with the prince. It struck me as being all rather formal and a bit pompous. No English noble would take kindly to being told what to do by a servant, however grand his designation. However, I was a stranger here, and one seeking refuge at that, so I waited my turn with as much patience as I could muster.

My companions had expected to accompany me, but they were rudely told to stay where they were. The prince only wanted to see me. That angered me but I tried not to show it as I followed the servant towards the throne.

'Ah, Lord Seofon, welcome to Frankia,' Charles said in Latin when it was my turn to walk up the steps. 'I understand that you were the last King of Northumbria's army commander. Why are you now an exile?'

'Northumbria is not a safe place for the friends of the last king, Domine,' I replied with a smile.

'So I understand,' he replied, but without returning my smile. 'In fact I have a letter here from King Alchred asking me to return you to Northumbria where you are wanted for regicide.'

My mouth dropped open in surprise and I felt physically sick. It sounded as if I and my family had walked into a trap.

'I therefore find myself in something of a quandary,' he went on. 'Offa of Mercia is growing too powerful and is charging too high a levy on trade between our two countries. I therefore need to cultivate Alchred and support him against Offa; at the same time I want him to lower the tariff he charges on trade between us so that we can export to Northumbria instead of the south of England. You understand my predicament?'

'Perfectly, Domine. In your shoes I wouldn't hesitate.'

He looked at me in surprise. At least I'd wiped away the look of disinterest he had effected up to now.

'Unless, of course, I had something more valuable to offer you,' I continued.

'And have you?'

'I think so. You have soldiers but not much in the way of fighting ships, I think.'

'And why should I need them?'

I lowered my voice so that the hovering servant, impatiently waiting to usher me away so that he could introduce the next man in line, couldn't hear.

'You father is dying by all accounts and he plans to divide the kingdom between you and your brother. In addition your uncle rules over part of Austrasia and Frisia – both of which have a long coastline on the German Ocean. If you wish to expand your part of the kingdom, you might find having the ability to land men all along that coast useful.'

I knew that the Franks had no warships to speak of. We had developed boats that could cross the sea when the Angles, Jutes and Saxons had first raided and then invaded what was then called Britannia. These had been craft that were rowed. We learned the art of sailing from the Scots who settled in Dalriada. They had adapted the old Roman galleys, which were unsuited to rough seas, into sleeker, more sea-worthy ships.

The trading ships that the Franks operated kept to the coast, as the Romans had. Sailing across large stretches of water in all weathers was a very different matter. I had learned all this, not from my time at Lindisfarne where study was almost entirely confined to the scriptures, but from my father who had an inquisitive mind and had talked to those who had studied ancient books and scrolls on the Continent, and in the libraries at Jarrow and Wearmouth.

However, I felt that the design of our ships could still be improved. They needed a higher freeboard and a broader beam to make them more stable but I had never had the time to develop my ideas.

My mind had wandered and I realised that Charles was speaking to me again.

'I will consider what you have said. In the meantime you may settle here under my protection for the moment; and you may operate as a merchant for now.'

The servant tugged at my sleeve to indicate that the audience was over. I nearly struck the man for his impudence but I managed to keep my temper in check. Once we had returned to the floor of the hall he was about to leave me to find the next man on his list, but I grabbed his upper arm and squeezed his feeble biceps so hard that the man squeaked in pain.

'Don't ever touch me again if you wish to continue to live. Where I come from, for a slave or a servant to touch a lord without permission is a crime punishable by death.' The young man looked shaken.

'I'm sorry, Domine,' he stuttered in poor Latin. 'But I'm not a servant, let alone a slave. My father is a noble; it is a great honour to be selected to serve the prince.'

I left thinking that things were done very differently here. For the first time I realised how much I already missed Northumbria.

~~~

The next four years passed uneventfully, at least for my family. Hilda and I were too much in love with one another for her to keep the silent treatment going for very long. I tried to behave towards her as normally as I could and slowly her frosty demeanour melted. We had one final heated exchange about the incident during the crossing after we'd landed and then made love passionately to celebrate our reconciliation.

We bought a place to live in on a small estate just outside Paris which resembled a small Roman villa. It was a vast improvement on our old hall as far as comfort went, but I could never bring myself to regard it as home. Octa, and later Uuffa, were accepted as students at the Monastery of Saint-Germain-des-Prés. At the age of fourteen Octa returned to the estate to start training as a warrior whilst I concentrated on building up my mercantile business. Renweard helped me on the maritime side and we prospered.

Both Hilda and I missed the boys when they left. When Octa returned he lived in the warriors' hall with the other young men under training. Some were Angles like us, mainly the sons of the warriors who had accompanied us, but many were Franks who were keen to learn how we fought. Most left me when they were trained and joined the army of King Pipin, but a few stayed and gradually I built up my warband, funded by profits from trading.

Pipin's brother died soon after our arrival, so that eliminated one problem for Prince Charles. I did wonder whether that would affect us as all of Austrasia and Frisia now came under his father's rule, but we heard nothing. No doubt he had other things on his mind. Frankia was engulfed by wars on a number of fronts; it was complicated so I didn't bother to try and understand what was going on until Pipin died and his two sons were elected by the Council of Nobles to rule Frankia jointly. It was an idea that was never going to work.

My knarr captains brought me news of what was happening in Northumbria. My shire of Islandshire had been given to a cousin of King Alchred. I hated to think of him living in my stronghold of Bebbanburg but there was little I could do about it for now. In 766 Archbishop Ecgbert died and a monk called Ethelbert was chosen by Alchred to succeed him.

Offa continued to expand Mercia's powerbase, taking over Kent, Essex and the Kingdom of the South Saxons as vassal states. His conflict with Wessex continued, as did the raids by the Welsh on his western border, but I heard nothing more about his demand that Luncæstershire be handed over.

I had also heard rumours that Alchred and Ethelbert were planning to send missionaries to pagan Germania, but it wasn't until King Charles sent for me that I discovered more. Thankfully he was in Paris on a visit and so I was spared the long journey to Aix-la-Chapelle.

This time I was conducted into a private chamber off the main hall rather than have to suffer the indignity of waiting in line for an audience. The room was warm, heated by a brazier in one corner, with wall hangings to take the chill off the stone walls.

Charles sat behind a table littered with scrolls. He waved me into the chair on the other side of the table and as I sat down I saw that the scrolls were all maps.

'How many men do you have now?'

'Warriors? Just over a hundred and twenty in my warband and another eighteen being trained. I also have enough sailors to crew my four knarrs and to helm and handle the sails on my four birlinns.'

I had built three more ships over the past four years and now each knarr was routinely accompanied by a birlinn. It was enough to warn off pirates and the like, especially as the knarrs and their escorts usually travelled in pairs if venturing into dangerous waters.

'I see. And how many men can you carry in your knarrs?'

'More than I have.'

'How many?' he asked again, impatiently.

'Each of my knarrs can probably carry forty men for a short voyage. I could probably squeeze another ten warriors into each of my birlinns. Another two hundred in addition to my own men.'

'I see. That's probably enough for what I have planned.'

'Of course, you could always hire some of the coastal trading galleys you Franks use: that is if your aim is to invade Frisia.'

He looked at me sharply. He was presumably under the misapprehension that noone knew that his brother, Carloman, had escaped from the stronghold in Burgundy, where Charles had imprisoned him, and had taken refuge in Frisia, the one kingdom in the Frankish Domain which had remained loyal to him. Frisia lay along the coast to the north of Austrasia and it was not unreasonable for me to think that our conversation was leading in that direction.

'You are more astute than I gave you credit for. You should know that Alchred has written to me several times asking me to either return you to Northumbria to face trial or to send him your head. I think that the fact that I have let you and your family live here in freedom, and allowed you to prosper as a merchant, is a favour that deserves one in return.'

'What favour would that be, Domine?' I asked with some trepidation.

'I want you to go to Marienhafe in Brokmerland, where Carloman is reputed to be living and kill him for me. Mind you it mustn't look like an assassination. I don't want people accusing me of fratricide.'

'That's a very tall order, Domine. Killing him might be accomplished without too much of a problem, but making it look accidental might be difficult, very difficult.'

'Why? I suggest you attack the place looking like English raiders and kill him during the fight. What's the problem with that?'

'Very well, Domine. It will take me time to gather my ships together. I will also need to buy or get more of our style of helmets and shields made for your soldiers. I can probably have everything ready by next spring.'

'I had hoped you could leave earlier than that, but it will have to do. I'll send one of my agents to you. He's a Frisian so he can spy out the defences of Marienhafe for you. The extra men will report to you at the beginning of March. Be ready by then. Oh, you can take your brother Renweard with you and your elder son, but leave the rest of your family here.'

I stiffened in anger. He obviously didn't trust me to do as he asked and wanted hostages to make sure I didn't abscond. I was about to say something unwise when he pushed one of the maps towards me so that I could see it.

'When you have done that I want you to find out what's happening in Saxony. I hear that Alchred has sent Northumbrian missionaries to convert the pagans living there to Christianity. Saxony is in my sphere of interest, not his. Find out what's going on and
report back to me.'

Chapter Nine – Frisia

Summer 771 AD

Much against his will, I persuaded Renweard to stay behind in Paris to look after my family and our business, although there wasn't much trading he could do until the ships returned. He said that he would try to rent cargo space on other merchants' knarrs, but we were all in competition so I wasn't too sanguine about that. At least he could go on recruiting boys to train as warriors so that we could, at least, replace our losses – hopefully - when I returned.

Uuffa was nearly seventeen by the time I set out and pleaded to be allowed to accompany me. He was a promising warrior and I was tempted to take him, but two things stopped me. King Charles wouldn't agree, even when I pointed out that my brother was now staying, and the fact that Hilda would have killed me had I taken both her sons on such a perilous mission.

'You're forty seven. It's time you took things easy instead of wandering off to play the hero,' she chided me one night. 'Let Renweard go.'

'I don't suppose that his wife would thank you for your suggestion.'

'Hah! I think she regrets marrying Renweard. You must know that he only wed her to get his hands on the vill. From what she tells me they have never made love.'

This came as a complete surprise to me. I had imagined that they had no children because she was barren. I thought about this. Hilda and I didn't cavort in bed as much as we had done when we were younger, but the thought that my brother just wasn't interested came as a shock.

'Has he never? Are you sure?'

'It would appear not. She suspects the reason but she has no proof.'

'What does she suspect?'

Hilda looked uncomfortable and I knew that she regretted saying as much as she had.

'I can't say.'

No matter how much I badgered her she remained adamant that she would not break a confidence. With that I had to be satisfied for now, but it nagged away at me. I had to know what my brother's secret was. We had always been close and I had never suspected that he didn't like women. For a moment I wondered if he had a clandestine passion for other men, or perhaps boys. I knew such relationships existed, although they were always kept secret, but I was certain that wasn't Renweard's vice.

The problem kept troubling me until eventually I realised what it could be. My brother wasn't unwilling, he was incapable of making love. I knew that there were men who had this difficulty. If it became known they were often teased and given the nickname soft sword. That had to be Renweard's problem. I felt for him, but it wasn't something I could ever talk to him about. It would ruin our close relationship if I queried his virility as a man. I put the matter out of my mind and concentrated on the task in hand.

A fleet of eight ships was always going to evince interest and we hadn't gone much beyond the mouth of the River Seine before a knarr crossing from somewhere on the South Saxon coast saw us and scuttled back whence it had come. By the time we reached the narrows between Kent and the western tip of Austrasia three warships had come out of Dover to inspect us, but they gave us a wide berth.

Being on board with my son gave Octa and me time to talk and get to know each other again. We had been close until he went away to be educated and then, when he returned, he spent his time with the other young warriors. I learned one thing which surprised me. Uuffa was not happy with his lot in life.

'Whilst Uncle Renweard seems content to be your deputy, Uuffa is ambitious,' he told me as we continued east along the coast of Austrasia. 'He wants to make a name for himself; being number four in the family pecking order is never going to be enough for him.'

I thought about what Octa had said as a group of islands appeared off our beam as we turned north. We were now in Frisian waters. The wind was coming from the north east and so we had to get the sails down and start to row. In any case it was time to slip below the horizon until dark.

My mind returned to the problem of Uuffa. I didn't want to lose him to the service of some mercenary captain or even to serve King Charles, but what could I offer him. Renweard was effectively my partner in our business and I intended to make Octa the captain of my warband soon. Cerdic was getting old and proposed to settle down in Paris for good. Then I had an idea. The captain of this birlinn was also in his fifties. Perhaps he could teach Uuffa what he knew and my son could take over from him.

Happy that I had reached a solution to the problem – hopefully – I began to think again about my strategy for eliminating King Carloman.

~~~

Leaving the rest of the fleet hidden to the north of one of the low-lying, sandy islands that lay offshore, I took the smallest of my knarrs and sailed towards Marienhafe. The sea was calm with just a few little waves lapping against the hull as we progressed slowly over the blue sea under a sky with scarcely a cloud to break the bright sunshine. The wind was coming from the east, which was a relief because it meant that we wouldn't have to tack on the return journey.

I took Charles' agent and Anarawd with me on the knarr. I distrusted the Frisian spy, whose name was Bavo and so, when I set him ashore to study the place's defences in more detail, I sent Anarawd with him.

From what I could see at a distance the port had a single jetty with several knarrs and smaller trading vessels tied to it, a few warehouses behind the jetty and a timber built church on a knoll behind them. A dozen fishing boats were beached on the sand beside the jetty. I could also see a few roofs either side of the church so doubtless these huts housed the fishermen and those employed at the port. There were three more substantial dwellings which presumably belonged to merchants.

A mile or so behind the port I could see a palisade on top of a low rise in the flat landscape. There were two towers either side of the main gate and the roof of what I presumed was a hall inside the compound. The palisade didn't look that high, perhaps ten or twelve feet?

Nothing was moving in or out of the port and the only activity I could see was one of the knarrs being loaded. Satisfied that I had gleaned as much as I could from the seaward side, we went about and sailed back to join the others.

~~~

'What happened?' I asked Bavo when they returned from their reconnaissance mission.

I had glanced at Anarawd when the two had entered the canopy erected over the aft deck to give me some privacy whilst we were at anchor. He had shaken his head imperceptibly to indicate that nothing untoward had occurred whilst the two of them were ashore.

'We landed on the beach to the north of Marienhafe and were unobserved as far as I could tell.'

He looked at Anarawd for confirmation, who nodded.

'We made our way into the port and found a place to grab some sleep until it was light. As you suspected, lord, the port has no defences apart from a small watch who patrol the streets at night and guard the jetty during the day. As far as we could see their main duty is to assess the value of every cargo that's landed or loaded and levy a tax on it. One knarr departed and another came in whilst we were there.'

'Did no-one question your presence?'

'No, lord. There was the odd beggar trying to cadge a coin and the odd boy offering his sister to pleasure the sailors, so I pretended to be one of the beggars with my mute brother.'

I looked a little sceptical. Anarawd was a blond haired, muscular youth whilst Bavo was small, skinny and dark haired. He reminded me of an undernourished rat.

'I said that we had different mothers,' he explained. 'Anyway, we waited until midday and went to a tavern for some bread and cheese. I listened to the chatter but there was nothing much of interest. A few mentioned the strange knarr that had sailed towards the port yesterday and then sailed away again but the general consensus was that it had a stupid captain who was lost. A few commented that he would be lucky not to get stranded on the numerous sandbanks that littered the sea offshore.'

That was more than useful, it was vital information. We would obviously have to sound the bottom as we made our way inshore. I began to revise my opinion of Bavo.

He looked at Anarawd who continued the report.

'We left the town by the only road out which took us close to the fortress. We tried not to seem too interested in it as we walked past but between us we managed to get a pretty good ideas of the defences. The palisade is about twice the height of a man but it is on top of a rampart of earth some four feet high with a ditch in front of it which is about the same depth.'

That was disappointing news. I had hoped to use ladders to scale the palisade.

'The gatehouse appears to be strongly defended,' he went on. 'The gates are kept closed unless someone wants to enter or leave and the two watchtowers either side of the gate are manned by two men in each.'

'Is that the only means of access?' I asked.

'No, there is a small postern gate on the west side; the side that the road passes the fortress. There may be one on the east as well, but I doubt it as there is no road or path there. There wasn't one on the north side.'

'Do you know if the postern is kept locked?'

'Perhaps not. There was someone walking ahead of us who turned off onto the path leading to the postern and he opened it and went inside without having to wait.' 'Did you form any estimate as to numbers in the garrison?' This time it was Bavo who answered.

'We could see the roofs of various buildings poking up over the top of the palisade. The one in the centre, the largest, is probably King Carloman's hall. We could only see the gable ends and they were built of dressed stone. There was another, larger wooden hall near the main gate, presumably where his unmarried soldiers live. I counted eighteen other buildings. Of course that would include stores, stables and so on but, from the number of huts and size of the second hall I wouldn't have thought that the garrison could number more than a hundred, probably less.'

'Thank you, you've done well – both of you.'

I gave them each a small pouch of silver coins and they bowed and left.

The most likely way in seemed to be via the postern gate, but I couldn't see how we could reach it with enough men to capture it and keep the main gates open long enough for my main force to reach it. I puzzled over the problem for the rest of the day and was no nearer a solution when night fell.

I tossed and turned for half the night, unable to sleep, then I had an idea.

~~~

Although the land was flat and devoid of undulations deep enough to hide our approach, there was a small wood about a quarter of a mile to the south-east of the stronghold. By dawn I was studying the place for myself, having been dropped off on the beach that Anarawd and Bavo had used the previous day. They had come with me, as had Octa and two more of my warband. Although I was now less suspicious of Bavo, I wasn't about to risk being betrayed.

I calculated that it would take fully armed men between eight and ten minutes to reach the main gates from here. It was a long time to expect a small infiltration party to keep the gates open once the garrison had been alerted.

I sucked my teeth in frustration. Suddenly the gates swung open and a group of ten horsemen rode out and headed down towards the port. Eight of them were heavy cavalry such as I'd seen in Paris. They were different to the mounted warriors in England in that they sat on bigger saddles with something the Franks called étriers hanging from leather straps attached to the saddle. This gave them a much more secure seat from which to fight on horseback than our horsemen had, whose legs hung free. It was an idea I intended to copy when, or perhaps if, I ever returned to Northumbria.

Rather than chain mail, they wore padded linen jerkins to which overlapping metal plates had been sewn. A leather under-helmet protected their ears and neck, over which they wore a round metal helmet shaped like a pot. They carried a small round shield and a spear intended for stabbing rather than throwing. A long sword hung from a baldric over the right shoulder and they all wore a dagger on a belt around their waist.

Their trousers were tied around the calf with leather ribbons and they had spurs attached to their shoes, another idea I intended to copy. Unlike King Charles' heavy cavalry, who all wore blue tunics under their armoured jerkins, Carloman's horsemen wore any colour other than blue. Otherwise they looked identical to them.

The man who led them was dressed in yellow trousers and a thick green tunic trimmed at cuff, neck and hem with rabbit fur. Over this he wore a red cloak. Beside him rode a more sombrely dressed youth carrying a banner. It was swallow tailed with red roses on a green background, which I knew was Carloman's personal standard.

Another idea began to form in my mind.

'Walk down to the port and see if you can find out the reason for Carloman's visits and how often he makes them,' I told Anarawd and Bavo.

They nodded and made their way through the woods so that they would emerge unseen by the sentries in the two watchtowers.

I waited impatiently for their return but it was late afternoon before they reappeared. 'Well?'

'He went into the church, lord, or at least we arrived in time to see him come out again,' Anarawd replied.

'We found out that he visits the church twice a week, once to see the priest and once for the service on Sunday,' Bavo added.

From what they had said I was fairly certain that Carloman went to make confession of his sins on the Saturday in order to purify himself for mass on the following day. All I had to do, therefore, was to attack him on his way to mass tomorrow.

'Did you find out when mass is said on a Sunday?'

'Just after dawn and again when the sun is at its zenith,' Bavo told me.

'I doubted that Carloman would want to attend the first service; the midday one seemed much more likely and I made my plans accordingly.

~~~

As we marched into the port the streets suddenly emptied as the inhabitants ran for the safety of their homes. This time Carloman had brought an escort of twenty men all of whom, except four who had been left outside to look after the horses, had entered the church for the service.

Those guarding the horses had sat down to play a game of dice and didn't notice my men until a dozen of them surrounded them. They made short work of cutting their throats. Octa took a hundred warriors and surrounded the church while Cerdic secured the side door with another twenty. I then led the remainder in through the main entrance.

Without a word my men rapidly lined the inside walls of the church and faced inwards whilst I strode up the aisle with ten men, pushing the worshippers out of my way as I went. When I reached the open-mouthed priest standing beside the altar I turned and surveyed the congregation.

Carloman stood with his hand on his sword in the front row with half a dozen of his men. The rest stood behind him. Like their king, they were uncertain what to do in the face of overwhelming force. I nodded at Bavo, who recited the little speech I'd made him learn.

'The first man to draw a sword dies,' he told them. 'We have no wish to defile the interior of a church with blood. You are heavily outnumbered; quite apart from the warriors you can see there are another one hundred and thirty outside.'

'What's the meaning of this?' spluttered Carloman. 'This is sacrilege! You are in the presence of your king, drop your weapons now.'

'I'm afraid I don't answer to you, Carloman,' I told him in Latin. 'You will accompany me outside. If you do so and your men remain where they are, no one need get hurt.'

He glared at me and barked out an order. I didn't speak Frisian but the meaning was obvious. His men immediately drew their swords and gathered around their master. This provoked panic amongst the rest of the congregation and they made a rush for the two doors. Of course, when they got there they found their exit blocked by more armed men and the women started screaming, believing they and their children were about to be killed.

However, this left the score of men around their king isolated. I didn't believe in wasting my warriors' lives and so I signalled to the dozen archers I'd brought in with me. Four were hit but the rest of Carlomen's bodyguard charged forward. The church was small and only a few yards separated the two sides. The archers dropped their bows and drew their swords whilst the rest of my men lowered their spears. The fight was fierce but short. Unfortunately, I lost some of my warband – mostly the young, hotheaded, newer members - but within ten minutes the last of the Frisian soldiers lay dead or wounded, including their king.

The priest had hidden behind the altar during the fight and now cautiously peered over it to see if it was all over.

'I regret the defilement of your church, father,' I told him in Latin and handed him a purse of silver. 'This is to pay for the clean-up and re-consecration.'

When I turned back to my men I saw Bavo kneeling beside the dead king sawing off his head with his dagger. I learned later that Charles had offered to pay him a hundred sous, equivalent to five pounds of silver, if he brought the head back.

As I made my way towards the door one of the men Charles had loaned me came running in babbling away in Franconian.

'Now you will pay for your crimes, Englishman,' the priest told me with relish. 'King Carloman was gathering an army to launch a

176

reprisal raid into Saxony. The first five hundred have arrived at the fortress and are hastening here to deal with you.'

Evidently one of the inhabitants of the place had run to the fortress when we appeared. I had no intention of facing so many men in battle and I had to think quickly how I might escape the rapidly closing net.

I thought of trying to convince them to swear allegiance to King Charles now that his brother was dead, but quickly dismissed the idea. He had been adamant that this was to appear like a raid by Northumbrians or Mercians. If I tried to involve him he'd only deny it and I'd probably lose my head as the leader of the raid just to prove his innocence.

There was only one thing to do and that was to make a run for it. However, if we attempted to reach our own fleet beached in the bay five miles away we'd be seen and cut off before we got there. On the other hand there were a few knarrs and other boats in the harbour, so that's where we headed.

We piled aboard the various craft and pressed the surprised sailors on board to cast off and get us under way. Unfortunately, there wasn't room for all two hundred of us and with alarm I saw that Octa was one of those still standing helplessly on the jetty.

'Make for the fishing boats on the beach over there,' I yelled across at him, pointing to where they lay on the sand.

'He nodded and led his thirty men along the coast towards the boats. Just at that moment the first of the Frisian army entered the port and tried to cut my son and his group off. As I watched helplessly Octa led half a dozen towards the small group of the enemy as they emerged beside a warehouse. The rest of his men ran towards the fishing boats and started to haul them down the beach into the sea as my son battled increasing numbers of the enemy.

I couldn't stand by and watch him die so I ordered the helmsmen of the knarr I was on to head back to the jetty. I and the sixty men on the knarr piled ashore but I had the presence of mind to leave four men behind to stop the sailors taking the knarr out to sea and safety.

By the time that I reached him Octa had lost his helmet and had a flesh wound on his head as well as cuts to his thigh and right biceps. I told Anarawd to get his former master back on board the knarr and then waded into the fight.

There were some thirty of the enemy fighting the last of Octa's men but our arrival forced them back into the narrow streets, leaving several dead and wounded behind them. A few of my men carried the dead and helped the wounded back to the knarr whilst we held the growing numbers of our foes back.

I raised my shield to ward off an axe blow and stabbed its owner in the stomach.

'Get a few archers ready on the jetty,' I panted to Cerdic, who was fighting at my side.

He nodded and slipped away, to be replaced by the man behind him. I raised my sword to parry a thrust by another Frisian then smashed him in the face with the boss of my shield. His nose burst like an overripe tomato and he yelped in pain. For a moment he was unable to see so I thrust the point of my sword into his neck.

'All ready,' Cedric panted as he re-joined me.

It was the last thing he ever said. A Frisian thrust his spear at him and he was too slow in deflecting it with his shield. The point aimed at his chest ended up in his eye instead. He fell without a sound and for a moment I stood there stunned. So much for the comfortable retirement I had planned for him. In a rage I slashed my sword at his killer, cutting through the haft of the spear, and tearing a long gaping wound through his leather jerkin and on into his belly. His grey, slimy intestines spilled out like worms and he fell to his knees. I lopped off his head and called on my men to push the enemy back.

We launched one last frenzied attack, driving the Frisians back, and then turned and ran, leaving our dead where they'd fallen. I bitterly regretted it but there was no possibility of taking them back with us. As it was it was a mad dash with the enemy right behind us. Suddenly the front row toppled to the ground as we ran past the archers and scrambled over the gunwale and onto the knarr's deck.

Two volleys of arrows had halted the Frisians for an instant but more and more of them were spilling onto the jetty now. After firing one more arrow each the archers made for the knarr. Someone – I later learned it was Anarawd – had had the presence of mind to have a few more archers ready at the knarr's side. As the other archers climbed aboard they sent a few more arrows into the leading pursuers, which made those behind them pause for a moment.

Seeing us getting away, the Frisians made one last rush to get at us but the ropes fore and aft had been cut with axes and the seamen were pushing us away from the jetty with the oars by the time that the front rank got there. Such was the pressure of the men behind them that the first score or so were unable to stop and were pushed into the sea. Those weighed down by a mail byrnie or steel plates sewn to a padded jerkin sunk like stones. Most of the others couldn't swim and splashed around until they too sunk beneath the water. A few managed to cling to the jetty supports until someone lowered a rope to haul them up.

One managed to swim to the side of our ship and we hauled him aboard. He looked to be about fourteen or fifteen at most. I was conscious of the fact that, with Cerdic dead Octa would become my captain and he would need a body servant instead of sharing the group of boys and men who served the warband in general. But I dismissed the thought as soon as it came to me. We were supposedly raiders from England so we could hardly take a Frisian captive back to Paris.

179

My next thought was to cut his throat and throw him over the side but there had been enough killing for one day. I left him whilst I thought about what to do with him and went to check on Octa. I found Anarawd bandaging his head, having sewn up his other cuts with catgut.

'How are you?' I asked as I knelt beside the sailor.

'I'll live,' he grinned, then grimaced as Anarawd tied off the bandage. 'I'm sorry about Cerdic though. How many others did we lose?'

'About twenty I think. I haven't had a chance to do a count yet.' That was something that Cerdic would normally have done.

'Had Cerdic lived he would have retired after we returned to Paris, so I've been thinking about a new captain in any case.'

'Who's in the running? Stigand is a good warrior and the men like him.'

'No, I think you're ready for the responsibility.'

'Me?'

My son obviously hadn't expected me to even consider him. It was true that he was only nineteen but he was my heir and the men respected him.

'Don't you want it?'

'Yes, of course. Thank you father; I won't let you down.'

'I know you won't. You haven't done so yet and I don't suppose that you're about to start. The only problem is Uuffa. I thought about what you said earlier and I intend to make him the captain of one of the birlinns, once he has learned enough seamanship and got some experience.'

'Hmm, it might be sufficient to satisfy him but it will take him a long time to become a sailor, then a helmsman, before learning all that a captain needs to know.'

'You don't think he has the patience?'

'I don't think he has enough patience,' he replied, with the emphasis on the enough.

'My brother is a doer, not a thinker. He likes to achieve things.'

'That's true, I suppose.'

Like most parents I tended to be blind to my children's faults.

'If you're looking for a new captain you probably couldn't do better than Anarawd,' he went on.

I looked at Octa in a new light. I already had a high opinion of his qualities but now I realised that he was a shrewd judge of character as well. I nodded. It was a sensible suggestion, but it didn't solve the problem of giving Uuffa a fulfilling role. For the moment I put the problem to the back of my mind. I'd only completed half of the mission that King Charles had given me.

We left the ships and fishing boats we didn't need stranded on the beach on the north coast of the island offshore and divided the fleet into two. I put Stigand in charge of the ships returning to Paris, with Bavo and Carloman's head sewn in an oiled leather cloth with pungent herbs to hide the inevitable smell. The basket in which it was placed was put in the bilge to keep it cool. I just hoped that it would still be recognisable when Bavo presented it to the king.

The Franks that Charles had loaned me returned to Paris as well, leaving me with ninety men in three birlinns to continue onto Saxony. If the Saxons had been raiding Frisia recently I wondered what sort of a reception I was going to receive there.

Chapter Ten – Saxony

761 – 762 AD

I was sailing blind, not knowing where the sandbanks were, so I breathed a sigh of relief when the low-lying sandy islands of Frisia receded into the distance. After two miles in which the man dropping the weighted line over the bows found no bottom, I decided we now had deep water under our keel. We stopped rowing and hoisted the sail.

The wind was from the north-east so it was hard work tacking to and fro, covering five miles for every mile we made in the direction of travel, but I didn't want to exhaust the men by making them row. They needed to be fresh in case we sighted a hostile sail.

I was confident of being able to outrun any Saxon warships we encountered. From what I'd seen of the typical ships the Saxons of Wessex used they were smaller and weren't as heavily built as my ships. They may have carried our ancestors over the sea to England, or Britannia as it was then, but they suffered in comparison with my warships, which were based on those used by the islemen of Dalriada.

Ours might be heavier but, because they were longer and could take the strain of a taller mast and a bigger mainsail, birlinns were faster than the Saxon ships; at least I hoped so.

My other problem was our destination. King Charles' advisers had told me that my best option was to head for Geestendorf, the port of Bremen, a little way down the River Weser from its mouth. I'd been given all the other information that the Franks had gleaned about Saxony, which wasn't very much.

Saxony consisted of a broad plain, except in the south where there were some low mountains. The inhabitants were pagans who worshiped a divine tree that connected Heaven and Earth. Eighty years previously two monks called Ewald the Black and Ewald the Fair set out from Northumbria to convert them to Christianity. However, they received a hostile reception and the missionaries were tortured and torn limb from limb. Afterwards the two bodies were cast into the River Rhine.

Their reluctance to accept Christianity and their tendency to raid their neighbours had brought them into direct conflict with King Charles. Our mission to discover the present state of affairs was, I was to discover later, a necessary reconnaissance prior to his long war of conquest and eventual subjugation of the Saxons.

Even after the murder of the unfortunate pair of monks called Ewald, my nemesis, Alchred of Northumbria, had sent another mission under a priest from Eoforwīc called Willihad to convert the Saxons. He had landed at Geestendorf and had established a church at Bremen. When I set out to find him I didn't know whether he was still alive or had suffered the same fate as the two Ewalds.

However, I did have one piece of luck. Amongst the crew of one of my knarrs was a sailor who had been the helmsman on another ship which had traded between Geestendorf and Lundenwic before he joined us. I gather he had fallen out with his captain and had been stranded in Paris. His misfortune was my gain. He didn't know exactly where it lay but he did say that he would recognise the mouth of the River Weser when we came to it.

Two hours after hoisting the sail we sighted another low lying island to the south of us. Our pilot got excited and told me that we should turn after we passed it and head south-east. Night was only a few hours away and I was doubtful of reaching a safe anchorage before dusk. Nevertheless, I did as he suggested.

Now we were on a broad reach and the birlinn flew along before the wind. My other two ships kept close station on us and two and a half hours after passing the last island we saw the mouth of the river ahead of us. There were a number of small islands that littered the estuary and I could see reeds growing around many of them; a sure sign of marshland. Our pilot told us that Geestendorf lay on a small island near the east bank and had its approach marked by sticks stuck in the mud to show the deep water channel; not that it needed to be that deep as our birlinns didn't draw more than four feet.

An hour later we tied up alongside the wooden jetty where there were several knarrs already moored. As I stepped ashore a rotund little man in a red tunic and brown trousers came strutting along the jetty accompanied by four armed men. The latter were indistinguishable from my own warriors, except none wore a byrnie and their helmets looked cheaply made.

Octa and several of my men picked up their spears and shields and came to join me. None wore armour as only a fool would try to sail wearing chainmail and a helmet. Still, they had the look of men who knew their business and both the official and his escort looked nervous. I told my men to put down their weapons and, accompanied only by my son, I walked towards the small, fat man with a smile on my face.

'Greetings,' I said warmly. 'We are Northumbrians come to visit Father Willihad. I trust he is well?'

'You mean the Christian troublemaker? Yes, he is well as far as I know. He lives in Bremen, not here though.' His eyes narrowed in suspicion. 'Why have you come in such strength? Have you come to make trouble? If you and

Willihad think you can convert us Saxons by force you are sadly mistaken.'

'No, not at all. The sea crossing is not always safe. There are Mercian pirates and Frisian ones too. It is better to be safe than sorry.'

'I see,' he said doubtfully. 'Well, you can stay here overnight but there is a fee to do so, and if your men make trouble in the taverns you will have to pay a stiff fine.'

'I understand. There won't be any trouble. How much to moor for one night?'

'Three pounds of hack silver.'

That was extortionate. I had expected him to say a few copper coins or an ounce or two of silver at most.

'No, that's ridiculous. Three ounces and that's paying over the odds.'

'Three pounds or you can leave now.'

'It's getting dark. We're staying for the night. You can accept what I've offered or you can try and fight us for more.'

'I thought you said that you came in peace.'

'And so we do, but that doesn't mean we won't fight robbers and thieves.'

'We'll have to see what our eorl has to say about that. He has a lot more warriors than you have.'

The use of the title eorl surprised me. Its use had died out in England a century or so ago, to be replaced by ealdorman. An English eorl used to rule over a large area of land, often a former petty kingdom. If there was an eorl here I didn't think he would live in such a small place, more likely he was based in Bremen. I decided to take a gamble. 'Why don't you do that, and when I get to Bremen I will be sure to tell your eorl exactly how much you are fleecing visitors for. I suspect that he has no idea what you

are charging, or how much you are keeping
back for yourself.' The look of panic on the
man's face was almost comical.

'That won't be necessary,' he said hurriedly. 'Let's say six
ounces of silver.'

'Three and that's my final offer. If you argue I'll reduce it to two.'

'Very well, three ounces; but I want it now.'

Octa brought it to me and handed it over with a grin. I let the
men to go ashore but only allowed them to take a seax or a dagger
and I warned them that, if there was any trouble, I would fine them
myself. I also put a strong guard on the ships. In the end the night
passed with no more than the odd fist fight and the next morning
we set off rowing down the River Weser.

~~~

Bremen was something of a disappointment. The banks of the
Weser were marshy and the jetty built out over the reed beds was
even smaller than the one at Geestendorf. It was full and two
knarrs were anchored out in the river waiting for their turn to
unload. The settlement itself – it was hardly large enough to be
called a town, although the locals called it a burg – consisted of
timber or wattle and daub huts with thatched or straw roofs. It
looked primitive by comparison with a similar sized place in
England.

I could see one timber building that was larger than the rest but
I couldn't see any windows, just double doors facing the river.
Presumably that was the eorls' hall. Smoke emanated from a hole
in the roof although it was a warm day, presumably so that a meal
could be cooked.

Streets led up from the jetty which even at this distance looked
as if they consisted of mud, debris and the usual unpleasantness. I
sighed when I thought of how clean we had managed to keep the

186

land inside the fortress of Bebbanburg. Even the settlement below the stronghold was cleared of rubbish, offal and faeces daily. It wasn't difficult; it just required a little organisation.

At least there shouldn't be a language problem. I had no trouble understanding the inhabitants of Geestendorf. Although the Saxon dialect they used was a little different to the English I spoke, it wasn't difficult to get the gist or to make them understand me. We had all spoken the same language two centuries ago but words, idioms and accents change over time.

We had no option but to anchor out in the river and, after we'd been there for a while, a small boat rowed out to us. It was yet another official but this time he was apologetic.

'Lord,' he called across when he was near enough, 'I regret that there is no room at the wharf but there is another jetty around the bend for those who don't have a cargo to unload. I presume that is the case?'

'Yes, we have come to visit Father Willihad.'

The man nodded. 'I'm a Christian but few are as yet. When you've moored you'll have to walk back to the burg. You'll find the priest's hut near to the eorl's hall. You will need to visit him and explain why you have arrived here.'

I nodded and expected him to row back to shore again, but he came alongside.

'How long are you staying?'

'I'm not sure, but at least two nights.'

'That will be twelve ounces of silver then, please.'

It seemed that all these port officials tried to make money on the side. 'Six, and I shall check with the eorl what the correct fee is.' He looked disappointed.

'Very well, one ounce per ship per night is the correct rate.'

I later found out that was the fee for knarrs who were unloading. The correct fee for visitors who just wanted to tie up alongside was half that. I hadn't been as clever as I'd thought.

Later that afternoon I walked back into Bremen with my son and two of my warband. Octa and I were dressed in the best tunics and trousers we'd brought with us; a sword and a seax hung from the belt at our waists but, in order to look nonthreatening, we wore no armour nor carried a shield, but at least we could defend ourselves if the need arose. I was wrong, of course.

I had no reason to hide my identity, or so I thought. No-one would have heard of Seofon of Bebbanburg here. When we got to the hall the sentry outside insisted we leave our swords with him but allowed us to keep the seaxes.

When the door opened all I could see was a smoky haze. There were no windows and no source of light, other than the open doors and a dying fire in the central hearth.

'Come in, whoever you are, and make yourselves known,' a voice boomed at us from the darkness.

'I would if I could see, lord,' I replied, which drew a chuckle.

'Wulfgang, go and fetch a torch for our visitors.'

A few minutes later a boy of about twelve or thirteen appeared with a torch and led us to the far end of the hall where a man and a woman sat behind a table. We passed other men and a few women sitting at other tables who gazed at us curiously before resuming eating and drinking. We had evidently arrived at a meal time. We ate in the morning and again just before dusk. As it was now halfway between the two I wasn't sure which meal they were having unless, of course, they ate three meals a day. If so, that seemed rather indulgent to me.

When we arrived at the eorl's table the boy put the torch in a sconce on the wall before sitting down beside those already seated.

'Come, sit and join us. Hilda, fetch three more trenchers.'

I started at hearing my wife's name but realised he was speaking to a servant girl. She darted away and came back with three scooped out trenchers of stale bread on a wooden plate which were filled with vegetable broth. In England this would be the food eaten by villeins and the poorer ceorls. Nobles usually had meat of some sort, as did their warriors, unless it was scarce.

We had eaten some bread purchased the previous day and hard cheese for our midday meal on board, but we set to with a will and ate in silence. Not so the rest of the occupants of the hall who were chattering away. I heard some teasing banter such as my own men would utter.

'Now, you look like a lord of some kind. What brings you to my humble hall?'

'I'm Seofon, an ealdorman from Northumbria sent by King Alchred to visit Father Willihad and report back on progress with his mission.'

'Alchred sent you? Strange, I heard that he had offered five hundred pounds of silver for Seofon of Bebbanburg. You are accused of regicide, I believe.'

~~~

I cursed myself for a fool. Had I not used my own name two of my men would still be alive and my son and I wouldn't be chained to a post in this hovel of a hut. Obviously the local eorl, whose name I didn't even know, intended to sell Octa and me to Alchred. He had no use for my warriors so he had them killed out of hand. At least one of them had managed to draw his seax and plunge it into the chest of a Saxon before he was cut down.

My one hope was my men who had remained with our ships. If all the Saxon warriors in Bremen had been dining in the eorl's hall, there couldn't be more that forty of them. There would be other, married warriors, of course, but they would live in their own huts.

Obviously he could muster a lot more than that, given time, but I had ninety men scarcely more than a mile from the burg. The only problem was they might realise that something was wrong when we didn't return, but they wouldn't know what had happened to us or where we were being held prisoner.

'Why are we here, father?'

Octa's question took me by surprise.

'What do you mean? You know that King Charles made it a condition of allow us to trade out of Paris.'

'No, why are we in Paris. We aren't merchants, or at least not primarily so. We are nobles of Northumbria.'

'You know why. Because Alchred has accused me of complicity in Oswulf's murder in order to put Æthelwold Moll on the throne.'

'Yes, I know all that,' he said impatiently. 'But why aren't we doing something to regain Bebbanburg?'

'Like what? Don't you think that is what I dream about every day? It's not going to happen as long as Alchred is on the throne though.'

'Then we need to remove him and put someone in his place who is well disposed towards us.'

'Such as?'

'Moll's son, Æthelred.'

'But he's only eight. Even if we did manage to unseat Alchred somehow, the Witan is hardly likely to vote for a child as king. Look what happened the last time we had a boy on the throne.'

'They might if they had a strong regent to rely on to bring him up properly, someone who is already his guardian.'

'You're living in a dream world, Octa. Why would they choose me?'

'They might if you were their leader and deposed Alchred. You yourself have said that he's proving to be more and more unpopular.'

'That's mainly because they blame him for doing nothing to counter the attack on Cumbria.'

'If you promised to drive Eugien out they may well rally to you.'

I had recently learned of significant events in Northumbria. Ciniod, the new High King of the Picts, was a weak man who had internal problems to contend with. Some said that his kingdom was on the point of splitting up again. The north had long since ceased to acknowledge the control of the high king and now the other mormaers were acting more and more independently of the centre.

As a result Strathclyde had seized their opportunity two years ago to regain their independence and King Eugein had declared that he was no longer a vassal of the Picts. In the spring of this year he had retaken the coastal strip of Galloway, which had long been part of Cumbria. Now he was said to be advancing further and further into Cumbria itself and had captured its capital of Caer Luel. Alchred's reaction had been to sue for peace in the hope of getting Caer Luel back in exchange for his recognition of the new border along the Solway Firth.

Eugein had rejected his overtures and sent the messenger's head back in a basket. As far as I knew, Alchred had done nothing further to counter Strathclyde's aggression and dissatisfaction with his leadership was growing as a result.

However, there was nothing I could do, even if I could think of what action to take, stuck here as a captive of some Saxon lordling.

~~~

We were woken the next morning by a boy who came in to empty our shit bucket and bring us some stale bread and hard cheese.

'We need more water too,' I pointed out as he went to leave.

He nodded and left with the stinking leather bucket.

Ten minutes later the door opened and I thought the boy was back with our water, but instead two men came in. One pointed his spear at us whilst the other went to undo our shackles.

'The eorl wants to see you,' the man with the spear grunted and gestured for us to precede him out of the hut.

Four more warriors waited outside to escort us to the hall and the man who'd released us kicked Octa to indicate that we should get a move on. When we entered it took some time for my eyes to adjust; then I saw with surprise that one of my birlinn captains, a man named Beadurof, stood there talking to the eorl and his son. The hall was full of Saxons warriors again but this time they were not eating, just drinking. I frowned in disgust. Any man who was quaffing ale at this time of the morning instead of practicing his fighting skills wouldn't prove much opposition to a real fighter.

'Ah, Lord Seofon. Good morning; I trust that you and your son slept well.'

Perhaps he thought he was being funny. Some of his men laughed dutifully at any rate.

'Thank you, yes. The hard earth is always preferable to a ship's deck, apart from the rats and the lice, that is. What do you want?'

'Your man here has offered to equal the reward offered by your king. It's not enough though. I want six hundred pounds of silver.'

Charles had been reasonable generous when funding our expedition, but not that generous. I had brought along some of my own money as well, but I doubted if what I had on board amounted to much more than three hundred pounds in total.

I saw Beadurof nod imperceptibly and I guessed what he had planned.

'Very well, I agree. He'll have to fetch it from my ship though. Will you send an escort?'

We were left standing there whilst we waited. I watched the eorl and his son, Wulfgang, carefully as they seemed to be arguing. I couldn't hear what was being said but the father evidently had enough of whatever his young son was protesting about and he clipped him about the ear. Thereafter the boy sat in sulky silence.

An hour later Beadurof reappeared with four men struggling to carry a large chest. The escort waited just inside the door, which I thought was a little odd. The eorl only had eyes for the chest though and, as it was dumped in front of the table, he rushed around it and lifted the lid.

The men in the hall had got up to crowd around, eager to see more silver than they ever had done before in their lives. Their lord threw back the lid – to reveal a load of stones.

One of the four who had carried the chest into the hall stabbed the eorl in the chest and the other three gathered around Octa and me protectively. At the same time the ten men by the door rushed forward and started to kill the unprepared warriors. Most had their swords on them but that was all. Half drunk, ill-trained and faced with enemies in armour with spears and shields, my ten men had killed more than half of them when the hall filled with the rest of my men, some of whom were carrying torches so they could see what they were doing.

Wulfgang had stood stunned at first but had drawn his dagger and, screaming with rage, he had launched himself at his father's killer. The man was so surprised that he was slow to react and the point of the dagger pricked at his byrnie before he brought up his arm to knock it away. It had broken several rings in the chain mail and the tip came away red with blood, but it had done no real damage. I stepped forward and drove my fist into the boy's jaw. He dropped like a stone.

Within ten minutes the only Saxon men left alive were the unconscious Wulfgang and several terrified servants. The eorl's wife had more gumption than the rest and picked up a discarded sword to attack me. Octa stepped in the way and knocked her out with the haft of a spear.

'Thank you men. I owe you my life and that of my son. Is anyone hurt?' A few had flesh wounds but nothing serious.

'Kill the wounded but not the eorl's son. Someone pick him up; he's coming with us. Empty my sea chest and bring that too. Whoever devised this plan deserves some of my silver. The rest of you can keep whatever you can find on the bodies.'

'We found three chests of silver and a small one of gold hidden in the eorl's chamber,' Octa told me ten minutes later as we were preparing to leave.

'Well done. We can divide that up later. I don't think we need to visit the priest after all. I'm sure that young Wolfgang can tell us all that Charles needs to know about Saxony. Let's get out of here.'

A group of armed Saxons were standing outside the hall when we emerged but they hastily disappeared when they saw how many we were. The only incident on the way back to the ships occurred as we were leaving the burg. An archer appeared on a roof top and sent two arrows our way. Both were caught on shields and a well-aimed spear took the bowman in the chest. An hour later we were underway.

~~~

'What do you intend to do with me?' a tearful and dejected Wulfgang asked me after he'd been sick over the side for the second time.

I wasn't sure if he was just a bad sailor or if his vomiting was due to concussion.

'That rather depends on you.'

'What do you mean?'

'Well, you can tell me everything I need to know about Saxony, or I can hand you over to the King of the Franks and he'll torture it out of you.'

He was silent for a long time. He kept wiping away the tears that leaked unbidden from his eyes. Eventually he made up his mind.

194

'If I tell you all that I can what happens to me then? Will you just throw me over the side?'

'No, you have my word that, if you co-operate, I'll not only let you live, but I'll take you into my household, and not as a slave. How old are you?'

'I was twelve last month.'

'Very well. I'll send you to a monastery to be educated until you're fourteen and then you can train as a warrior, or you can stay and become a monk.'

'Monk? My mother was a Christian but my father and I worship Odin and the old gods.'

'Would you be prepared to be baptised?'

He shrugged. 'My mother always wanted me to become a Christian but my father wouldn't hear of it. He only put up with Father Willibad and his efforts to convert us because my mother insisted.'

'That doesn't answer my question.'

'Yes, I suppose so. Is everyone here a follower of the White Christ then?'

'Yes, there are very few pagans left in England or Frankia now.'

'Strange, my father always said that being a Christian made men into cowards who couldn't fight, but your men fight like devils.'

'That's because we train hard and many of my men have stood in the shield wall in battle; not the younger ones though. Your father's men were indolent and over indulged themselves with ale. Have you no enemies?'

'We have no king so the eorls and chieftains sometimes squabble amongst themselves. Sometimes the Jutes and the Danes raid us but usually they just come to trade.'

'The Danes?'

'Yes, that's what we call the people from the islands to the east of Jutland.'

'And they are warlike?'

'Very. They have several kings who fight amongst themselves and they raid the Norse.'

'Norse?'

'Yes, the people to the north of us. I've not been there but those that have say that it's a wild land of steep sea inlets called fjords, mountains and poor land for farming.
That's why they raid.'

I realised that Wulfgang was likely to be a fount of useful
information, not just about
Saxony, but about lands I didn't even know existed. I wondered if Charles did.'

'Tell me something that's been puzzling me. Why didn't your father try to attack my ships? He must have known that they were full of warriors.' The boy shook his mop of dirty flaxen hair.

'No. That's what we were arguing about. I said yours were fighting ships, though we hadn't seen any similar before. He said that they were a type of knarr; fighting ships would be larger and have shields hanging along the sides.'

That explained why he was taken unawares by my warriors, but I was mystified by Wulfgang's reference to larger warships with shields placed along the gunwale.

'What warships are you referring to?'

'The Danes and the Norse. They have big ships they call dragon ships or longships which can hold fifty or sometimes as many as eighty warriors.'

They certainly had to be much bigger than my birlinns which typically could hold about thirty plus a few seamen and ship's boys.

'They look different to your ship too.'

'In what way?'

'Yours has a lower freeboard with a gunwale that slopes outwards at the top to stop water breaking over the side. The longships are broader in the beam with a higher side which ends up vertical for the last few strakes. You couldn't hang shields from the

196

side of your ships if you tried. They have anything between thirteen
and thirty four oars a side, or so I've heard. It would require
seventy men just to row the larger longships.'

'Do they use knarrs for trade?'

'No, they often use longships for that as well but they do use
karves as well. It's a type of longship, but shorter and wider in the
beam with a deeper draft.'

I left him to sleep and recover from his bout of sea-sickness
whilst I pondered what he'd told me. As we turned west on a
course to pass the treacherous Frisian islands to the north the
lookout yelled that there was a sail on the horizon. His hail had
roused Wulfgang and he came to stand beside me at the stern.

'It's a longship, probably a Dane,' he said.

'How can you tell?'

'The size of the sail and you can just make out shields along the
gunwale if you look.'

The hull had appeared over the horizon by then but it was
something of a blur to my older eyes. It was difficult to judge size
with nothing to compare it with out on the sea but it did seem to be
much bigger than our three ships. Luckily it didn't come to
investigate us but continued to head south.

'Where is it making for?'

'Into a bay called the Jadebusen.'

'To trade?'

'There's no trading ports in the Jadebusen. He's going to raid the
settlements around the bay.'

'You don't seem very bothered.'

'Why should I be? They're not Saxons, they're bloody Frisians.'

For a moment I considered going to the aid of people who were,
after all, now subjects of King Charles, but it wasn't my fight. As my
son had pointed out, we should be concentrating on regaining
Bebbanburg, not acting as Frankish mercenaries.'

Chapter Eleven – The Regent

773 – 779 AD

'Uuffa's knarr is back,' Wulfgang said as he hurried into my hall in Paris.

Æthelred bounced excitedly by his side. The two boys had seemed to bond as soon as they met. Perhaps it was because both of them lived with my family, but were not part of it, that they were drawn together. When Wulfgang had left to be educated at Saint Dennis the younger boy was dejected for a long time, but now that he was back and training to be a warrior they spent what little spare time Wulfgang had together.

King Charles had been pleased with my report on Saxony and intrigued when I told him about the Danes and the Norse, about whom he had heard very little. As a reward he had given me the title of count, which I supposed corresponded to ealdorman in England. Unfortunately no land came with the title and so I became even more determined to regain what I'd lost in Northumbria.

I had started to plan for this eventuality by sending Uuffa on a spying mission to Northumbria. This satisfied his craving for more responsibility too, but Hilda had not been very happy and she let me know it in no uncertain terms. She felt I was sending our son into very real danger.

He went disguised as a monk. His task was to travel through as much of the kingdom as he could gathering information, especially about attitudes to the king. I had also given him the name of several ealdormen who I trusted with instructions to sound them out about deposing Alchred.

I knew that I had to win the majority of the nobles over to support Æthelred as king if there was to be any chance of success. I had already come to the conclusion that the bishops and the abbots were likely to support the scholarly Alchred.

He was due to return before the winter storms started but the knarr on which he was supposed to return came back without him. I was worried and Hilda was so upset that she stopped speaking to me. At the start of November I sent another knarr to the pickup point – the fortress of Dùn Barra on the north-east coast of Lothian – whose ealdorman I knew I could trust. Indeed, if I couldn't trust him I could trust no one in Northumbria.

I was relieved that the knarr had returned safely and prayed that my son was on board. The boys had brought me the news of its arrival before it had finished docking, so I sent them down to see if my son was on board. I looked at Hilda but she was quietly weeping and wouldn't meet my eye. The wait until they returned seemed like an age, but when they did they brought my son with them.

We are not a demonstrative family but I was so pleased to see Uuffa that I started towards him to enfold him in my arms. Thankfully Hilda beat me to it only to be pushed away.

"Mother! I'm not a little boy anymore to need cuddles from you. Besides I stink and need a good wash.'

This was said with good humour, however, and he smiled at both of us.

'I won't pretend that I'm not glad to be home though.'

'We are grateful that you are returned unharmed, Uuffa. Why don't you go and wash and get changed out of that tattered habit? Then you can come back and tell us about your travels over a goblet or two of wine.'

Wine had taken me some time to get used to. It had been the drink of the Romans and the Franks had continued to produce it from their vineyards, but I still preferred ale or mead; the problem was I had to import it if we wanted to drink it and that made it expensive. We had gradually got used to drinking wine instead and now I quite liked it.

'Some think that giving up Cumbria, or at least the northern part of it, is a price worth paying for peace, but the majority expressed concern over having an appeaser as king. It makes Northumbria appear weak and, as Offa grows more and more powerful, they worry that he will seize Luncæstershire; something he continues to threaten to do,' Uuffa began once we were all seated around the central hearth of my hall.

'Up to now he has been preoccupied with making himself Bretwalda of everywhere in England south of the Mersey and the Humber. With the subjugation of Essex, Kent and the Kingdom of the South Saxons, only Wessex now resists him. However, he has now embarked on a project to keep the Welsh from raiding Mercia. He is building an earthen rampart all the way from near the mouth of the River Severn in the south to
Prestatyn on the north coast.'

To my mind such a project was futile. To be effective a fortification needed to be effectively defended; even Offa didn't have the manpower to man something that must be nearly two hundred miles long. Perhaps, though, it was no more than a grandiose gesture or a boundary marker.

'The project is not quite as difficult as it sounds. There were previous efforts to build such a dyke along part of the border which have fallen into disrepair, but even so he will need to build another hundred miles of rampart.'

'So hopefully Luncæstershire is safe for now,' I said. 'What about Cumbria?'

'Eugein still holds the north of Cumbria but, with the resolution of the dispute over the throne of Dalriada, he is now threatened by King Áed mac Echdach on his western border. He has withdrawn back into Strathclyde but Alchfrith has refused to take the opportunity that this gives him to retake Caer Luel. This has caused some of the ealdormen to name him a coward.'

'Is there any talk of disposing him?' I asked.

'Yes, very much so,' he said. 'The problem is that no one can agree on who should replace him. Some are in favour of getting him to abdicate in favour of his son, but he is only sixteen and inexperienced; other have suggested the late King Oswulf's son, Ælfwald. The restoration of Æthelwold Moll was muted as a possibility until he died two months ago.'

It was the first I'd heard that Æthelred's father was dead. I would have to tell the boy before the news reached him from other sources and so I told Uuffa that we would continue shortly and went to find my ward.

He and Wulfgang were practicing with wooden swords and small shields in the open area behind the house where the stables were. The older boy passed on what he was learning to his eleven year old friend every afternoon as soon as his own training was over. I called Æthelred to my side and Wulfgang came over, curious as to what I wanted. I was about to send him away but I thought the boy might need someone to console him and I wanted to get back and hear the rest of Uuffa's report, so I let him stay.

'Æthelred, I have some bad news about your father,' I began.

'My father? I haven't thought about him for ages. You are my father now.'

'I'm your guardian, Æthelred, your real father doesn't change just because some misguided people made him become a monk.'

'Nevertheless, he abandoned me. He should have taken me with him. I could have become a novice.'

'You were very young at the time, though it's not unheard of for small boys to become novices, it's not usual. Would you have wanted to be brought up as a monk?'

The boy looked at the sword and shield he was carrying, then looked at the ground and moved the dust around with the toe of his left shoe.

'No, I suppose not.'

'Your father wanted what was best for you; besides your life was in danger as his heir. He felt that you would be safe with me and that I would look after you.'

'Why are we speaking of him now? Has something happened to him?'

'Yes, I'm afraid that he's recently died.'

'Oh! I see.'

He said nothing more but stared at me as if he disbelieved what I was telling him. A tear escaped from the corner of his eye, which he wiped away with his sleeve.

'You can leave him with me now, lord,' Wulfgang said. 'I know only too well what it's like to lose a father. I'll look after him.'

I nodded my thanks and put a hand on Æthelred's shoulder to give it a gentle squeeze before returning to my hall. I glanced back as I entered the door and saw the two boys in each other's arms. Both were visibly sobbing.

'How did he take it?' Hilda asked when I rejoined her and our two sons.

'Not well. I think he's tried to forget about his father, but the news of his death shook him. Wulfgang's looking after him.'

'Those two are close, perhaps too close,' Octa said.

'You think their friendship is unhealthy?'

'They are more than friends, I think.'

'How so?'

'Perhaps I'm wrong.'

'You must have grounds for saying that, Octa,' Hilda said.

'Only rumours, but perhaps there is substance to them.'

This was greeted by silence as we all thought of the implications. Of course, it could be perfectly innocent but even gossip of that type could ruin Æthelred's reputation and deprive him of his chance at gaining the crown. If it were other than innocent few would understand, or forgive, such a relationship between males.

'We need to find Wulfgang a girl,' Hilda said.

'A wife you mean?' I asked, thinking him a trifle young for marriage.

'No, just a pretty wench to bed him. I'm sure their friendship is just that, after all Æthelred is still eleven, but once word gets around that Wulfgang has slept with a pretty maid people are less likely to think he likes boys.'

I looked at Hilda gratefully. It was an awkward situation and what she proposed seemed a good solution. However, at present I was more interested in what Uuffa had to say.

'Did any speak of Æthelred as a contender for the crown?'

'A few, but most were against the idea of a boy king until Beorhtmund suggested you as regent. The idea circulated rapidly and many seemed to consider it an option.'

Beorhtmund was the Ealdorman of Dùn Barra, the son of the father of the same name. He was, I hoped, my friend because where he led the other ealdormen of Lothian would follow; perhaps others too.

'Thank you, Uuffa. You've done well, I'm proud of you.' He smiled his thanks at me.

'Yes, well,' Hilda said with a frown. 'I suppose all's well that ends well, but don't you dare send him on any more dangerous missions on his own.'

'The question is,' Octa said, 'what do we do now?'

'We daren't delay,' I replied. 'If we do we'll find Ælfwald or Osred on the throne and our chance of getting Bebbanburg restored to us will have vanished.'

'So what do we do?'

'We take Bebbanburg back by force and then declare Æthelred as king in succession to his late father. However, that will have to wait until the spring when it's safe to cross the German Ocean. In the meantime I'll send messages to all those who might support us asking them to rally to Æthelred's side when the time comes.'

'Won't that risk Alchred getting to hear of the plot against him?'

'It might, but I won't include any details - just say that they will know when the time to act comes.'

~~~

I stood at the prow of the leading birlinn with the breeze blowing my hair around my face as Bebbanburg appeared over the horizon. I had adopted the Frankish fashion of shaving all my face whilst we lived in Paris but I'd decided to grow a moustache again over the past winter. However, it had appeared as a mixture of white and grey hairs instead of the black one I had shaved off years before. I hastily shaved my incipient moustache off again and then noticed how many grey hairs there were on my head, especially around my ears. I was growing old.

At the age of fifty I felt as fit and strong as ever I did but I did tire more easily. My ambition now was to see Octa in a position to inherit Bebbanburg and become the Ealdorman of Islandshire before I died. Not that I expected that to happen for a while yet.

My brother Renweard had remained behind in Paris to oversee the business and Hilda had stayed with him for the moment. I hadn't told King Charles, who people were now calling Charlemagne – Charles the Great – in case he prevented me leaving with my warband, which now numbered one hundred and twenty. Renweard planned to follow me and take up his old position as shire reeve if we were successful. If we weren't, then he could stay where he was.

With no children of his own he would be the last of the House of Catinus in that eventuality. I had thought of leaving either Octa or Uuffa with him but neither would hear of it.

Uuffa had preceded me by two days in our smallest birlinn, landing with Anarawd in a cove to the north of the Isle of Lindisfarne. They were dressed as monks and their role would be crucial to our success.

On the twentieth of March 774 I set foot once more on Northumbrian soil. I lifted Æthelred down from the side of the birlinn. He had just turned twelve and we had agreed that he should be treated as the king as soon as we landed.

'Welcome back to your kingdom, Cyning,' I said to him.

His reply surprised me.

'Thank you, heræswa, may God be with us.'

It was a long time since I had been the Heræswa of Northumbria and it felt good to be accorded the title once more. However, we could call each other what we liked, it would mean nothing unless we could depose Alchfrith and get the boy accepted in his stead. The first step would be to capture the stronghold below whose fortifications we had just landed.

We planted my wolf's head banner and that of the House of Æthelfrith, from whom Æthelred claimed descent, in the ground and my men started to set up camp around them.

What I hadn't expected was that the man who now commanded the fortress would sally forth and attack us within an hour of our landing. Thankfully Octa, as captain of my warband, had put out sentries as soon as we had agreed where to camp.

We had landed ten of the horses we'd brought with us by that stage and they had been saddled ready for a group of my horsemen to patrol the surrounding countryside.
I had no intention of being surprised by reinforcements loyal to Alchred.

As the force from the fortress charged out of the main gate and around the side of the rock on which it stood my men hastily stopped what they were doing and grabbed their helmets, shields and weapons. There was no time to pull on byrnies or other protective covering as they rushed to form a shield wall.

When I'd been master of Bebbanburg my warband were trained horsemen. However, the new lord evidently didn't see the need to train his men to ride, or couldn't afford the number of horses required. The men making their way towards us as fast as they could were on foot in the main. They were led by eight mounted men. One was wearing a very expensive byrnie which covered his arms as well as his torso and which had been gilded to look like gold.

His helmet was ornate with a crouching animal of some sort as its crest. This was made of gold and the helmet itself was inlaid with gold patterns. Instead of the fixed visor with eye holes that I favoured, his was open-faced. Beside him rode a man bearing a green banner. There was a strong breeze off the sea in which the banner fluttered so I could make out its emblem – a bear on all fours.

As I mounted and gathered nine other horsemen around me, Octa took command of the shield wall. Behind them the archers formed up and sent a couple of volleys at high trajectory towards the enemy.

They did little damage, although one horse was wounded and threw its rider, but the arrows striking shields made the attackers nervous and they slowed their pace. I smiled grimly; experienced fighters would have speeded up to reduce the length of time that they were vulnerable to arrows. These men were not battle-hardened. The next volley was more successful with several men suffering wounds to their legs and right arms.
Another horse was hit, which reduced their mounted force to six.

They had drawn ahead of those on foot by a hundred yards or so and the gap was widening as the panting men behind them struggled to keep up. I led my nine horsemen around the right flank of my shield wall and headed for the richly dressed enemy leader. He saw me coming and turned his horse's head to meet me.

I saw that he was riding like all Anglo-Saxons up to that time – in a saddle with no stirrups. I had learned from Charlemagne's heavy cavalry and had bought new saddles like theirs. The stirrups which hung from the new saddles gave us greater agility when fighting from horseback, better control of our mounts and we were more difficult to unseat.

The man in the gilded byrnie thrust his spear at me as we closed but I ducked and it went over my shoulder. I sat up again as he passed me and stabbed my spear in the rump of his horse. It reared up and he fell backwards over its hind quarters. I had no more time to worry about him as another rider wielding an axe had it raised ready to chop down at my horse's head. I yanked the reins to the left and the axe missed its target. The impetus of the swing unbalanced its owner and he started to fall off his horse to the side.

I looked around for another opponent but my men had disposed of the rest. I saw with alarm that the warriors on foot were only a few yards away so I yelled for my men to retreat and whirled my horse around to follow them. However, I had forgotten the two dismounted riders. The ornately dressed man ran at me with his sword whilst the other grabbed my shield and tried to pull me from my horse.

Because my feet were in stirrups I couldn't kick the man holding my shield away so I kicked my spurs viciously into the side of my horse and it leaped forward in reaction to the pain. I let go of my shield and the man holding it fell away. His leader's sword missed me and struck the rump of my horse just as I hit him a back handed blow with the haft of my spear. He stumbled and fell just as my horse reared up, neighing loudly because of his wounded rear. My stirrups meant that I was able to stay on the bucking horse. Then suddenly he started to bolt.

I clung on for dear life as he raced, not back towards my own men as I'd hoped, but towards my advancing foes. Those in front scattered out of the way but the press of men behind was too great and my fleeing steed was forced to a halt. I had dropped my spear and tried now to draw my sword, but to no avail. Hands grabbed me and my horse and pulled us to the ground.

My wounded horse fell onto its left side with my leg trapped under it. I felt a massive blow to my helmet and then everything went black.

~~~

I awoke feeling sick and my head felt as if a blacksmith was using it as an anvil. I lifted my head and vomited, then fell back into blessed unconsciousness. The next time I woke up it was dark. My stomach lurched but all that came out of my mouth was yellow bile. I felt dizzy and my head pounded as if someone was banging it on a rock.
Gradually the nausea faded and the room stopped spinning around me.

My eyes were accustomed to the dark but all I could see was a very faint line under where I supposed the bottom of the door was. There didn't appear to be any windows and the floor under my hands was hard earth. I knew where I was – in the small stone built hut that was used for prisoners in Bebbanburg. I was back in my ancestral home, but not in the way I had envisaged.

As I lay there, drifting in and out of consciousness, I tried to think of a way out of my predicament. I was certain the man who had worn the gilded byrnie was Beagnoth, the man Alchred had made Ealdorman of Islandshire in my place. I was equally certain he knew who I was. The only mystery was why was I still alive?

I had expected to find myself chained or tied up by rope, but presumably my captors thought that a stone prison with a stout wooden door made such additional measures unnecessary. As time wore on my head cleared and I felt a little better. I felt the side of my head gingerly. There was a large lump there and my hair was matter with dried blood. Otherwise I seemed unharmed, apart for a few bruises and a pain in my side – presumably a cracked rib or two.

I got to my feet slowly and immediately felt faint, so I sat down again with a bump. A few minutes later I tried again and, although I felt dizzy, I managed to stay on my feet. I took a few tottering steps and banged into the cold stone wall. My breath rasped in my throat with the effort and I held onto the wall until I was breathing normally again.

I cautiously took a few more steps with one hand against the wall for support and my breathing became less ragged and my balance improved. After what seemed like an age, but which was probably in reality no more than half an hour, I could stand and walk normally; not that there was far to walk in any one direction. My cell was, if I remembered correctly, no more than about eight feet square.

Either my mind was playing tricks on me or the faint light under the door was getting brighter. The sun must be rising and a feeling of dread overcame me. Dawn was the traditional time for executions. I jumped when I heard the bar outside the door being removed and the light of a new day flooded into my prison. A figure stood in the doorway, silhouetted against the pale sunlight reflected off the stone wall of the lord's hall behind him.

'Get up you heap of dung. Ealdorman Beagnoth invites you to join him on the parapet overlooking your camp,' he said with a sneer. 'Not that you'll enjoy the view for long. He intends to hang you from the palisade where your men can watch you twitch and kick as the life ebbs out of you.'

'How kind of the usurper who sits in my hall drinking my mead to ask for my company, but I fear I'm not feeling too well. Please convey my regrets to Beagnoth and tell him to go and copulate with himself.'

The man stepped into the small room intending to punch me for my insolence, but I stepped out of the way and his fist hit the far wall with a sickening crunch. He yelled in pain and clutched his broken hand with his left one. I swiftly kicked him behind his right

210

knee and the leg gave way. I grabbed his head from behind and twisted it savagely to the right. I heard his neck break and let the body drop to the floor.

I stepped over it and peered cautiously out of the door, only to find myself standing in front of two monks. It was only then that I noticed the daggers dripping blood and the two dead warriors at their feet.

'It seems that you didn't need our help after all, father,' Uuffa said standing beside a grinning Anarawd.

They had managed to enter the stronghold the day before my fleet arrived in the guise of monks from Lindisfarne on their way to Jarrow and had stayed with the chaplain overnight. The idea had been for them to open the sea gate at dawn, but they had watched the sally the previous day and seen me brought in as a captive. Their plans had then changed.

'Did the chaplain suspect anything?' I asked as we left the cell and stood in the narrow alleyway between it and the hall.

'Yes, he soon realised that we weren't proper monks when he found out we didn't know that Higbald was now the prior of Lindisfarne Monastery. We left him tied up.'

'I'm pleased for Higbald. He's done well for someone who could well have ended up as a slave or worse,' I said, thinking of the Mercian boy I'd saved from King Eadbehrt's torturers nearly twenty years ago.

'You two can catch up later,' Anarawd hissed, 'for now we need to worry about getting out of here alive.'

I was about to reprimand Anarawd for his insolence when I realised that he was right. We moved to the end of the prison wall and I risked a quick glance up to where Beagnoth was waiting impatiently up on the parapet which ran around the inside of the palisade. Just at that moment he sent a man to find out what was causing the delay in fetching me. I had less than a minute to come up with a plan.

~~~

What I didn't know until later was that Beagnoth had lost nearly half his men in his abortive attempt at the sally to take us by surprise. Octa's shield wall had held firm and, being composed of twice as many men as Beagnoth had, it had managed to outflank his men. They had turned and fled moments before being trapped and had lost more men during the rout that followed. Beagnoth had led the flight back into the fortress and the only horseman to escape had been the one carrying my unconscious body.

Now he only had twenty two men, some of those wounded, to defend Bebbanburg. However, even that would be enough as the only points vulnerable to assault were the two gates and the palisade either side of them as it ran up onto the basalt plateau on which Bebbanburg was built.

I was naturally concerned about all three of us staying alive, but that would be irrelevant if I couldn't capture the stronghold before a relief force arrived.

'Quick, drag those two bodies back into the cell.'

We did so and shut the door. I prayed that the man sent to see what was happening didn't notice the blood stained grass but the ground in the alleyway was in shadow so there was a chance that he wouldn't.

It was a tight squeeze in the cell with three bodies and the three of us. I was standing closest to the door and so Uuffa handed me a sword he'd taken from one of the dead men. As soon as the door opened I thrust the point into the man's neck and we pulled his body inside as the last of his blood pumped out of the gaping wound.

We left the door open to let in some light as we sorted through the leather and linen padded over-tunics and found helmets that would fit. Then, arming ourselves with their weapons and shields, we left the hut, closing the door and barring it; not to keep the dead men inside, but so that all looked normal to anyone walking past.

We made our way to the sea gate. Octa had drawn up our warriors in expectation that his brother and Anarawd would be successful in getting them open, unrealistic as that original plan seemed to me now. Beagnoth stood on the parapet beside the gate with a dozen men, four more stood inside the gate and, having killed four of the remaining garrison, presumably the remaining two were guarding the main gate.

Several of the men I could see had bandages around arms or legs.

I knew that the only way up to the parapet where Beagnoth stood was via the nearby ladder or the steps over a hundred yards away. I calculated that it would take the men on the parapet well over a minute to cover that distance, descend the steps and reach the gate. It wasn't long but it would have to be enough.

We had brought thirty horses with us and I suspected that Octa would have his horsemen ready just out of arrow range to charge up the incline as soon as the gates started to open. I hoped so at any rate.

'Where's the damned prisoner?' Beagnoth called down to us, thinking that we were the men he'd sent to fetch him.

'He's still unconscious, lord,' Uuffa called back.

'I don't care if he's bloody well dead, go and fetch him so I can hang him from the ramparts.'

'Yes, lord.'

But instead of turning around I ran as fast as I could towards the four men standing inside the gates with Uuffa at my heels, whilst Anarawd ran over and pulled the ladder down. For a moment Beagnoth and his men stood there in stunned silence, then he realised what was going on.

'Get them!' he yelled, his face going puce with rage.

By this time Uuffa and I had reached the four at the gate. They were slow witted and only one managed to lower his spear before we were amongst them. We each killed one man before they could react and then I felt the spear point strike my borrowed shield. Uuffa killed my attacker whilst I warded off a sword cut at my head from the last man. He never stood a chance against two of us and a moment later we lifted the bar that held the gates closed.

We tugged at the heavy right hand gate trying desperately to open it before the pounding feet I could hear behind me reached us. As the gate opened, our horsemen started up the slope. They were a hundred yards away and closing fast but our foes were much closer. By now Anarawd had joined us and each of us levelled a spear at the onrushing warriors.

'Good odds eh? Four to one,' Anarawd laughed.

He was excited and his blood was up. Uuffa and I were more concerned about surviving for the next few moments.

Most of the men on the parapet had been off duty and were only there to watch an execution. All had swords and seaxes but only a few wore any form of protection and only one man, presumably one of those on duty, had a spear and shield. Then an arrow struck my shield. I looked up to see an archer in the watchtower, however I didn't have to worry about him for the moment as he couldn't send any more arrows our way without hitting his fellow warriors.

The first to reach us were armed with sword and seax and they stabbed and hacked at us but to no avail. We stood together in the narrow gateway, which was a mere four feet wide as we'd only had time to open one of the two gates. As one man raised his sword to strike at me I blocked it with my shield and thrust my spear into his belly. He fell and I was forced to let go of the spear as it was well and truly embedded in his body. Thankfully the man behind him tripped over it and I had time to pull out my seax and cut downwards into his neck, severing his spinal cord, before he could recover.

At that moment I heard the pounding of hooves behind us and the three of us darted out of the way and stood to one side just in time as Octa led his horsemen through the open gate in single file. They scattered the remaining warriors, cutting them down with their swords and skewering them on the end of their spears as they went. We three followed the last of the horsemen through the gate just in time to see Beagnoth fall to my son's blade.

But I'd forgotten the archer in the watchtower. I watched horrified as Octa toppled from his horse with an arrow in him. I headed for the tower to wreak my revenge on the sentry but I was too slow. Uuffa beat me to it and two minutes later I saw the man thrown from the top of the tower to land in a mess of blood and broken bones on the ground below.

~~~

Beagnoth was dead and Bebbanburg was mine once again, but that mattered not at all if it had cost me my son. I rushed to where he lay with the arrow sticking out of his chest. He groaned, so thank the Lord God that he was still alive. I pushed those clustered around him out of the way and knelt by his side.

The arrow had broken the links of his chain mail and had cut through the leather and his clothing, piercing the skin. Thankfully it had been deflected by a rib bone and hadn't hit his heart or any other vital organs; at least I didn't think so. He was breathing unevenly and he was unconscious, probably because he had banged his head inside his helmet when he hit the ground.

I got some of my men to carry him carefully into the hall and I followed. Uuffa went to join me but I stopped him.

'Someone had to take care of the men, make sure the wounded are looked after and take care of the corpses. Our foes can share a common grave but our dead need preparing for a proper burial.'

I looked at the women weeping over Beagnoth's corpse and those of his men.

'Let them take care of their dead, then they are to leave this fortress, together with his reeve and servants. I want them all gone by dusk. The slaves stay. Understand?'

'Yes, father. Will Octa be alright?'

'I hope so. We'll pray for his recovery later.'

'What about the chaplain?'

'You stayed with him. Is he Beagnoth's man or can I keep him on?'

'I don't think he liked Beagnoth; he was a hard lord and the ceorls and villeins hated him. I think you can trust him.'

'Very well, he can stay for now. Go and free him. I'll let you know as soon as there's any news about your brother.'

He nodded and hurried away as I went into the hall.

Once the blacksmith had cut through the rings of his byrnie around the wound, the old slave who knew something about healing removed Octa's clothing to expose the wound. She washed it clean of blood, though it continued to well out of the wound, and then used a sharp knife to cut around the barbed head so that it could be removed. After that she poked around and removed all the bits of cloth and leather she could find, then washed the blood away again. That done she turned to me.

'It hasn't done too much damage as far as I can see, lord. However, if I sew the hole up it'll stretch the skin and the stitches will probably tear out again. I need to cauterise it.'

'Go ahead, but be careful. I've seen men die of shock when the hot iron is applied to a wound.'

'Your son is unconscious so he shouldn't feel a thing,' she said, giving me a smile that exposed her gums and few remaining blackened teeth.

I suppose it was meant to be reassuring but it was more like a horrible leer.

She heated the iron and, whilst men held Octa's feet and arms just in case, she applied it to the wound. The blood boiled and there was a stench like burnt pork. Octa arched his back and groaned but didn't wake up. Then it was all over. I went outside to tell Uuffa.

Two days later the burials were over, the signs of fighting had been removed and it was as if I and my family had never left, apart from the absence of Hilda who was still in Paris. Seward had cleared out Beagnoth's possessions, all except his chests of silver and a small one of gold, and brought my sea chest up from the ships. Octa had regained consciousness and seemed to be recovering. He did nothing but complain, more about his forced inactivity than about the pain he was in, which had to be a good sign.

Æthelred had moved into the king's hall, a separate building constructed some time ago for royal visits, with Wulfgang and a few other young warriors under training who would be his companions and the nucleus of his gesith. The boy was pleased to have his own hall, but he tried not to show it. After all, if he was going to be a king he'd better start behaving like one.

Meanwhile I had sent messengers out to every ealdorman, bishop and abbot announcing Æthelred's return and calling for the Witan to meet to formally depose Alchred and elect his replacement. I deliberately didn't refer to Moll's son as king or to myself as hereræswa. I wanted the Witan to have the appearance of choice, though only an idiot wouldn't realise where this was heading.

I had chosen Yeavering as the meeting place. It was within my shire and it was the ancient summer palace of the Kings of Bernicia, so it had symbolism. It also had the advantage that the nearest ealdormen were all supporters of a change in regime. Those from Lothian were definitely in our camp, as were the ealdormen of the two shires on the west coast. I was less certain of the rest of Bernicia but there was a good chance that most could be persuaded to support Æthelred. The one who certainly wouldn't do so was

Sigca of Hexham. Alchred might well have supporters in Deira as well but I hoped that enough of them could be won over.

Beorhtmund was the first to arrive followed by Bishop Cynewulf of Lindisfarne and the Abbot of Melrose. I had brought eighty warriors with me and Beorhtmund had thirty. Slowly more nobles and churchmen arrived. Both Godwyn of Cumbria and Wynstan of Luncæstershire pledged their support for Æthelred as soon as they arrived. Both had good reason to distrust Alchred; in Godwyn's case it wasn't an exaggeration to say that he hated the man.

Gradually the rest drifted in. The last to arrive were the king and the archbishop. He had brought a small army of a thousand men with him, including the fyrd of Eoforwīc. I had asked Cynewulf to chair the Witan and he immediately asked the king to send the fyrd home. Alchred refused until I asked the ealdormen on whom I could rely to surround the Eoforwīc camp and disarm the fyrd.

The archbishop's men and the king's army had slightly greater numbers but the fyrd weren't minded to fight for Alchred and they had started to desert on the way to Yeavering. That first night the trickle turned into a flood and Alchred was left with fewer armed men that we had.

The day started with the two sides jeering and yelling insults at one another but many of Alchred's men refused to join in the usual prelude to a fight and that was enough to show the rest in which direction the wind was blowing. An uneasy calm descended on the various armed camps and I asked Cynewulf to take advantage of it and convene the Witan without delay. I had a feeling that, whatever the disparity in numbers, fighting might break out later, especially if the men started to drink, so I was determined to resolve matters before nightfall.

Cynewulf, usually a mild mannered man in my experience, grasped the bull by the horns as soon as everyone was seated in the king's hall.

'We are here because Alchred has proved to be an unsatisfactory ruler in the eyes of some of his nobles. In particular Godwyn of Cumbria accuses him of cowardice for not coming to his aid against Eugein of Strathclyde and Wynstan has no confidence that Alchred would support him if Offa of Mercia renews his claim to Luncæstershire.

At this Alchred, who had remained silent up until now, got to his feet.

'That is a lie, but that should not be the first business on the agenda bishop. There is one here who is an outlaw accused of regicide and now he has foully murdered Beagnoth of Bebbanburg. He must be arrested and held for trial by the Witan, together with his accomplices – his son Uuffa and the boy Æthelred.'

'Thank you, Alchred, I think we can resolve that matter first, as you say.'

For a moment I wondered whether the bishop was playing some sort of double game but my thoughts were interrupted by Alchred screaming at Cynewulf.

'You will call me Cyning, Cynewulf, and I want him arrested. I'll convene the court at which he is to be tried.'

'I'm sorry, Lord Alchred, but your fitness to be our king is one of the matters we are here to resolve,' the bishop said calmly. 'Now please sit down so I may put the matter of whether Ealdorman Seofon is to be arrested to the vote.'

'He is not an ealdorman, he's a murderer!' Alchred screeched at him.

Cynewulf sat there in silence calmly regarding the erstwhile king until Alchred calmed down and realised that he was making a fool of himself. He sat down and glared at the bishop.

'Thank you. Now please stand if you think Lord Seofon should be arrested.'

Alchred, the archbishop, several of the abbots and three ealdormen got to their feet. All of the latter were Alchred's appointees. Looking around them, two of the abbots sat down again then the rest did likewise, leaving just five men on their feet.

'Well, that seems to have resolved that little matter. You may sit down again; the decision of the Witan is that Ealdorman Seofon is not to be tried for murder. Now we proceed to the matter of the arraignment against the king for cowardice and his unsuitability to rule.'

At that Alchred was on his feet again crying treason.

'Please sit down. You and your supporters will have the opportunity to put your case once we have heard the accusations against you. I will say this though. Your continual interruptions against the conventions under which the meetings of the Witan are held is doing your case no favours. Godwyn, would you like to speak first?'

Wynstan followed Godwyn. Their opinion of Alchred was well known and they had nothing new to add, then Wihtgar of Elmet voiced his concerns about Alchred's ability to protect his shire from the increasingly powerful Offa of Mercia. Beorhtmund got to his feet next and said much the same thing about the threat from the Picts. The Ealdorman of Selkirk supported him. He too was worried about having the Britons of Strathclyde on his western border and wanted Eugein driven back across the Solway Firth. As expected, the Ealdorman of Berwicshire sided with his fellow Lothian nobles. They didn't believe that Alchred was likely to act and so he had to be replaced.

Next Cynewulf invited Alchred to respond.

'War is not the answer,' he began. 'That has led to disaster in the past. We need to resolve these problems through negotiations.'

'What has that achieved so far?' one of the ealdormen who hadn't spoken until now called out. 'Your messenger's head came back in a basket. Unless we fight for what is ours our foes will think we're a bunch of cowards.'

There was a growing murmur of agreement with that sentiment and Cynewulf had to bang his fist on the table to restore order.

'Be quiet! Let the speaker be heard in silence. You can have your say later.' 'We've heard enough. Let's put it to the vote,' another called out.

'No, not yet. We must conduct ourselves in accordance with the rules or people will say the decision of the Witan was invalid.'

That silenced everyone and Alchred was allowed to continue.

'Would you rather lose your lives in a futile war on the far side of the Pennine Mountains? Northumbria has been at peace under my rule and you have all enjoyed prosperity. Going to war would put all that at risk. The Bible say we should turn the other cheek; I'm not advocating that, but we do need to reach a peaceful compromise. In the previous century Northumbria included Lindsey. It lay south of the Humber and we lost many lives in a futile war to hold it. In the end it became Mercian, where it belonged geographically.'

'So are you saying we should surrender the shires on the far side of the Pennines and reduce Northumbria to Lothian, Bernicia, Deira and Elmet?' Godwyn asked incredulously.

'Perhaps you'd give up Lothian to the Picts too, and consolidate our border on the Twaid?' Beorhtmund enquired sarcastically, ignoring Cynewulf's repeated thumping of his fist on the table.

Uproar ensued and I thought for a moment that Alchred might be physically attacked. It didn't happen though. Archbishop Ethelbert got to his feet and glared at everyone until the uproar subsided.

'May I, Bishop?' he asked Cynewulf who waved his hand wearily for him to speak.

'You are forgetting one thing. Alchred is your crowned king, anointed by me in the name of God the Father, Christ the Son and the Holy Ghost. He cannot be unseated by a mere vote of this assembly. He will still be your king in the sight of the Almighty.

Now forget this nonsense and reaffirm your oaths of loyalty to the king.'

He sat down amid a stunned silence. I realised that I was in danger of losing the massive gamble I'd taken, so I looked at Cynewulf for permission to speak. He nodded, looking thoughtful.

'What the archbishop says is true. However, no king who has lost the confidence of his nobles and his people, as this one has, can continue to be an effective leader. There are therefore two alternative courses of action open to us to resolve this issue. As Ethelbert has so eloquently reminded us, we cannot depose Alchred, but he can abdicate of his own free will.'

'Why on earth should I do that?'

Alchred asked derisively. 'Because the other alternative open to us is to kill you.' The king's face went white and then red with rage.

'You would threaten to kill your king. That's treason!'

'If you leave me no other option, yes I'll kill you. Now will you abdicate and go into exile voluntarily?'

'You wouldn't dare kill me,' he blustered.

'Why not? You already accuse me of organising the killing of King Oswulf?'

'And may you rot in Hell for it.'

'If Seofon doesn't kill you, I will,' growled Godwyn.

One look around the hall apparently convinced Alchred that there was no shortage of nobles who were prepared to see him die, if that's what it took to get rid of him.

'Very well,' he said, his shoulders slumping. 'I'll abdicate.'

Once the deed of abdication was signed, I had the former king escorted to Bebbanburg where he would await his family before leaving on one of my birlinns to wherever he elected to settle. His gesith was disbanded and the other armed warriors who had accompanied him to Yeavering seemed content to accept the Witan's verdict.

I had thought that Alchred might decide to become a monk, but he chose to flee to the Kingdom of the Picts with his wife and two sons – Osred and Almund. There were those who worried that he would return with an army of Picts, but I wasn't. The man lacked the backbone to fight for his lost crown. I was more worried that his sons might do just that once they had grown up. However, they were just small boys at the moment and so I forgot about them for now.

We were not out of the woods yet. I still had to ensure that Æthelred was elected. The Witan met again the next day to hear the submissions of the candidates and this time I brought Æthelred with me. He was only twelve but you could already see his father in his face.

As captain of his gesith, Wulfgang accompanied him and they made a handsome pair. Both wore their fair hair down below their shoulders and were richly dressed in tunics made from the best wool, trimmed with wolf fur, trousers cut in the Frankish fashion - which was tighter to the leg than the English favoured - and fine brown leather boots. What I hadn't realised was that seeing them together like that would merely inflame people's suspicions as to the nature of their association.

By comparison his rivals looked like ceorls. Æthwald was the son of Oswulf, the king that the boy who was then called Bleddyn had killed and therefore the grandson of King Eadbehrt. The other claimant was Sicga, Ealdorman of Hexham and a cousin of Alhred's. He was one of those who had become a noble during Alhred's reign, in his case by marrying the only child of the previous ealdorman.

He had no blood ties to the sons of Ida, the first king of Bernicia, although he did to the defunct royal house of Deira. It didn't take the Witan long to rule that he was no true ætheling, which made the

223

man scowl and mutter imprecations under his breath. I disliked and distrusted him; he was a man who needed to be watched.

Æthwald was the next on his feet. As he was descended from two kings he had a good claim but he was only fifteen and inexperienced. The Witan knew that, if they elected him, he was just about old enough to rule on his own, the age of majority under Anglo-Saxon law being fourteen. No-one could see him as a war leader; if they wanted an incapable ruler they would have stuck with Alhred.

Cynewulf thanked him for outlining his claim and asked if anyone wanted to speak. I had hoped that I wouldn't have to get up to oppose him openly. Although I'd done my best to orchestrate the outcome I wanted, I wished to stay in the background as much as possible. I didn't want to make any more enemies; I had quite enough as it was.

Just when I thought I'd have to get to my feet Godwyn beat me to it. I wondered why Beorhtmund hadn't spoken, or one of the other nobles who had pledged their support to Æthelred. Perhaps each was waiting for the other, then another thought came to me, and not a pleasant one.

What had united us was the need to get rid of Alchred. Now that he was gone they didn't want to hand me the power that would accrue to the king's guardian, especially if he was also the regent and the hereræswa. I would be king in all but name and, as my great-uncle had sat on the throne, albeit for just a few months, it seemed likely that they thought I had ambitions over and above regaining my former status. The fact that I could trace my descent back to Ida, albeit through the female line, gave some credence to their fears, if I was interpreting their silence correctly.

Having Æthwald on the throne, an impressionable youth with scarce a hair on his face as yet, might suit some of them better. He wouldn't be able to control them and they could then act as petty kings in their own shires. Of course, that would spell the end of

Northumbria as a powerful kingdom and it might even split back into its original constituent parts. Unless I was overthinking this, those who thought like that were being very short-sighted. All the petty-kingdoms of England – and there had been over twenty of them at one stage – had been swallowed up by their more powerful neighbours.

Whilst I had been thinking Godwyn had sat down and Wynstan was on his feet saying much the same thing, but about the threat from Mercia. After he had had finished Cynewulf asked if anyone else wanted to add anything. No-one did.

'Very well, the last of the notified candidates is Æthelred, son of King Æthelwold Moll.'

As we had agreed, the boy got to his feet, much to the surprise of everyone who had expected me to speak on his behalf as his guardian. We had rehearsed what he would say and how to respond to those who questioned him, of course.

'I'm the only son of King Æthelwold and Queen Æthelthryth and, as such, the last of the line of Æthelfrith, the first king of a united Northumbria. I am well aware that some doubts surround my father's lineage. Yes, he was a bastard, the product of the detested Osred raping a novice nun, but neither he nor I are anything like my wretched grandfather.

'I have been brought up for the past nine years by Ealdorman Seofon, an honourable and loyal man who was shamefully treated by King Alchred. I've been tutored by a scholar from the Monastery of Saint-Germain-des-Prés in Paris and have met the famous Charlemagne. I mention this, not to boast, but to demonstrate that I have had a wide and varied upbringing and, despite my years, I do not think like a little boy.

'I have yet to start my formal training as a warrior, but I practice daily with members of my gesith and I have started to learn about strategy and military tactics from the former hereræswa, Seofon of Bebbanburg; a man whose reputation you all know. But what you

may not know is that he conquered Frisia for Charlemagne and defeated the
Saxons of Bremen, the son of whose eorl is now the faithful leader of my gesith.' To call me the conqueror of Frisia, or even to imply that I defeated the Eorl of Bremen in battle, was stretching the truth more than a little, but it sounded impressive and what these people needed now was a war-leader.

'If I am chosen to be your king I know I will need regents to help me until I am fourteen, or even sixteen. If the choice were mine I would ask the archbishop to be my spiritual teacher and tutor in administration and the Ealdorman of Bebbanburg to lead my army and continue my education in warfare.'

I was proud of Æthelred. Not only had he delivered what we had rehearsed perfectly, even embroidering it skilfully when it came to my prowess, but he had sounded like a king, despite his high pitched voice. Wulfgang clapped him on the shoulder and Æthelred blushed as they exchanged a smile.

My relief was short lived. The Bishop of Hexham got to his feet next and unsurprisingly he was in the camp of Sicga. Despite the fact that his candidate had been ruled ineligible he went on the attack.

'You say that Æthelfrith was your ancestor, descended in the male line, but what proof do we have of that?'

The boy looked floored by the question and so I got to my feet.

'If I may, perhaps I can answer that. Those of you who were present at the Witan when Æthelwold Moll was elected will know that irrefutable proof was presented at that time. If you doubt my word, bishop, you only have to look in the records.'

'Thank you Lord Seofon. I was present and I can confirm that is correct,' Cynewulf said with a smile and his fellow bishop sat down looking annoyed.

Both Godwyn and Wynstan stood to confirm their support for Æthelred provided I was confirmed as hereræswa. The next man on his feet was the archbishop and I held my breath.

'Much as I dislike Seofon personally,' he began, 'I can see that a combination of Æthelred the Ætheling as king and Seofon as hereræswa will give us the strong leadership Northumbria so badly needs at this time. However, I cannot accept a king who is suspected of being a catamite. I refer to rumours about his relationship to the captain of his gesith...'

He got no further. A furious Æthelred leaped to his feet and, ignoring Cynewulf's instruction to sit down he launched into the archbishop.

'Who says such a thing?' he demanded. 'How dare you call me a catamite? Yes, Wulfgang and I are close, but to suggest that our association is anything other than blameless is not only untrue but it is a slur on my character that demands satisfaction. Let anyone here who believes such a slander stand now and my champion will fight him to the death in defence of my honour.'

The vehemence with which Æthelred reacted to what the archbishop had said cannot have been fabricated. It was plain to all that the rumours about the two boys were untrue. Not only had the exchange cleared the air about Æthelred and Wulfgang, but it had also shown the putative king as a strong character, despite his young age. What had been a potentially damaging situation had been set on its head and it had significantly helped Æthelred's candidature.

'Very well,' Æthelred said after a pause. 'Archbishop, you should be more careful about what you say. You wouldn't be the first bishop to be imprisoned.'

That struck home as Cynewulf himself had been incarcerated by King Eadbehrt decades earlier. There was a deathly silence as Æthelred sat down, his face still grim and suffused with anger. After a minute or two Cynewulf invited the archbishop to continue. He slowly got to his feet and faced Æthelred.

'I apologise if I have offended you, Æthelred, but I was merely raising a matter that troubled everyone here. However, I'm grateful to you for making it perfectly clear that the stories that have been circulating are no more than scurrilous lies.'

It was well said but the archbishop still appeared to be somewhat shaken by the boy's vehement reaction. He took a deep breath before continuing.

'Like many here I suspect, I worry that we might be giving Seofon too much power as he is the boy's guardian as well, but I see no alternative but to make him joint regent with me, if you will have us. However, I suggest that I should become the king's guardian until such time as the Witan grants him full powers as our monarch.'

'No, that's not acceptable to me,' Æthelred said, rising to his feet again. 'I don't remember my own parents and Seofon and the Lady Hilda have been mother and father to me for as long as I can recall. They will move to Eoforwīc with me. Renweard is the shire reeve of Islandshire; he can look after things there.'

'The whelp speaks as if he is already king,' one of the ealdormen, a man I didn't recognise, said with a sneer.

'And you are?' Æthelred asked.

'Sentwine of Beverley,' he replied, flushing with annoyance at not being recognised.

'One of Alchred's appointees,' I whispered to Æthelred.

'I should tread carefully Sentwine. If I am elected by the Witan I would know who my friends are and who are my foes.'

That wasn't something I had coached the boy in and I was very proud of the way he'd handled himself today. His warning, coupled with his earlier outburst, certainly gave others who were thinking of challenging him pause for thought.

'Does anyone else wish to say anything?' Bishop Cynewulf asked.

Beorhtmund stood up and I wondered what the man I had thought of as a friend until today would say.

'I wish to endorse Æthelred the Ætheling as our king and to support both the nominations of Seofon to be hereræswa and for him and Archbishop Ethelbert to be joint regents. I also think that Seofon and Hilda should remain as the king's legal guardians until he is fourteen.'

He sat down and smirked at me. I smiled back, more in relief than anything. However, one thing I had learned from today was that powerful men did not have friends, they had allies if they were lucky.

~~~

My first task as hereræswa was to retake Caer Luel and drive the Britons of Strathclyde out of northern Cumbria. I settled my wife and household in Eoforwīc in time for Christmas and as soon as the weather improved I set off for the muster point for the army – Hexham. It was not only a convenient base for operations in Cumbria but it would put Sicga to the expense of feeding the king and his household whilst they remained as his guests. It was some way from Caer Luel but the route there was easy; all we had to do was to follow the valley of the South Tyne River.

I sent Uuffa and Anarawd ahead to the border with an escort of twenty horsemen to reconnoitre the area.

'We went all the way along the river as far as the confluence with the River Irthing and saw no sign of any enemy,' my son told me two days later.

Where the two rivers met was on the boundary between Cumbria and Bernicia, although the division between them wasn't always clearly delineated.

'The local thegn hasn't had any problems with raids from Cumbia,' he went on, 'so I suspect that they are concentrated around Caer Luel and the settlements nearby.'

'Good. Thank you. Nearly everyone who I'm expecting has now sent contingents so we'll move out along the valley tomorrow. We'll camp there in two days' time. In the meantime I want you to cross into Cumbria and see if you can find out what's happening at Caer Luel, but don't get caught. Quite apart from the fact that I want you back safe and sound, I don't want the enemy to know we're in the area.'

It was twenty miles to Cumbria and large armies on foot don't cover more than about ten miles a day, even when the going was good. We set off on a cold but bright day in early March. The normally muddy road was still crisp with frost as I rode ahead of the main body with my horsemen at a steady walk whilst we waited for Uuffa and Alwyn to report back. It was mid-morning the next day before Alwyn appeared on his own. By then we had reached the campsite for the second night at the confluence between the South Tyne and the River Irthing on the border between the two shires.

'Uuffa and the scouts are keeping an eye on Caer Luel. Everything seems normal so far. Farmers are coming in to the market as usual and there's some traffic along the river out towards the Solway Firth.'

'What about the settlements between here and there?'

It's difficult to tell without talking to the occupants, but one or two have been burnt down. The rest appear to be functioning as normal, but I suspect that the original inhabitants are now slaves and the new owners are Britons.'

I went out of the encampment to think. So far only my horsemen had arrived, the rest would camp down river when they arrived. One of the advantages of being there first was you got the clean water.

The banks were gravel, rather than mud and bog, with grass and bushes rising up to low hills. I climbed to the top of one and looked out along the valley. I could see in the distance that the valley narrowed with tree covered slopes coming down to the river. The going tomorrow wouldn't be as easy and the army would, of necessity, be more strung out. That would make it more vulnerable if the Britons knew we were there.

I sat down to think. I was uneasy about the apparent normality of Caer Luel and the surrounding countryside. Of course I hoped that the Britons would be unaware of our approach but it would be a miracle if we could assemble an army and march towards them without Eugein, or whoever he'd left in charge, hearing about it. The more I thought about it the more I began to smell a rat.

I was only dragged from my reverie when a spot of water hit my cheek, soon followed by several more. The blue sky dotted with fluffy white clouds had vanished and grey clouds were scudding in from the west as the wind picked up. My guess was that we were in for a stormy night and I was glad my tent and those of my mounted warband were already erected.

It started to rain in earnest and the sky grew even darker as the first of the main body arrived. They tried to find what little shelter there was as they waited for the baggage train to arrive with their leather tents. By the time everyone had them erected they were soaked to the skin and those who had chain mail would have to get rid of the rust as well as dry out as best they might.

I was also sopping wet as I eventually made my way back down the hill from my observation point, still having no plan for recapturing Cumbria. My servant, Seward, chastised me, saying that I would catch a fever, as he stripped me, got me dry and gave me clean, dry clothes. They were something that few others would have with them.

The storm passed in the night and the next morning dawned bright and clear. I decided to delay that day's march by a few hours so that everybody could dry their clothes. We had posted sentries, of course, and I had sent scouts out to warn us of any enemy approach so the men felt free to wash in the river whilst their clothes dried.

It also gave me the opportunity to call a war council. Every ealdorman except those from Beverley, Luncæster and Loidis were present. They had stayed behind with their warbands and fyrds just in case Offa decided to take advantage of the situation. The Bishops of Lindisfarne and Hexham and a number of priests and monks had also accompanied the army, the latter mainly to deal with the wounded, and the archbishop joined us as joint-regent.

Æthelred stood on a makeshift dais so that he could see everyone and I turned to him now.

'Cyning, I am uneasy about the very normality of northern Cumbria,' I began, 'I suspect that we are being drawn into a trap. I have no evidence of this, merely an intuition. I had expected our foes to have heard of the muster at Hexham and to be preparing to meet us in battle.'

'What do you suggest, Seofon. That we sit here and wait to see what happens?' 'No, not at all.'

I was slightly annoyed by the boy's response. It seemed to imply that I was bereft of ideas.

'However, I do think we need to scout further into the hills to the north of the river. If I was Eugein I would try and trap us between his army and the river. If he attacks us on the march we could be in serious trouble. I propose to send scouts into the hills whilst we construct a defensive position here, just in case. That does mean a delay in our advance which, if my suspicions prove unfounded, may well mean that the enemy have a little more time to make preparations to resist us. I would like to hear what others think.'

'It seems to me that we risk little by staying here whilst we learn more of the enemy dispositions,' Godwyn said. 'Once we reach the coastal plain around Caer Luel the enemy will know of our presence in any case.'

232

Others thought that we should press on and strike whilst we had the element of surprise, dismissing my suspicions as fanciful. Sicga even came close to suggesting that I was a coward.

'To even suggest that Seofon's proposal is anything other than prudent shows what a fool you are, Sicga,' Beorhtmund said, making the other man put his hand on his sword before the archbishop interrupted.

'To start calling each other names is less than helpful. I am far from a military man but it seems to me that we need as much information about the Britons as possible. I would remind you that previous kings have led their armies to annihilation because they walked blindly into a trap.'

That swung opinion in my favour. I had no intention of doing anything other than what my common sense told me, but I did need to take this disparate group of nobles with me. Division rather than unity had been Northumbria's curse for decades and we were the weaker for it.

By mid-morning my scouts were ready and I sent them out in three groups of twenty, all mounted, under the command of Octa, Uuffa and Anarawd. My choice of the latter surprised everyone except those who knew him. To those who queried my decision I merely said that he had served me as an agent on the Continent. No-one would connect him with the Bleddyn who was suspected of murdering King Oswulf sixteen years previously.

It was Anarawd who found the Strathclyde army. He estimated their numbers at three thousand, rather more than the two and a half thousand I had with me, but a fifth of my men were trained warriors whereas few of the enemy host would be. They were camped all along a small valley two miles north of the River Eden, which ran west from the confluence with the South Tyne and the Irthing to Caer Luel and on into the Solway Firth. Now I knew where they were I could turn their ambush into a trap of my own.

~~~

At dawn the next day I watched as a few men in the valley below me got up, stretched and went to relieve their bladders. The move into position at night had been difficult, but in the end only a handful had got lost. Now we were ready. I signalled to the man just below the skyline and he waved my wolf's head banner to and fro. It was the signal for the attack to begin.

I mounted my horse and led a hundred and fifty horsemen in a charge down the hillside into the Strathclyde camp. At the same time seven hundred warriors formed a shield wall to prevent escape from the entrance to the valley. I had divided the fyrd into two groups, one commanded by Octa and one by Beorhtmund. They now swarmed down both the opposite slope and the one behind me.

Another hundred men under Uuffa had moved into position at the head of the valley to cut off escape that way. I'd left Anarawd with the king, Wulfgang and the ten other companions who formed his gesith to watch from the top of the hill from where I'd led the charge. The clergymen had joined this little group too, which added the archbishop's bodyguard of thirty warriors as additional protection. I felt that it would be enough. That didn't prove to be the case but I didn't find that out until later.

I had opted for an axe with a long handle rather than a spear which could only be used to kill one man before I'd have to let go of it. I brought the sharp axe head down on a man who was trying ineffectually to get out of my way instead of fighting me. The Britons were scattered and disorganised. As we cantered through their camp my axe became coated with gore as I chopped down man after man. Then I was through the camp and I pulled my horse to a halt as Octa's men ran past me, eager to join in the slaughter.

I rode a little way up the opposite slope so that I could get a better view of what was going on. My horsemen gathered around me and I was pleased to see that I hadn't lost more than a handful. Then I saw something that chilled my blood.

Someone had spotted the yellow and red banner of Northumbria and that of the Archbishop of Eoforwīc flying amongst the group with Æthelred. A large group of Britons had fought their way clear of Beorhtmund's men, who were now busy fighting those still in the encampment, and they were clambering up the hillside towards the king. I estimated their numbers at several hundreds, many times more than those with Æthelred and Archbishop Ethelbert.

'Follow me at the gallop,' I yelled, digging my spurs into my mount's flanks so sharply that it reared up slightly before tearing off back through the camp, scattering friend and foe alike.

I didn't look back to see if the others were behind me. All my attention was focused on what was happening at the top of the hill. I was relieved to see that someone had ordered the forty warriors to dismount and form a shield wall to protect the king and the clergymen. It might be enough to hold the enemy until we could get there, although ten of the warriors – Æthelred's gesith - were boys still under training.

My heart lurched as I saw that Æthelred himself was standing in the middle of the front rank. It was brave but foolhardy in the extreme. Then I sighed in relief as Wulfgang pulled him back into the second row and took his place.

By now our horses were labouring up the steep slope. Their gait had inevitably slowed to little more than a man's walking pace and I watched helplessly as the first of the Britons ran into the shield wall. The Britons were in no sort of formation and had to be struggling for breath after their climb. Certainly their charge would have no momentum behind it, but I could no longer see what was going on as the defenders had disappeared behind a mass of their foes.

I started to yell to attract the Britons attention and my men joined in. Those at the back turned to see us a mere hundred yards from them and panic quickly spread through their ranks. Dozens started to break away and flee along the hillside in both directions. I ignored them and lifted my bloody axe to strike down at the Britons still fighting the king's shield wall.

I don't know how many I killed but afterwards my arm was so stiff I could hardly lift it. As more and more of my men arrived to join in the slaughter the Britons broke and fled. I jumped off my horse whilst my men set off in pursuit and rushed to check on the king. Of the thirty who had formed the shield wall scarcely a dozen remained alive and many of those were wounded.

One of the latter was Wulfgang and I saw with tremendous relief that the boy attending to the cuts to his arms and legs was Æthelred. He was covered in blood but it must be someone else's as he appeared to be unharmed. He was cleaning the wounds as one of the monks prepared to sew them up. As I reached him I saw that he was sobbing with relief at Wulfgang's survival.

~~~

It took the rest of the year to recapture Caer Luel and drive the last of the Britons back into Strathclyde. Unfortunately King Eugein was one of those who had escaped but he had lost nearly a thousand men killed or captured during the battle in the unnamed valley.

We celebrated Christmas at Eoforwīc that year. I was away from Bebbanburg more often than I was there now. Renweard looked after the fortress and the shire whilst I assisted the archbishop to rule the kingdom.

That wasn't to say that Æthelred didn't play his part. He insisted on being involved in all the important decisions, held court each day and toured the kingdom with us, but he was also busy with his education and weapon training.

He and Wulfgang remained close friends, so much so that one or two others at court appeared to be jealous of the Saxon youth and the odd scurrilous remark reached my ears. It seemed that what had happened at the Witan hadn't entirely put paid to the derogatory gossip about the pair. As time went on I was more and more convinced that they did love one another, but only in the platonic sense. After all the king was only twelve with no sign of incipient manhood as yet. Wulfgang was nearly fifteen though. I decided to have a discreet word with him about my fears for Æthelred's reputation.

'Sit down, Wulfgang. I trust your wounds have healed now?'

'Thank you, lord. My right arm troubled me for a while and I walked with a limp, as I'm sure you noticed, but exercise to build up the muscles seems to have cured me. I assume that concern for my health wasn't why you wanted a private meeting though?'

'No, not entirely. I've been meaning to speak to you for some time now. My concern is for the king's welfare and the high regard in which he is held by most people.' 'As is mine, lord, I can assure you,' he said quickly.

'Yes, I know. Look, Wulfgang this is difficult for me. Please let me say what I have to and then think before you say anything in response. The last thing I want is for a gulf to grow between us but I am increasingly concerned about what some nobles and others in positions of influence are saying or insinuating.'

'You are referring to my friendship with the king, I presume.' I gave him a pained look.

'I'm sorry I interrupted, please go on.'

'Yes. Some are jealous whereas I fear that a few have misinterpreted your closeness as an unnatural vice,' I said uncomfortably.

To my surprise Wulfgang laughed.

'I thought for a moment you might have wanted to see me in order to accuse me of getting one of the Lady Hilda's slaves pregnant.'

'Have you?'

'It would appear so. It doesn't show yet but she tells me that she is late. I'm sure you know what I mean.'

The confident, almost cocky, way he said that annoyed me but I realised that the boy was proud of showing what a virile young stud he was. At least it would seem that I didn't have to worry about his friendship with Æthelred in that way.

'I'll talk to my wife about that, but you won't be the first noble to get a slave pregnant. You're a bit young as yet but perhaps we ought to think about you getting married.'

'To a slave?' he asked aghast.

'No, of course not! You'll need to do something for the child in due course, but that's not my concern at the moment. No, I mean marry the daughter of a thegn perhaps.'

'No, I'm sorry lord,' he said with some vehemence. 'I'm not ready to settle down with one girl, not by a long way. I like them well enough to spend a night or two with them, but that's it. I know it would squash the stupid rumours about me and the king but I'm not prepared to saddle myself with a girl I don't love just to do that.'

'Very well. But I think it would do no harm if gossip about you getting this slave pregnant were to circulate.'

He nodded. 'And I'll try to explain to Æthelred that we need to behave more circumspectly in public.'

'Good.' I sighed. 'I suppose I'd better go and talk to Lady Hilda about this wretched girl. It's another conversation I'm not looking forward to.'

He grinned at me but it soon disappeared when I added that she would no doubt have a few choice words for him too.

~~~

Life continued without further significant dramas for two more years. Octa met and married Cynwise, the younger sister of Godwyn of Cumbria, and Æthelred reached the age of fourteen, at which age he was officially regarded as a man rather than a boy.

Octa and Cynwise had a son at the end of 777 who they called Eafa. From the start he was a lusty child and he thrived. It was a bad winter that year and a number of babies, young children and old people died during it, but thankfully Eafa survived.

Wulfgang got three more girls pregnant to my knowledge. This didn't add to his popularity in certain quarters, but it did quash the speculation about him and the king. However, the rumours had weakened Æthelred's reputation.

Nevertheless, the Witan decided, unwisely in my opinion, that Æthelred was now fit to rule on his own. At least it meant that I was no longer a regent and I was free to return to Bebbanburg. Renweard wasn't exactly overjoyed to hand over the reins of power to me and made no secret of his feelings. We didn't have an argument – there was nothing to argue about. I was ealdorman and he was the shire reeve. But the atmosphere was strained and, after two months, he decided to return to Paris to take charge of our business interests there. I watched his ship as it set out for Frankia with a heavy heart. When we were younger we'd been very close, but time changes things. I turned my back on the receding ship and went to tell Uuffa that he was now the shire reeve.

He got married to Beorhtmund's younger daughter of at the beginning of 778 and decided to move into the vacant hall at Alnwic. Otherwise life was unremarkable until early September. Then Æthelred discovered a plot against him and dealt with it badly.

Chapter Twelve – A Kingdom Divided

778 to 786 AD

Ælfwald had never really accepted the verdict of the Witan in 774 that he was too inexperienced at fifteen to be king. When Æthelred reached the age of fourteen in 777 and was allowed to rule without regents he was outraged. I dismissed the reports I heard as the ravings of a jealous and immature young man. However, it did appear that he had found a few ealdormen to support him – Sicga of Hexham, Sentwine of Beverley and Cynric of Leyburn in particular. They were natural allies of his as all three had been appointed by King Alchred and consequently Æthelred didn't go to any great lengths to hide his dislike of them.

They felt, probably with some justification, that their position was precarious. Soon the court was rife with rumours that they were conspiring with others against the king. As soon as he got wind of the plot Æthelred should have had them arrested and brought before the Witan for trial. He didn't. Instead he issued warrants for their execution.

Had I still been by his side I would have told him that, whatever the loyalties - or the lack thereof - of individual ealdormen, condemning them to death without a fair trial was likely to incense every one of his nobles. He might be king, but he needed their support to rule, especially in today's day and age when kings came and went with alarming regularity. Oswiu's uninterrupted rule of twenty eight years was but a distant memory.

The other mistake he made was in not inviting the three traitors to Eoforwīc where they could be arrested with little fuss. By sending out fifty warriors from his warband to bring back each of the three was crass. Of course, they got wind of what was afoot and fled into Mercia.

Unsurprisingly, Offa welcomed them with open arms. Fortunately for us Ecgbert of Kent had recently raised the standard of rebellion against Mercian dominion and had defeated Offa's forces at the Battle of the Medway. Otherwise I'm certain that he would have invaded Northumbria on the pretext of supporting the aggrieved ealdormen. The condemnation of three of the seventeen ealdormen without consulting the Witan had further damaged Æthelred's standing in the kingdom. A few blamed me for poor advice, though I had nothing to do with the matter, and others thought that they saw the archbishop's hand in this. Some even blamed Wulfgang who, as captain of the king's gesith, had the king's ear.

As a Saxon, Wulfgang wasn't popular in a land where practically all the nobles and most of the thegns were Angles by descent and his womanising didn't help. Consequently he became the scapegoat for the king's error of judgement. A more cynical and pragmatic monarch would have blamed Wulfgang and have exiled him, at least pro tem, but Æthelred wasn't like that. He stood by his friend and accepted the blame.

'What do you think will happen,' Hilda asked me as we sat glum faced in our chamber the evening that we heard the latest news.

'I hear that the archbishop has called a meeting of the Witan against Æthelred's wishes. It is to meet at Eoforwīc in the middle of December.'

'December? Well, if the weather is as bad this year as it was last very few will be able to make it through the snow to get there.'

'That's probably what Ethelbert is banking on. Even if conditions are difficult many of the ealdormen and churchmen from Deira should still be able to make it. It's those like me from the north and from the west who won't be able to attend.'

Hilda nodded glumly. Ethelbert had fallen out with the king over the appointment of the new Bishop of Hexham. The archbishop had recommended the Prior of Hexham Monastery, but he was Sigca's cousin and Æthelred wouldn't entertain the idea. He wanted Higbald, the Prior of Lindisfarne. He was the Mercian whose life I'd saved all those years ago and I thought him a good choice. Unfortunately the old rivalry between Lindisfarne and Eoforwīc for supremacy in Northumbria hadn't entirely disappeared and Ethelbert was totally opposed to his consecration. Perhaps he thought that Ælfwald would be more amenable if he was on the throne.

Whatever the archbishop's motives in calling the Witan together, I was determined to attend and I persuaded Beorhtmund to come with me. We offered to take Bishop Cynewulf as well, but he was ill. Octa came with thirty of my warband and Beorhtmund brought another twenty.

Hilda said that, as I wouldn't be able to make it back in time for Christmas, she would travel down to Alnwic to be with Uuffa and his wife, who was expecting their first child quite soon now. Cynwise and baby Eafa didn't want to stay at Bebbanburg on their own and went with them.

We all travelled together for the first stage of our journey overland and, although the road was muddy and the weather miserable, at least it wasn't deep in snow as it had been last December. From near Alnwic Beorhtmund, Octa and I travelled the rest of the way to Eoforwīc by ship, or rather ships – a knarr and a birlinn.

Beorhtmund was dubious about the wisdom of a sea voyage due to the prevalence of storms in the winter, but the thought of travelling all that way on a horse in rain, wind and mud appalled me. I was no longer as young as I used to be and long periods on horseback made my joints ache.

The first day after we left the mouth of the River Aln was uneventful. The sky was cloudy and the wind had the chill of approaching winter about it but the sea was little more than choppy and we made good progress. It would have been foolish to sail on after dark so we anchored in the mouth of the Tyne overnight.

The next day the sea was a little livelier and the wind was stronger. We flew along with the wind coming from the north east. That night was more comfortable and we managed to reach Whitby just as the sun was sinking in the west. Sleeping in the guests' dormitory wasn't quite like being at home in my own hall but it was a damn sight better than sleeping on the open deck of a ship.

We hoped to reach the entrance to the inland sea on which Eoforwīc stood by nightfall but our luck had changed. The day started with barely a breath of wind. Gradually it picked up and we started to move through the water at a reasonable pace, but the wind, from the north now, kept increasing in strength and we were flying before it. Both ships had to take in a few reefs by midday and the waves kept on increasing in size. The air was now laced with salt water and the size of the following sea began to concern me.

When the headland near the Black Rocks hove into view through the rain and sea spray I breathed a sigh of relief. Beyond it there was a sandy beach and the headland would protect us from the worst of the wind. Large waves crashed onto the beach but we made it to the shore safely. It took us some time to haul the ships far enough up the beach so that the hulls weren't being thumped onto the sand by the waves, but by midafternoon I was satisfied that we would be able to see out the storm in safety. The problem was that we might not now make it to Eoforwīc in time for the meeting of the Witan two days hence.

The storm raged for most of that night and the next morning but by early afternoon it had blown itself out. There was still a swell on the sea but that would just make sailing uncomfortable, not dangerous. The problem was that the wind had died away and moved round to the east. We would be lucky to make more than three of four miles each hour under sail and knarrs weren't intended to be rowed on the open sea. Their six oars a side were only intended for manoeuvring in port.

We set out nevertheless and reached Filey Bay that evening. With any luck we could now make it to Eoforwīc by the day of the Witan.

~~~

A combination of light winds and a broken steering oar delayed us further and we didn't tie up alongside the quay at Eoforwīc until midday. Leaving Octa to sort things out with the port master, Beorhtmund and I hurried up to the king's hall, only to find that the Witan was meeting in the church. We arrived just in time to hear a furious argument in progress.

'I'm your king,' Æthelred was saying with some vehemence. 'I have no intention of abdicating and, as we know from what was said when I was crowned, you cannot legally depose me. Especially as less than a quarter of the Witan are present.'

It was true. Apart from the archbishop, only the abbots of Ripon and Eoforwīc were there to represent the Church. There were also six ealdormen present, but three of those were the men that the king had issued death warrants for.

Everyone turned around to see who had entered as the door opened to admit us along with a gust of rain laden wind. Æthelred seemed to be the only one present who was pleased to see us.

The Ealdorman of Eoforwīc, a man called Sigered, was presiding. As the Witan was being hosted by Ethelbert and this was his church I had expected him to be in charge. Perhaps he thought that this rump of a Witan would have more credibility if he didn't chair it.

Sigered was looking harassed and for a moment he welcomed the interruption but, when he saw who it was, he scowled.

'You're late,' was all the welcome we received.

'As we got caught in a storm we are lucky to be here at all. Good day, Cyning,' I said bowing towards the king. 'What's going on?'

'If you'd been here on time you'd know,' Sigered replied.

He was still a youth struggling to grow his first moustache and his attitude irked me.

'I'm your hereræswa and I suggest you pay Beorhtmund and myself some respect unless you want to earn my displeasure.'

I might be old but I still had a good reputation as a warrior.

'Er, I apologise. Please come in and sit down.'

The only vacant seats were on a bench beside Sicga, Sentwine and Cynric, the three ealdormen who Æthelred had accused of treason.

'Thank you, I'll stand. I'd rather not associate with traitors.'

The three muttered amongst themselves but said nothing out loud in response.

'Please yourself,' Sigered said with a sniff.

'Perhaps it would be helpful if I brought Seofon and Beorhtmund up to date,' Æthelred said smoothly.

'This Witan was called, not by me as king, but by the archbishop. There are, of course, insufficient nobles and senior churchmen here for it to be regarded as legitimate but, nevertheless, the majority voted to proceed anyway. I am, apparently, too young and inexperienced to continue as king, as evidenced by my issuing a warrant for the heads of these three conspirators. I acknowledge now that I should have had them arraigned before the Witan – and by that I mean a proper meeting not this farce – where they could have been tried and then executed.

'These men tried to make me abdicate and, when I refused, they said that they would depose me anyway. I think that is a fair summary of where we'd got to when you came in?'

He looked around the room but no one said anything in response.

'Good. I wouldn't wish to misrepresent the situation.'

The king sat down on his throne and I walked to the front of the nave and turned my back on Sigered.

'I agree with the king that this is no proper meeting of the Witan. For it to be regarded as valid over half the members would need to be present, as has always been the case in the past. Secondly, as most of you will know, the Witan held four years ago ruled that a king was anointed by God and therefore couldn't be deposed; he had to agree to abdicate. If I remember correctly, archbishop, it was you who made that very point.'

Ethelbert had the grace to look uncomfortable. He looked old and worn out. Perhaps he was too tired to stand up to the anti-Æthelred faction. It was only then that I remembered that he was related to the two men sitting beside him – Ælfwald and Osred. One was the son of King Oswald and the other was the son of King Alhred. Presumably one or other hoped to replace Æthelred on the throne. This was not looking good.

I glanced at Beorhtmund, who was looking grim. He moved alongside me, the hand on the hilt of his sword.

'I think the outcome has been decided long before we got here,' he whispered.

As if to prove his point Sigered looked at me with a smirk on his face.

'Lord Seofon has questioned the validity of this Witan. It's a pity, of course, that more couldn't attend in person, but I sent messengers to various ealdormen to determine their views before the Witan met. All those who replied agree that Æthelred is too young to lead us properly and should stand down. I have letters from six of them here. That accounts for all except those of Cumbria, Lothian Whitby and Jarrow who are too far away to have replied.'

'No doubt the rest agree with you? How much did it cost in bribes?' I said, unable to keep the sneer out of my voice. 'What about the other abbots and bishops?' 'I'll vote on their behalf as their metropolitan,' Ethelbert snapped.

'You know it doesn't work like that Ethelbert. This is a secular matter, not a spiritual one. Each member of the Witan has a vote.'

'Enough!' Sigered banged the table. 'All those in favour of deposing Æthelred stand.'

As Beorhtmund and I were already standing we promptly sat down on a bench, pushing the three traitors who had been sitting there out of our way. Everyone else except Æthelred stood, some reluctantly.

'I don't accept this; I am still your king,' he said, his face puce with rage, 'and you will pay for this.'

'I think not,' Sigered said. 'You are no longer our king. Guards, arrest Æthelred.'

As the four men by the entrance moved forward Beorhtmund and I drew our swords. They should have been taken from us at the door but our late arrival had taken everyone by surprise. The sentries hadn't expected resistance and I thrust my sword through the throat of one of them and Beorhtmund chopped into the neck of another before they realised what was happening.

The other two were slow to react. There was no space to use their spears and by the time that they had dropped them and half drawn their swords we had killed them too. Whilst this was happening Æthelred drew his dagger, the only weapon that was officially allowed in a meeting of the Witan, and thrust it through Sigered's neck, hissing 'traitor', before hastening to join us.

The others present were stunned at how quickly the meeting had turned into a charnel house and they were slow to get to their feet and draw their daggers. Beorhtmund and I levelled our swords at them and no one had the courage to be the first to attack, though they called us every name under the sun. Meanwhile the archbishop was yelling sacrilege and wringing his hands.

'Yes, you're right Ethelbert,' I told him, 'sacrilege has been done here today but, unlike your church which can be cleansed and re-dedicated, Northumbria has been dealt a blow by cowards and arrogant fools that it may not recover from.'

It was time to go and the three of us opened the door and left. I was vastly relieved to see Octa and our warriors in the courtyard outside. Several of the archbishop's warriors lay dead and the rest stood to one side, uncertain what to do. They were outnumbered, but I was certain that someone would have gone to summon the warbands of those nobles still in the church.

The door opened again and Cynric appeared in the opening with Sentwine behind him. An arrow took Cynric in the chest and he crumpled in a heap at the top of the steps. Sentwine hastily retreated inside and slammed the door shut.

'Think it's about time we left,' Octa said.

'I'm not leaving without Wulfgang,' Æthelred said stubbornly. 'I left him here; where is he?'

'I don't know,' Octa replied. 'He was here but someone called him away to deal with a problem. I didn't think anything of it at the time.'

Just at that moment Wulfgang and eight of the king's gesith appeared. Their byrnie's were splattered with blood and they had drawn swords and carried shields.

'We had to fight our way here, Cyning. It was a trick and two of our number are dead; what's happening.'

'The archbishop and the rest of the plotters tried to depose me,' he called back.
'Where is my warband?'

'They were taken unawares by the men who came with the ealdormen. They disarmed them and locked them up.'

'Come on,' I interrupted. 'There is no time to lose. We must get back to the ships.'

Our warriors formed a square around us and we headed back to the quayside at a fast jog. People scattered out of our way and we made it there without further incident. Whilst the rest embarked, I sent a few men to cut the rest of the ships tied up alongside adrift to slow any pursuit.

Just after we had cast off and were heading away from the quay, warriors started spilling out of the streets leading down to the port. Another few minutes and we would've been outnumbered and fighting for our lives. A few arrows struck the ships but no one was hit as we rowed slowly towards the open sea, the birlinn towing the knarr into the head-on wind.

~~~

We reached Bebbanburg safely and the next morning I set out for Alnwic to bring my family back to the security of the fortress. I had no idea what the new king would do, or even who he was. I would have gone south by ship as no one in Northumbria had a fleet to match mine, but a storm blew in from the north east and I didn't want to wait until it had died down. Consequently I set off with thirty mounted warriors whilst Beorhtmund headed north to prepare his two strongholds at Dùn Èideann and Dùn Barra for a possible siege.

He would warn the Ealdorman of Berwic en route and I sent two messengers to inform the ealdormen of Selkirk and Cumbria. We were certain that all three would join us in repudiating whoever the false Witan had chosen as king after we left.

My unease began when I saw smoke spiralling into the grey sky when we were still a few miles from Alnwic. I kicked my horse into a gallop and we arrived at the settlement to find the hall a blackened ruin. Even more disturbing, the place seemed deserted.

It was only when they saw my banner that people started to emerge from their hiding places. Then I saw the thegn and his family appear from a nearby wood with his six warriors.

'What happened?'

'The king's men came,' he replied, looking sheepish. 'There were thirty of them, there was nothing we could do.'

'Where are my family?' I asked, fearing the worst. 'Were they inside the hall?' 'No, lord,' his eleven year old son answered. 'I watched from the edge of the wood. They took your family captive and bundled them onto a cart. Your warriors tried to stop them but there were only ten of them and they were all killed. They threw the bodies into the lord's hall before setting fire to it.'

'I don't suppose you've any idea where they were taking them?'

'No, lord. I'm sorry. They headed south, that's all I know.'

'How long ago was this?'

'They came at dawn so I suppose they left three or four hours ago.' 'Thank you. You did well,' I told him.

The boy had more initiative and courage than his cowardly father. I thought of punishing the man but that would mean his family would suffer, including the boy, so I let it go.

I took one last look at the charred ruin of what had been my home for the past few years until my father died and headed south with my men. We were all mounted and the cart would slow the king's men down, so we had every chance of overtaking them if they were heading for Eoforwīc. However, we would need to do so quickly because we had few provisions with us.

It was only as we cantered on through the mud under the trees, bare now of their leaves, that I realised that I didn't even know which king these men served.

~~~

'They're camped in a clearing about two miles away, lord,' Anarawd told me.

'How many?'

'I counted thirty two, including the four sentries they've set.'

'And my family?'

'They've tied Uuffa to a wheel but the women and children were left in the wagon.'

'Did you hear a baby crying?'

'No, lord. Sorry.'

That could mean that either Uuffa's wife hadn't given birth yet or the baby was dead. In my concern I discounted the fact that he or she could be sleeping. Their encampment was on the north bank of the River Tyne. We were now in the shire of Jarrow whose ealdorman was an unknown quantity. I thought that he could be persuaded to remain loyal to Æthelred, but I wasn't about to take any chances. The sooner we were back in Islandshire the happier I would be. Beyond the Tyne lay the shire of Catterick and I was even less certain of their ealdorman. I decided that I needed to rescue my family before they crossed the river.

The camp was on the river bank fifteen miles inland from the sea. The nearest crossing point was a ford at a settlement called Wylam. I had two choices. I could either strike during the night, or I could set a trap at the ford. If it was just a matter of killing the warriors who had attacked Alnwic I would have opted for the former. However, I thought I had a better chance of protecting my family if we ambushed the column in Wylam.

The main disadvantage was that I'd need to secure the place first and their ealdorman might not take kindly to that, especially if people died. I therefore decided to go and see the thegn and ask for his help.

'Why should I help you?' the man asked belligerently whilst his wife and children cowered in the corner of their hall, gazing fearfully at the three armed strangers.

His small group of warriors stood around him in the large hut he was pleased to call his hall, fingering their sword hilts nervously. None of them looked a day under fifty and their paunches hung over their sword belts, indicating that it was a long time since they had last been in a fight.

I had only brought Anarawd and Octa with me but I was confident that we could kill the lot of them without breaking a sweat if we had to, and they knew it.

'Because you have two alternatives: either you help me and I'll leave you in peace and no one will ever know what happened here, or I will have to take your family hostage and force you to help us. Which is it to be?' I asked with a smile.

'But, if I help you kill the king's men I'll be marked as a traitor and killed anyway.'

'Not my king and not if you do what I tell you,' I said, and then I explained my plan to him.

~~~

I watched the light grow in the east under grey leaden skies. Nearly an hour later Anarawd rode into the settlement to tell me that the enemy were on their way. With the wagon it would take them at least another hour to reach us. Nevertheless I had my men get ready.

Thankfully, although it looked as if it might rain any minute, it stayed dry. I watched through the gap in a shutter of a hut on the outskirts as the first men came into view. They were two scouts who rode on through the huts, past the hall and down to the river bank. They didn't seem surprised that the place seemed deserted; anyone with any sense would avoid armed strangers.

The main body rode into the settlement next – a dozen men following their captain, a man dressed in a silvered byrnie over a richly embroidered tunic. An ornately decorated helmet hung from his saddle horn. I recognised him immediately. It was the eldest son of the late, unlamented Sigered who Æthelred had killed. Presumably this young man was now the Ealdorman of Eoforwīc.

Behind the first group came the wagon. Its occupants would be sitting or lying in it so I couldn't see them but I heard the faint cry of a young child and breathed a sigh of relief. Of course, it could be Uuffa's baby, if it was born yet, but it sounded more like that of my grandson, Eafa.

The scouts had now crossed the ford and disappeared into the trees on the far side. I waited until the ealdorman and his group were about to exit the settlement before I sprung my trap. I nodded to the man beside me and he blew three short blasts on his hunting horn.

The young man paid the price for not wearing his helmet when an arrow struck him in the head. The archer was on the roof beside him and, at that range, the point cracked open his skull before burying itself in his brain. He toppled from his horse just as a group of riders appeared from a narrow alley and attacked the group bringing up the rear.

At the same time my archers stood on the roof tops bringing down warrior after warrior in their leading contingent. A few tried to escape along the alleys leading off the main thoroughfare, but they soon found these blocked with furniture, or anything else the inhabitants could find to use as a barricade. The alleys were so narrow there wasn't space for them to turn their horses around and they were easy targets for the archers.

I led three of my men to the wagon and we clambered into it. I barely had time to check those crouching inside before two of the horsemen appeared alongside us. One tried to stab Hilda with his spear whilst the other fought with the pair of my men on that side. I brought down my sword with a roar of rage, chopping the point from the shaft, and then thrust my seax into his thigh.

He bellowed in pain and a moment later an arrow killed his horse. He was thrown clear but Uuffa leaped out of the wagon and kicked him hard in the face. My son's hands were tied behind his back but he kept kicking the warrior's head until the man lay still. I jumped down to join him and cut his bonds so that he could pick up the man's weapons and cut his throat.

We clambered back onto the bed of the wagon to find that the other horseman had also been killed. I cut my wife and the others free and Hilda threw her arms around me, hugging me so hard that I could hardly breathe.

'Is everyone alright?' I asked trying to look around.

'Yes, except for the poor baby. It was stillborn the night after these swine attacked
Alnwic.'

I looked at Uuffa's wife who was sobbing in his arms. Cynwise smiled at me as she suckled Eafa so I knew that they we fine.

'I have to go,' I told Hilda. 'I need to make sure that they are all dead.'

She nodded and I ran to find my horse, but by the time I'd reached the river I found that it was all over. The three men I'd sent over the river had disposed of the scouts and a quick body count established that we'd killed all thirty two men. One had managed to get clear, but an archer had brought down his horse and one of my warriors had ridden up and killed him as he lay trapped under it.

We loaded up the cart and took the dead – men and horses – five miles the other side of the river. We buried them in a clearing in the woods well away from the road. Even if they were discovered it would look as if they'd been ambushed there and not at Wylam. That way I'd kept my promise to the thegn that I wouldn't involve him.

~~~

When we returned to Bebbanburg I found out that it was Ælfwald who had been elected and crowned by Ethelbert. However, the Lothian lords, Godwyn of Cumbria and I continued to regard Æthelred as our king and he ruled our part of the kingdom from Bebbanburg. I had suggested that I should rebuild the hall at Alnwic and move there so that Bebbanburg could return to its original role as the seat of royal power, but the king wouldn't hear of it.

I had no illusions that we'd be left in peace but Æthelred delayed doing anything until the end of 780. The death of Archbishop Ethelbert that summer had been seen by some as God's retribution for illegally deposing Æthelred. It took some time before Eanbald was consecrated as his successor, mainly because the Pope's agreement had to be obtained first.

Just before he died Ethelbert had put Eanbald in charge of building a new church in stone at Eoforwīc and he now devoted much of his time to the enterprise. Eanbald had cynically seized the opportunity presented by Cynewise's death to take over the responsibility for sending missions to the pagans living in the lands to the north-west of the Continent. The new church was therefore to be called Eoforwīc Minster as it would be the church of a missionary teaching monastery.

My friend and mentor, Bishop Cynewulf also died that year, two months after Eanbald. The monks chose their prior, Higbald the Mercian, to succeed him and
Æthelred approved their choice. The only problem now lay in getting him consecrated. The Bishop of Hexham was in the enemy camp and Eanbald would never agree. My solution was to send him in a birlinn to Paris to be ordained as a bishop there.

Finally in late November Ælfwald managed to put together an army to invade Bernicia and capture Bebbanburg. We had already laid in supplies to last us the winter and, confident in my stronghold's ability to withstand a siege, I sent a messenger to tell Beorhtmund this, but also to say that if, in the unlikely event we were still being besieged at the start of spring, I would be grateful if he could send a relief force.

The reply which came back reminded me of the dangers of being over-confident. My friend and ally had died two weeks previously and now his nephew, Torhtmund, asked King Æthelred to confirm him as the new ealdorman. He didn't say anything about riding to the rescue after the winter was over and I suspected that he was waiting to see how the dice rolled.

I mourned the death of Beorhtmund. He had always been his own man but our interests usually coincided. Moreover, he was a leader and where he went the other ealdormen of Lothian followed. On my advice Æthelred replied regretting the death of his uncle. He said that he would gladly confirm him as ealdorman just as soon as he received the customary tax for the transfer of the title and he came to Bebbanburg to take the oath of fealty.

We heard nothing more before Ælfwald's army arrived. I had expected him to lead it but his banner was missing. Instead I soon learned that the commander was Sicga of Hexham, who it appeared was now his hereræswa.

It was an impressive host. Octa, Anarawd and I estimated the numbers the morning after their arrival and came to the conclusion that there were nearly two thousand of them. However, fourteen hundred or so appeared to be members of the fyrd. We had a hundred warriors and some two hundred from my fyrd who had taken refuge in the fortress with their families and animals. The rest of the people of my shire had withdrawn into the Cheviot Hills pro tem, though they wouldn't be able to stay there once winter arrived.

We had hidden the flour and other provisions laid by for the winter to prevent our foes getting their hands on them and to feed my people once the supplies they had with them were exhausted. I fully expected that they would have to kill and preserve some of their livestock too, much as they were needed for breeding and providing milk and cheese next year.

For the first time in my life I prayed for snow.

~~~

My prayers were answered a week later when the weather changed from cold and wet to bitterly cold. The first snow arrived overnight but there was only a few inches of it. Then it arrived, driven by a north easterly wind in billowing clouds that restricted vision to a few feet at best. The wind drifted it in great heaps more than the height of two men, one standing on the other's shoulders, by the time it ceased.

We huddled around our fires indoors, changing the sentries every hour to prevent them dying of the cold, but in truth there was no possibility of the enemy attacking in this weather. When the blizzard ceased the enemy encampment had all but disappeared under a blanket of pure white snow. We watched with amusement as their men dug themselves out of their tents and started to clear the snow away into tall heaps.

The snow was too deep for foraging or hunting – not that there would be much game around this time of the year and I wondered how long their supplies would last. Even gathering wood and lighting a fire required considerable time and effort. I could imagine that there would be multiple cases of frostbite and perhaps more than a few deaths from exposure.

That night the skies cleared and there was a hard frost – a very hard frost. Most of our water came from the well but the reeve had laid in dozens of barrels of water to be on the safe side, given the numbers now in the fortress. It proved difficult to break the ice on top of the water in the barrels when they were checked and it took several blows with an axe to break through it. It measured more than the length of a man's foot in depth.

There was, of course, no ready supply of water outside the fortress except for the one in the settlement, and I'd had that poisoned. It would mean digging a new well in due course, but better that than give the enemy a ready supply. They would have to cart water in from several miles away and it would take them a long time to clear the track to get there.

It stayed fine but intensely cold for three days before dark clouds filled the sky once more. They brought more snow with them, not as much as last time, but enough to block the track to the enemy's water supply again and cover their encampment with two more feet of the stuff.

I was fairly certain that by now Sicga's men would be starving. It was bitterly cold and they must have been exceedingly miserable. They hadn't made any attempt to storm my walls and I suspected that morale in the camp was at rock bottom.

He had brought six ealdormen and their warbands and fyrds with him and, as I watched, many began to pack up to return home. Sicga tried to stop them and there was a clash of arms in which several men died. They stayed one more night and then the next morning the great exodus began.

It was slow going for them as they had to clear the snow out of the way first. Octa begged to be allowed to follow them and kill the stragglers. It seemed to me that anything which discouraged a repeat of the attempt to capture Bebbanburg was a good idea and Æthelred agreed. He was fed up with being cooped up and wanted to go with Octa. It was only with great difficulty that I managed to persuade him that he was too valuable to risk.

It was two weeks before Octa returned. He had chased the enemy and killed over a hundred stragglers as they retreated as far as the Tyne. Many more hundreds had died by the wayside from exposure or starvation. Not all of them were from the fyrd either. He estimated that a hundred and fifty of the dead were trained warriors. He brought back pack horses laden with byrnies, leather coats, helmets and weapons to prove it.

At the Tyne the defeated army had split, the larger group crossing the river and the rest heading west towards Hexham. As the latter was Sicga's contingent he'd decided to follow them. He and his men had found the conditions very difficult, but at least the enemy had cleared the road for them and the packhorses were laden with supplies.

At Wylam Sigca's men had taken all the supplies the inhabitants had, leaving them to starve. Those who resisted were killed. It was hardly likely to endear him to the Ealdorman of Jarrow but Sicga was past caring. Octa said he gave the inhabitants of Wylam what supplies he could spare and told them to head for Jarrow and tell their lord what had befallen them. He added that they should mention that their saviours had been King Æthelred's men.

He had caught up with a band of fifty men left behind by Sicga to slow the pursuit. Octa said that he was outnumbered but his foes were in too poor a condition to offer much resistance and he slaughtered them to a man for the loss of three of his own. He had followed the rest as far as Hexham and managed to slay another twenty or more. However, the number of dead and dying by the side of the road as they passed numbered at least ten time that.

Of the two thousand men who had come north to besiege Bebbanburg I doubted if more than half of that number had made it home safely, and that included the hundreds suffering from frostbite. I suppose I should have been pleased that Ælfwald was unlikely to venture into Bernicia again, but I grieved for the loss of so many. Northumbria had lost a quarter of its fighting men, and for what? An argument over who should sit on a poisoned throne.

I would continue to support the king to whom I'd pledged my allegiance, but I was tired of the internecine warfare, the plots and the betrayal of oaths for political advantage.

~~~

It seemed that I was not alone. In 786 two papal legates arrived at Eoforwīc to see Archbishop Eanbald. With Ælfwald's agreement he summoned a church synod which all abbots and bishops in Northumbria attended, including Higbald of Lindisfarne once he'd received a safe conduct.

Among the measures adopted were laws that debarred illegitimate children from inheriting kingdoms, bishops must not involve themselves in secular affairs and tithes must be given by all men to the Church. It also laid down clear differences in dress between bishops, priests, monks, and laymen in dress. However, the most important edict was against regicide. Anyone found guilty of such a crime would be automatically excommunicated and condemned to the fires of Hell.

Whilst Æthelred and I both welcomed certain aspects of these decisions, two of his ancestors had been bastards and he wondered where that left his claim to the throne. I was, of course, worried about the edict on regicide. The prospect of spending eternity in Hell worried me considerably. So much so that I went to Lindisfarne and confessed my sins to Bishop Higbald.

'Any form of murder is enough to consign you to Hell, Lord Seofon. The murder of a king is, in my view, no worse or no better than the murder of the lowliest of his subjects. If you truly repent and have otherwise led a good life, then I hope that Saint Peter may admit you to Heaven, but it isn't my decision.'

With that I had to be satisfied. I was now sixty two, well beyond the age that most people lived and I was beginning to think about the past rather than the future. I decided that I would like to live out my days here at Bebbanburg. My fighting days were over.

Chapter Thirteen – The Restoration of King Æthelred

789 to 792 AD

It didn't work out like that, of course. I was watching Octa teach eleven year old Eafa the elements of sword fighting when a messenger rode in through the gate. He dismounted outside the king's hall and went inside. I was curious so I wandered over to find out what news he'd brought. At that moment Cynwise emerged from our hall with Hilda and our granddaughter, Osoryd, who had just turned five. These days my joints ached when I walked so I found it impossible to rush, much as I wanted to.

'What's happened?' Hilda asked.

The pretty girl I'd married thirty eight years before was now a matronly figure with grey hair, but she was ten years younger than me and more agile.

'I don't know, but the messenger seemed in a hurry.'

'I'll find out', Octa said, striding past me. He had now taken over most of my duties as ealdorman. Uuffa was no longer the shire reeve, which was now Octa's official title. My younger son was Æthelred's hereræswa, an appointment that I'd given up several years ago. He'd been building up the army, mainly using the wealth from our trading enterprise. Uuffa had a daughter following the loss of their firstborn but his wife had died giving birth to their third child, a boy. He had only survived his mother by a few days.

Uuffa had never remarried but seemed happy enough. He doted on his daughter, a girl called Odelyn, who was now six. He was away in Paris at the moment visiting Renweard and Odelyn had gone with him for the first time.

Ten minutes later Octa came out of the king's hall and asked me to join them.

'Tell Lord Seofon what you've just told me,'

'King Ælfwald has been murdered by Ealdorman Sicga,' the messenger said. 'He was visiting him at Hexham and they went hunting. They stayed the night at the old Roman fort called Cilurvum. In the morning the king was found dead and Sicga's warriors then appeared and slew those who had accompanied the king. Sicga has declared that Osred, the elder son of King Alchred, is now the king.'

'Obviously Osred was in on the plot,' Æthelred said. 'We cannot continue with two kings in Northumbria. The other ealdormen will be outraged that yet another king has been murdered, however irregular his election. We must be ready to take advantage of the situation.

'Octa, I want you to send messengers to our other ealdormen. Winter is nearly upon us so it's too late to campaign this year but in early March they are to muster their fyrds and be ready to march on Hexham. Once we have dealt with Sicga we'll march south. Either the nobles will join us or I'll replace them. Seofon, I want you to stay and defend Bebbanburg in case it all goes wrong.'

'Thank you for your consideration, Cyning, but I am not yet so feeble that I cannot sit on a horse, even it is a little uncomfortable.'

I wasn't about to miss this for the world.

'In that case, ride to Lindisfarne. I'd like Higbald and some of his monks, especially those trained as healers, to accompany us when we go.'

The weather for early March was good. It was freezing at night, but tolerably warm during the day, and it was dry. We waited for Torhtmund and his men before advancing to the southern end of Redesdale where the men of Selkirkshire and of Otterburn were assembled. We now numbered over nine hundred. When Godwyn and his Cumbrians joined us a few miles north of Hexham it took our army to fourteen hundred.

It was inevitable that Sigca would hear of our coming, but he thought himself safe behind his palisade. It took us a day to construct enough ladders and then Æthelred led the assault on all four sides of the palisade around his hall at Hexham. I and the other ealdormen tried to persuade him not to risk his life but he was adamant that he wouldn't ask his men to do what he wouldn't do himself. It certainly gave them heart, as did the open air mass celebrated by Higbald and his priests immediately before the attack.

Octa tried to stop me, but I too insisted on leading one of the groups. Godwyn led the third group and Torhtmund the fourth. At seventeen he was young for such a responsibility but, as the most powerful ealdorman in Lothian, the others automatically deferred to him.

My heart was racing as I lined up with the three hundred men I was to lead. Octa was by my side, as we started the advance. We went steadily with twenty men to a ladder. Even with his fyrd Sigca couldn't have more than three hundred to defend all four sides of his perimeter. That meant seventy five at most along the stretch that we were attacking.

Those with bows went ahead of us with a companion to hold his shield in front of the pair. I had thirty bowmen – a mixture of hunters and warriors trained as archers who used a more powerful bow. Our constant barrage of arrows kept the defenders heads down and very few arrows came back at us. I saw several of the defenders hit as they incautiously tried to see where we were.

The ground was uneven, which dictated our slow pace, but it hadn't rained for some time - unusual for that time of year - so the ditch when we came to it was almost dry. I slid down into the bottom and waited with my shield over my head as half a dozen men pushed a ladder into place. My bowmen were now joined by those boys from the baggage train who had slings. They and the archers kept up a steady rate of fire aimed at the top of the palisade to prevent men from pushing the ladders away.

As soon as my ladder was in place I started up it, followed by the other men in my small group. There was only room for four or five men on the ladder at once so the others had to wait impatiently at the bottom with their shields raised to ward off the odd missile and rock that came down at them.

I was really feeling my age as I climbed up the ladder but adrenalin gave power to my aching leg muscles and allowed me to ignore the pain in my hips and knees. When I reached the top an axe man swung his massive weapon at my head. I ducked and it whistled over my head to imbed itself in the shield I carried on my back. It stuck fast and I grabbed the dagger I had between my teeth and stuck it under the hem of his byrnie into his groin. He screamed and fell back, knocking the defender behind him off the parapet at the far side.

That gave me time to clamber over the top of the palisade, breathing hard, draw my sword and swing the shield round to my front. I knocked the imbedded axe free with my sword and turned just in time to confront a spearman who was intent on gutting me.

For a moment I was worried about my unprotected back but then I heard Octa say he was behind me and I concentrated on the spearman.

He was a youth who looked to be no more than fourteen and I wondered if he had even started his training yet. His only protection was a leather cap and one of the small round shields used by young boys to practice with. I nearly made the mistake of sparing such an unworthy opponent, but then he made a jab for my eyes and I brought my shield up to deflect the point and I stabbed forward with my sword at the same time. He managed to get his shield in the way and my sword slipped off it to the right.

The lad looked both pleased and relieved that he had survived so far, but my next move – to punch the boss of my shield into his unprotected face – took him by surprise. His nose was smashed and probably his jaw too. The pain blinded him, which gave me enough time to bring my sword back into play and gut him. Dying of a stomach wound can be a long and painful process so I stabbed down into his throat to spare him that before stepping over him to meet my next opponent.

An arrow ricocheted off my helmet with a loud thunk and I looked round to see where the archer was. He was up in the tower beside the main gate but, as I watched, one of our men climbed into the top of the tower and stabbed the man before throwing his body out of the tower to crash onto the ground below in a bloody mess of broken bones and torn flesh.

I was brought back to the battle for the ramparts by a blow on my shield but it wasn't delivered by a weapon. An enemy had backed into me whilst fighting off two of my men. It was hardly playing fair, but that isn't something you do in a fight if you want to survive. I whipped my sword round into his neck, half severing it from his body and he collapsed onto the walkway. I pushed him off into the courtyard and out of the way and looked around, ready for my next opponent. Only then did I realise that there were no more men left to fight.

A quarter of the garrison had perished by the time that the rest surrendered. Of course, there was little point in fighting on after Torhtmund had killed Sicga. The news spread and his men threw down their weapons. A few were still killed until the bloodlust died, but that always happens.

It was only then that reaction set in. Every muscle in my body screamed in agony and I was hardly capable of moving. I collapsed wearily against the side of the palisade and sat there thinking that I would never, ever be able to move again.

~~~

It took me two days to recover and even then I was still stiff and sore. By that time Æthelred had appointed a new ealdorman from amongst the thegns of the shire who had sworn fealty to him and the dead had been buried. The Bishop of Hexham, a man called Tilbeorht, had died during the attack and the king appointed a priest called Æthelberht, who had previously been Bishop of Whithorn in Galloway, to replace him. That meant that the only bishop who didn't support him now was Eanbald, Archbishop of Eoforwīc.

Typically the weather broke just as we prepared to leave and the rain came down in torrents. I climbed wearily into the saddle, clutching my cloak tightly around me, as we headed south east towards Durham. The Ealdorman of Jarrow marched south to join us and we arrived outside the stronghold of Durham on its steep hill with over two thousand men. Thankfully the Ealdorman of Durham accepted Æthelred as king. I wouldn't have wanted to have to assault the place, especially in the wet. It might not be quite as impregnable as Bebbanburg, but it wasn't far off.

At Catterick we found that the ealdorman had fled with his family, presumably to Eoforwīc. A new ealdorman was appointed and he mustered his men to swell the numbers in our growing army by another four hundred. Æthelred sent to Whitby for its ealdorman to join us and, whilst we waited, word of what had happened at Eoforwīc reached us.

The sons of the late King Ælfwald - Ælf and Ælfwine, aged ten and eight respectively - had sought sanctuary in the new minster but Osred had secretly ordered Eanbald to expel them just after the celebration of Christmas. As soon as they emerged they were seized by a crowd of men, taken down to the river and drowned. The story which then circulated was that this was done on the orders of Æthelred. It was obviously intended to turn people against him, but Osred ruled Eoforwīc and most people realised that it was a crude attempt to discredit Æthelred. The rumour persisted though.

When we reached Thirsk we were met by Osred's army. It consisted of the men of the six shires who supported him - Eoforwīc, Beverley, Loidis, Ripon, Leyburn and Luncæster. They were more populous than the more northern shires but I counted no more than two thousand men against our three thousand. Nearly every man entitled to bear arms in the whole of Northumbria must have been gathered there. Had we fought each other the kingdom would be finished as a military power.

The morning had dawned fine and clear but clouds gathered as we moved into battle formation. By the time we were ready drops of water had started to splash my cheeks and patter on my helmet. A stream with boggy banks lay between the two armies. It was no place to try and form a shield wall. The more you pushed at the enemy the more your feet would slip and slide, gaining no purchase.

It wasn't my place to offer advice unless it was asked for; my son was the hereræswa, but thankfully he too saw the disadvantages of the place as a battlefield. He went to talk to the king and minutes later we were withdrawing back up the slope we'd just come down to take up a new position on the ridge. Now Osred's men would have to cross the boggy brook and struggle uphill before attacking us. They would arrive tired and have to fight uphill against superior numbers.

I was put in charge of our two hundred horsemen; something that I welcomed. I wasn't certain that I had recovered sufficiently from Hexham to face another long fight on foot. I sat next to Æthelred and his gesith, the numbers of which he'd now expanded to thirty. As we watched, Osred and his six ealdormen rode forward and floundered through the mud and the stream before stopping at the bottom of the slope.

'Perhaps he wants to surrender,' Æthelred said, more in jest than in hope. 'Come on, let's see what he wants.'

He, I, Octa, Wulfgang and three of his gesith walked our horses down to meet him, stopping just out of arrow range of his men.

'What do you want, Osred?'

'I want to talk terms. There is no point in wasting the lives of Northumbrian men. That only benefits the Mercians and the Picts. You can keep Lothian but I want the rest of Northumbria.'

'What gives you the right to demand anything? No Witan has elected you as king as they did me.'

'These nobles chose me to succeed Ælfwald after you had arranged his murder and Eanbald crowned me in the new minster.'

Æthelred flushed with anger and I had to put a restraining hand on his sword arm as he went to draw it.

'That's a lie and you know it. Sigca of Hexham killed him on your orders.'

'Not my orders, yours; and then you killed him to stop him from talking.'

'You're deluded,'

'Cyning, Osred, this isn't getting us anywhere. We all know that Sigca killed Ælfwald and he has paid for his crime. We should be talking about the future, not the past,' I said before things got out of hand. 'You are heavily outnumbered, Osred, and the lie of the battlefield is also in our favour. You must know you cannot win.'

'Nothing is certain in war, Seofon, you should know that. If Æthelred is killed your people will have nothing to fight for.'

'The same is true for your men,' I pointed out. 'Would you allow Æthelred to reassume the crown which is rightfully his if you are allowed to go into exile unharmed?'

I looked at Æthelred for confirmation as I said this and, thankfully, he nodded his agreement to my proposal.

'No, I'm the crowned king, it is for me to lay down the terms under which you traitors might be permitted to live.' He replied, getting visibly worked up.

At that moment one of his nobles, Osbald who had succeeded Sigered as Ealdorman of Eoforwīc, broke in.

'He's right, Cyning, we can't hope to win today. You should take what terms you can negotiate.'

'Traitor,' Osred hissed at him. 'I'll have you executed for disloyalty.'

Ealdorman Osbald stared at him for a long moment before riding back through the boggy ground to where his men stood in line. Moments later he led all four hundred of them back through the cloying mire and up the hill. For a moment I thought that the man was mad and was going to attack our shield wall, but then I noticed that his men had their shields on their backs. They weren't attacking, they were joining us.

Abruptly another of his ealdormen, Eardwulf of Ripon, turned his horse and followed Osbald's example. The other four nobles looked nervously between their shrunken force and our enlarged one before one of them spoke.

'I'm sorry, Osred. I'm joining Æthelred.'

The man who'd spoken was Sentwine of Beverley, the last of the conspirators who had put Ælfwald on the throne ten years ago.

Before he could move, Osred drew his sword and thrust it into his throat in a blind rage. Before the man had hit the ground Wulfgang had ridden forward and banged his axe against the would-be king's helmet. The blow dented it and knocked Osred out.

'Go back to your men and take them home.' Æthelred told the remaining ealdormen. 'The Witan will meet at Catterick in one month's time to swear their oaths of fealty to me as king. No election is necessary as I never ceded my throne to Ælfwald and both he and this piece of offal,' he said indicating the unconscious Osred, 'were false kings.' 'What will you do with Osred, Cyning,' Eardwulf asked.

'Enough kings have been killed. He'll be tonsured and exiled, probably to Iona, if they'll have him.'

~~~

Unfortunately Osred hadn't learned his lesson. Two years later he landed on the coast of Luncæstershire with what was purported to be an army of Manxmen, but which was in reality a Mercian army. I learned later that Offa had offered him his men in exchange for the promise that the shire would become part of Mercia as soon as he was crowned King of Northumbria.

The campaign in 790 had been a great strain for me and I was now two years older. I knew, with a great deal of regret, that I wouldn't be straying far from Bebbanburg from now on. My mortality was weighing heavily on my mind in any case.

My younger brother, Renweard, had died in Paris at the beginning of the year and Anarawd had gone over to replace him. I'm not ashamed to say that I missed him. I missed Æthelred and Wulfgang too. They had been a part of my life for a long time but the king rarely came to Bebbanburg now. But most of all I missed Hilda. She had died two months after Renweard. She had been my companion as well as my wife and I often found myself talking to her before I realised that she wasn't there anymore.

Even Octa was away much of the time. As hereræswa he spent a lot of time at Eoforwīc or traveling around the kingdom with the king. Of course, Cynwise and my granddaughters were still here but she thought I spoilt Osoryd and Uuffa's daughter, Odelyn, too much. She was probably right.

Eafa had left to attend the monastery school on Lindisfarne in the summer of 790 and I couldn't even look forward to his return to train as a warrior later this year. Octa had decided that he should go to Eoforwīc instead, where he would be mixing with sons of other nobles. There he would make friends that could be useful to him later in life; he wouldn't do that at Bebbanburg.

As a result I grew closer to my younger son, Uuffa and on good days, when my joints didn't ache so much, he took me hunting. It took me days to recover afterwards and Cynewise scolded me for being an old fool, but it made me feel as if I wasn't ready for the cemetery quite yet.

During my recovery I felt well enough to embark upon a hunt and we brought back a fine stag for our larder. My feeling of euphoria vanished, however, when a messenger arrived with news of Osred's return. Uuffa immediately started to gather the fyrd and prepare the warband to march to the muster point at Durham.

I was left in charge at Bebbanburg with a garrison of old men and boys under training as warriors; scarcely twenty all told. If by some miracle Osred won I didn't see how I could hold the fortress if we were attacked in any strength. But at least preparing for such an eventuality gave me something to do, and it took my mind off the fact that my sons had gone off to war without me for the first time in decades.

It was September before we had news. The two sides had met at a place called Aynburg west of Durham. Yet again Osred's men deserted him as soon as they saw the size of the host that Æthelred had brought against him. He fled but he'd been caught near Tynemouth and killed. I hoped that would be the last of the rebellions against Æthelred's rule. Unfortunately I was destined to be disappointed.

I had expected Uuffa to return to Bebbanburg, but his men came back without him. He had gone to attend the wedding of the king to Elfflaed at Catterick. She was the daughter of Offa of Mercia and the union surprised me, especially as Offa was thought to be behind Osred's attempt to take the crown. Perhaps he needed to placate Æthelred, who can't have been very pleased at Offa's interference in Northumbrian affairs. No doubt Offa realised that he'd made a mistake. He certainly didn't want trouble in the north; he had enough of that in the south.

Raiders had landed on the coast of Dorsetshire in 789 and had killed the shire reeve. The men responsible were said to be Northmen by some or Norsemen by others. I'd heard of them before when I was in Saxony. I thought that they might be Danes, but rumour had it that these raiders came from elsewhere in Scandinavia. Other raids had occurred in the last two years against Kent, East Anglia and Essex, all of which were independent kingdoms, but they acknowledged Offa as bretwalda. Consequently he was busy trying to devise ways of countering these raids.

Wessex had supposedly acknowledged him as overlord as well and their king, Beorhtric, had married another of Offa's daughters to cement the arrangement.

Nevertheless the peace between the two kingdoms continued to be a fragile thing. I also heard from Anarawd in Paris that Charlemagne was playing politics in England, having approached both Offa and Æthelred with offers of a treaty which included an attractive trade deal. I was glad that I no longer had to get involved in such machinations, but I did worry about what the future held for my sons and grandchildren.

Chapter Fourteen – The Coming of the Vikings

793 to 795 AD

The year so far had been noted for its freak weather. We had unseasonably hot weather at the end of March and a snow storm in early May. Two days before this we had thunder and lightning that continued intermittently for twenty four hours. Then this morning we had a hailstorm. The superstitious were saying that the end of the world, when Christ would raise the dead, was nigh.

I didn't believe these doom-mongers, but what happened later gave some credence to those who said that these unusual happenings presaged disaster.

I had good days and bad days. The eighth of June in 793 was one of my better days and I even managed to make it up the steps to the walkway along the top part of the palisade. I gazed out over the German Ocean thinking about the past. After a while I was conscious of someone coming to stand beside me and I smiled when I saw it was Octa. He had come on a visit with his son Eafa to see his family and to try and persuade Cynwise and Osoryd to return with them to Eoforwīc. His daughter was now nine and he thought it was high time that she was introduced to life outside Bebbanburg.

Not that it was the small settlement it used to be. Trade with the Continent had brought all manner of craftsmen to live there – jewellers, gold and silversmiths, armourers to make weapons, wood carvers and furniture makers. There was also a regular livestock market and we had recently started to export fleeces and wool yarn. There were others centres similar to Bebbanburg, but only a few were as large. It made what was to happen all the more worrying.

'You're feeling more like your old self today, father?'

'Yes, thank the Lord. Such days seem to be increasingly rare, I mustn't complain though. There's no one who grew up with me who is still alive. Although there are days when I think that's more of a curse than a blessing; this isn't one of them though.'

I looked up at my eldest son. He was forty one now and the odd grey hair had started to appear in his long brown locks. Just at that moment there was a clatter as Eafa ran along the planking of the walkway. He arrived somewhat breathless beside us and pointed to the north east.

'What's that ship, father?'

At fifteen his eyesight was a lot better than either of ours.

'What ship? The lookout hasn't spotted anything,' Octa replied.

'That's probably because the idiot is looking the other way,' Eafa said impatiently.

'Look, there's another one now.'

'Heardred,' I called up to the lookout. 'Can you see anything to the north east?'

'No, lord. Yes, wait a minute; there's a faint smudge on the horizon. I can't make out any details yet though.'

It seemed that his eyesight wasn't as good as Eafa's either. A few minutes later he called down again.

'I can see a second one now. The sails seem larger than they would be on a birlinn or a knarr.'

'Larger?'

'Yes, when our own ships appear over the horizon I can usually tell whether it's a birlinn or a knarr by the size and shape of the sail; but at the same distance these two sails seem to be bigger.'

I was intrigued and waited impatiently for the two ships to come closer so that Eafa, who'd I'd sent up the watchtower to join the lookout, could tell me more.

'The sails have a weird device on them,' he shouted down a few minutes later. 'It looks like a black bird of some sort on a dirty yellow sail. It appears as if it lying on its back with its wings outspread and feathers like long fingers hanging down.'

I looked at Octa and he shrugged his shoulders. It wasn't a device that either of us had seen before.

'The ships are turning in towards the coast now,' Eafa called. 'They are longer than any ships I've ever seen. There are blobs of colour all along the sides, perhaps shields?'

That surprised me. Our ships had sides which were built out at an angle so it wouldn't have been feasible to hang shields along the gunwale. The top strakes of these strange ships had to be vertical for that to be possible.

'They're lowering the sails and putting out their oars. I can count fifteen, no eighteen of them.'

Eighteen a side meant at least thirty-six rowers. With sailors, ships' boys, helmsman, captain, archers and warriors as spare rowers it probably meant a crew of fifty or more on each ship.

'They've rounded the point and are heading into the beach below the monastery,' Eafa shouted, clearly puzzled.

I wasn't. I suddenly had a premonition that the arrival of a hundred warriors on Lindisfarne could only mean one thing. They were pirates or raiders intent on plunder. It had been a place of pilgrimage for a hundred and fifty years as the resting place of two famous saints – Aidan and Cuthbert – not to mention other relics such as the saintly King Oswald's head and arm. Consequently Lindisfarne had grown rich. The church was full of gold artefacts: candlesticks, the large cross on the altar, dishes and chalices; even the lectern was inlaid with gold.

Word of the monastery's wealth must have somehow reached these strangers. No Christian would dare to pillage such a holy place so they must be pagans, perhaps the Danes that Wulfgang had spoken of? I wished he was here now. He might have been able to help identify them. Whoever they were, there was no time to lose.

'Octa, sound the alarm. Get the warband mounted and ride as fast as you can for

Lindisfarne.'

He looked at me in shock for a minute, then ran towards the steps yelling for the lookout to ring the bell in the tower. Eafa started to descend until I shouted at him to stay.

'I need your eyes up there,' I told him. 'I need to know what's happening.' 'Heardred can tell you that, grandfather,' he called back, continuing his descent.

'Damn you, boy. I'm your ealdorman as well as your grandfather. Now do as you're told. Heardred, go and saddle your horse.'

'But, grandfather,' he replied, 'I need to go with my father.'

'You're not a trained warrior yet, boy. You'll stay here.'

Dispiritedly he turned and slowly climbed back up to the platform. We both knew that it wasn't his eyes I needed. He might have better sight than most, but he wouldn't be able to make out much detail at a range of six miles. No, I was keeping him safe.

I doubted that my warband would get there in time to be of much use. It was sixteen miles by land to the monastery. At least the tide was out which meant that Octa could ride across the sands to the island. If only my ships were here they could have crossed by sea, but they were all away at the moment.

My heart sank as Eafa called down sullenly that he could see a spiral of black smoke, and then another. By the time my son and my warband got there it could all be over. In a way I hoped that would be the case. He had taken every warrior who could ride with him, all fifty five of them, but they would be heavily outnumbered and I didn't know what sort of fighters these raiders would be.

Less than an hour had passed when Eafa yelled that he could see something happening on the sands. At that distance, even though the air was crystal clear, it would be difficult to make out any detail, however good his eyesight. The disappointment disappeared from his voice as he got excited by what he saw.

'I think it's a group moving across the sands.'

'Can you see if they are monks or islanders?'

'Not at this distance, they're just a blob, but they're probably both. Oh!' he exclaimed, 'they're being pursued by another group of men. I can see the sun glinting off helmets and weapons. It must be some of the raiders.'

'How many?'

'Difficult to say, grandfather. Perhaps a score or more.'

I grunted in satisfaction. Octa should be nearly at the point where the path across the sands started. He would be able to both save the monks and islanders and hopefully slaughter the enemy. That would leave fewer for him to tackle on the island.

'I can see some sort of movement. It looks like a group leaving the mainland to cross to the island. I wish I could see more clearly. Yes! I can see the sun reflected off helmets now,' he called down. 'It must be father and his men.'

Although he couldn't possibly be certain, it seemed most likely.

'They should get there before the raiders catch up with the others,' he yelled, his excitement palpable.

'How many monks would you say there are?'

'I can't distinguish monks from islanders, or even see individuals, grandfather; they must be six miles away, but I'd say it's a sizeable group.'

In addition to the sixty or seventy monks and novices, the bishop and few priests, there were over a hundred men, women and children who farmed the rest of the island. The group of escapees probably only represented around a third of the total.

'The cowards are turning back,' he shouted.

I couldn't make out anything at that distance and was confused as to who he meant.

'Our men?'

'No, grandfather, of course not. The raiders, but they won't get back to the island before father reaches them.'

Before long after that he told me that our horsemen had now merged into the other group with the sun glinting on helmets and weapons. I imagined the horsemen cutting down the fleeing enemy, but perhaps the latter had turned to make a stand.

'I can't make out what's happening,' Eafa cried out in frustration. 'No, wait. I think our men may have overcome the enemy. At any rate I can't see the sun reflected off metal anymore.'

'What of the monks and the islanders?'

'I can't see any movement on the sand now grandfather. They must have reached the mainland.'

Then he shouted out that the longships were being pushed back into the sea.

'I can't make it out clearly but groups appear to be going to and fro between the monastery and the shore.'

More smoke snaked up into the sky and then he shouted with excitement that the raiders seemed to be lining up on the beach because our horsemen had appeared on the skyline above the beach.

'I think that some must be trying to drag their ships back into the sea whilst the rest hold off father and his men,' he said.

The beach was a mile or so nearer than the sand so Eafa could make out a little more of what was happening. Of course, the tide was going out still and so their ships would be further up the sand than when they'd beached them. I knew that, if it was our birlinns, their bottoms would be stuck fast and we'd probably have to wait until the tide came in, but these ships must have a protruding keel which acted like a sled because Eafa told me ten minutes later that they'd managed to float them.

'Their shield wall has broken I think, at any rate they're running for their ships. Father can cut them down before they can get there,' he cried gleefully. 'Oh, no.'

'What is it?'

'Our men have halted and they're retreating. They must have archers on the ships and they're preventing us from closing with them. In fact I think a few of our horsemen are down and the rest are retreating out of range.'

Even my poor eyes could make out the two ships as their rowers turned them and headed back out to sea. The wind was against them now and so they their crews rowed them to the north east until even Eafa couldn't see them anymore.

It was now late in the day and I expected Octa to stay the night on Lindisfarne. Eafa and I would have to wait until tomorrow before we heard more of what had happened. I fretted over how much damage had been done to the monastery and to the vill outside it. Most of all I wondered if Higbald was safe and how many monks had been slaughtered.

We got the answers to some of those questions earlier than I'd thought. A messenger arrived during the night to tell me something that broke my heart. We had lost ten dead and a dozen wounded, who would hopefully recover. However, one of the dead was Octa. He'd been hit in the throat by an arrow just before the raiders left.

~~~

We were all stunned by Octa's death. I had always been closer to him that to Uuffa, who had grown to resent the fact that he wasn't the first born. Now he would have to reconcile himself to seeing his fifteen year old nephew as my heir.

He wasn't the only one who felt bitter. Cynewise blamed me for sending her husband to his death whilst I stayed safe and secure inside my fortress. I couldn't really blame her. I felt the same way. I cursed my old age; it should have been me who died. I'd lived a full and long life and it was my time to go. For a while I sunk into a state of maudlin self-pity which Cynewise had no patience with.

'You are his father, you need to get his funeral organised, and those of the brave men who died with him,' she told me. 'Bishop Higbald needs help to rebuild what the raiders destroyed, and you need to see what you can do about finding out who they were and how to contact them.'

'Contact them? Why?'

'They took six men hostage, four monks and two novices. Perhaps you could ransom them back.'

Much of the wealth of Lindisfarne had been stolen during the raid. Instead of being one of the richest monasteries in Northumbria it was now the poorest.

'How can I find out who they were? No one seems to know.'

'They were from the north, or at least that's what everyone is saying. You have a prisoner. Find out from him.'

Suddenly I felt a fool. Cynewise was right. Instead of feeling sorry for myself I should be doing something. I was still the ealdorman after all. The boy my warriors had captured could tell us who he was and where he came from. The problem was language. There was the odd word he seemed to understand, but it was impossible to converse with him.

Then I had an idea. I needed to send a messenger to tell the king what had happened; he could also take a letter to Uuffa asking him to bring Wulfgang back with him. He'd had contact with the Danes when he lived in Bremen and, if the boy was a Dane, Wulfgang might be able to interrogate him.

It was nearly mid-summer and we couldn't wait for Uuffa to arrive before we held the funeral service. Octa's body was already beginning to smell. The other warriors who'd been killed had been brought back to Bebbanburg and buried there but Higbald had accorded my son the honour of burial in the monastic cemetery.

The shell of the church had been cleared of the debris but work had only just started on a new roof, so the service was held in the open air. Higbald read from one of the beautifully illustrated copies of the Lindisfarne Gospels. The monks had carried them and other precious artefacts away when they fled. They may have lost the gold ornaments and the bishop's hoard of silver, but those could be replaced in time. The gospels were irreplaceable.

After we had seen the coffin lowered into the grave and had each thrown a handful of dirt onto it, we returned to Bebbanburg. Cynewise had invited me to ride in the covered carriage with her, Osoryd and Odelyn but I was too proud to do so. I couldn't mount on my own so my body servant cupped his hands together so he could lift my foot. Even so swinging my leg over the saddle was painful. Once there my joints still hurt, but at least I could ride back to the fortress with some of my dignity intact.

Four days later Uuffa and Wulfgang arrived.

'The king has agreed to let me stay for a while to act as the shire reeve until Eafa has completed his warrior training and can take over.'

I nodded gratefully and told him in more detail how his brother had died. Wulfgang listened and asked questions about the ships the raiders had used. 'They could be Danes but they could equally be Norsemen.' 'What is the difference?' I asked.

'The Danes include the Angles and the Jutes, your ancestors, and the people who live in the archipelago of islands to the east of the peninsula north of Saxony. The Norse live still further north in a barren land of mountains and deep sea inlets they call fjords. Where is this prisoner of yours? Let's see if we can understand one another, though the
Danish I learned as a boy is a bit rusty now.'

When the boy was brought in it was evident that he'd been treated well. He was clean and wore new homespun trousers and a tunic. He stood sullenly between two warriors who towered over him. I put his age at twelve or thirteen. He had long fair hair but no incipient beard showed on his face as yet. I saw that his eyes, when he glanced up occasionally, were a vivid blue. He reminded me in many ways of Wulfgang when he was a boy.

The latter started to talk to him and the boy's surprise at hearing a language he understood was evident.

'He understands me, or enough for me to interrogate him,' Wulfgang said after a few minutes of conversation. 'He's asking what will happen to him if he tells us what we want to know.'

'First ask him his status. Is he a noble's son who can be ransomed for the return of the monks they kidnapped, or a slave?'

Following a few more questions Wulfgang said that the boy was no thrall, what they called slaves, nor was he the son of a king or jarl. Jarl was apparently the equivalent to our ealdorman, but what it really meant was chieftain or leader. He was a bóndi's son who was serving his jarl as a ship's boy.

'Bóndi?' I queried.

'Our nearest equivalent is ceorl; bóndis are freemen who are farmers or artisans such as smiths and merchants. However, the term also includes wealthy land owners who we would term thegns.'

'And what sort of bóndi is the boy's father?'

'He's a tenant farmer who pays rent for his land to a rich bóndi. The boy's name is
Erik, by the way.'

I was disappointed; the boy would be no use as a hostage who I could exchange for the monks. I remembered that I'd promised to decide the boy's fate once I knew his status.

'Tell Erik that I will spare his life if he tells me all that I want to know.'

'He asks if that means he will become a thrall – a slave – if so, he would rather die.'

'What is so terrible about being a slave? Tell him we treat our slaves well.'

'He says that in his country thralls are forced to wear an iron or a wooden collar and are scarcely regarded as human. Even the dogs are treated better.'

'I see. Very well, explain that I won't enslave him but I expect him to become a servant.'

Then I had an idea. As a warrior in training, Eafa had no body servant of his own. My own body servant could train Erik so that he was ready to serve Eafa when the boy became sixteen in a few months' time. I put the idea to Eafa who studied the boy, then smiled and nodded his head. Wulfgang then gave Erik the option of a slow and painful death or becoming my grandson's body servant.

'He agrees,' Wulfgang said after a lengthy exchange.

'Good of him,' I muttered, annoyed at the time it had taken the boy to accept my offer.

'Now ask him where he comes from.'

It appeared that Erik wasn't entirely sure. He said he wasn't a Dane, with some contempt, but Norse. He lived in a small settlement a few miles from the head of the fjord where the jarl who had led the raid had his hall. The place was called Hladir. His father and elder brothers worked a smallholding which they rented off the bóndi who owned all the land in the valley where he lived.

He was the youngest of six children: four boys and two girls. His mother had given birth to nine in all but three had died whilst still babies. This had been his first voyage as a ship's boy and two of his brothers had sailed as warriors on his ship, which he called a drekar.

He explained that it was more properly termed a skeid, meaning that which cuts through water, and had roughly thirty oars a side. The term drekar came from the carved and painted dragon's head which was placed on the prow before a fight.

He went on to say that there were other types of longship: the snekkja typically had twenty oars a side and the karvi was the smallest warship with between six and sixteen oars a side. Jarl

Haraldr, the man who owned the two drekar used in the raid, owned two snekkja and several karvi as well. His jarl owed allegiance to a king somewhere but he didn't know his name.

He described his drekar as being about a hundred feet long and eighteen feet in the beam. It was built of oak and, unlike our ships, it had an external keel. The mast carried a sail which measured some forty feet across and, like ours, was made from rough woollen cloth. They were woven as one piece and that made them stronger than ours, which consisted of several lengths of cloth stitched together.

Their voyage had lasted for nine days. They had followed the coast south for four days before they came to the tip of a peninsular dominated by a mountain the jarl had called Gullfjellstoppen. There they turned out to sea, leaving the coast behind. Their only guide was the sun, when it appeared. He didn't know how it worked but the helmsman said that they were heading south west. The wind was variable; some days they barely seemed to moving through the water. On other days the wind whipped the crests of the tall waves into horizontal sheets of spume and the drakars flew along, almost leaping down into the troughs and shooting up the far side of the wave. Erik had found it exhilarating rather than frightening, which said something about the boy.

Then they sighted land and went ashore to find out where they were. They sought Lindisfarne because, even at Hladir they had heard stories of the wealth of the monastery there. The local inhabitants they had captured didn't speak their language, of course, but at the mention of Lindisfarne they pointed south. They had taken a man who appeared to be a priest with them to guide them and then, when they had found Lindisfarne a day later, Jarl Haraldr had thrown him over the side to drown.

Erik's tale rang true. A boy his age could hardly make up that sort of detail. At least now I had a rough idea where these raiders had come from. One other interesting thing the boy had said was that they called their piracy going *a-viking*. It appeared to be the common pursuit of their warriors in the summer months.

Normally they raided closer to home but this year Haraldr had been tempted to risk the long and perilous voyage across the open sea to find the fabled Isle of Lindisfarne. The men who came with him were all volunteers and all would share in the plunder, as well as the proceeds from selling the unfortunate monks as thralls.

~~~

The story of the attack on Lindisfarne spread throughout the whole of Christendom and men began to say that the Northumbrians had been punished by God for their many crimes, especially regicide and the general fondness of the people for material wealth at the expense of their spiritual welfare. It was unfair as both Mercia and Wessex had experienced their fair share of infighting for their respective thrones.

In due course Eafa became a warrior and Erik became his body servant. The boy had learned English rapidly and he carried out his duties diligently, but he had a streak of mischievous which could have made him a nuisance; instead it made him interesting.

I spoke to him occasionally and grew more interested in these northerners. I learned that there were three distinct peoples, though they all spoke roughly the same language. They were the Danes, the Norse and the Swedes. His people, the Norse, lived along the coast which was dotted with fjords like his. He didn't know how many there were but he did know that very few lived in the hinterland. They were seafaring folk who eked out a living from the land as best they could when they weren't raiding.

He was adamant that they didn't raid for pleasure, but because they needed to in order to survive. There was no overall king of the Norse but many petty kings, each of whom derived his power from the number of jarls sworn to him. Jarls in turn depended on their success at rewarding their warriors to keep their position. The more successful a jarl or king was at raiding and providing for his people, the more powerful he became.

Internal blood feuds and struggles for power were almost a way of life. The only thing that would unite them was the promise of plunder. Their class structure wasn't as rigid as ours. Although kings tended to come from one family, that wasn't always the case. A jarl would hope to hand over to his son when he grew too old or was killed but, if he lost his popularity any of his bóndis could challenge him for the torc he wore around his neck; the torc being the symbol of his status.

'What about the Swedes?'

Erik shrugged and settled his bony posterior more comfortably. He was sitting cross legged beside the hearth whilst I sat on a chair covered in a thick fleece to give me some comfort. Normally a servant would never sit in the presence of his master but I found it more comfortable if the boy sat so I didn't have to crane my neck when I looked at him.

He was growing into a tall, if gangly, youth now he was approaching fourteen.

'All I know is that they live far to the south of us, further along the coast. Perhaps to the north east of the Danes,' he added helpfully.

'Do they raid as well?'

'Yes, but I've heard they confine their raiding to the Baltic Sea. That's all I know.' I'd heard of the Baltic. It was an almost completely inland sea to the east of Denmark.

'Well, I hope that we don't get any more raids like that on Lindisfarne.'

Erik look as if he was uncertain whether to reply or not but in the end he said something that troubled me greatly.

'Because Jarl Haraldr's raid was such a success, word will spread,' he said. 'Soon every king and jarl seeking treasure and prestige will want to launch a raid across what you call the German Ocean.'

~~~

The boy's words proved to be prophetic. In 794 Vikings attacked the monastery at
Jarrow but this time their ealdorman's warband was closer at hand and they drove the Vikings back into the sea. They escaped in their three longboats but returned that night. The warband was drunk after celebrating their victory and the Vikings succeeded in looting the monastery.

In 795 they rounded the north of Alba and attacked the Isle of Skye before proceeding to loot the Holy Isle of Iona and several Irish monasteries.

These events seemed far away and peace had returned once more to Bebbanburg. I had stationed part of my warband in a small fort on Lindisfarne where the monks could take shelter if there was another attack. I also made sure that at least two of my birlinns were available in Budle Bay at any one time. That said, I had doubts that they would be a match for one drekar, let alone two.

Eafa grew older but he was still very young to be my shire reeve. He made mistakes but he wasn't afraid to admit them or to seek my advice. I grew more and more incapacitated and I could only get around now with the aid of a stick and the shoulder of a servant to lean on. I knew my days were numbered and then came the news that made death seem like a welcome release from this world.

Epilogue – The Year of Three Kings

796 AD

When I was told that Torhtmund was waiting in the hall to see me I knew that something serious had happened. With great difficulty I got out of bed with the help of my body servant and young Erik. The Norse boy was fifteen now and had developed into a muscular youth; such a change from the scrawny boy he'd been three years before.

My body servant was no longer the faithful Seward. He had died the previous year and I had been depressed for some time by his demise. It seemed that everyone that I'd been close to had gone before me. My new servant was a Frisian slave called Bernard. He was sixteen and had been bought by Anarawd in Paris as Seward's replacement. He was dutiful and eager to please, almost too much so. His obsequiousness made me miss Seward even more.

I hobbled into the hall and sat down in my chair with relief. Eafa was present, as was Cynewise. Osoryd had left Bebbanburg the previous year to become a novice at Coldingham, twenty miles up the coast in Lothian. It was her choice to become a nun and, although I had hoped that she would marry and unite our house with one of the other great houses of Northumbria, I didn't try to dissuade her. Cynewise had less sense and forbade her. Of course, this only made Osoryd more determined and Cynewise never forgave me when I sided with her daughter.

'Torhtmund, welcome. Don't stand there, someone fetch a chair for the ealdorman, and refreshments. Have you come far?' He nodded and then sat down.

'From Hexham.'

'If you've come to tell me that Offa of Mercia has died, I've already heard.'

'No, not Offa. The king was visiting Hexham and decided to go hunting. I was with him, as was Uuffa and the ealdormen Ealdred and Wada. When we brought the stag to bay we all stepped back to let Æthelred have the honour of killing it. As he went forward those two traitors threw their spears into the kings unprotected back, killing him.'

'No! Not again. Poor Æthelred. Why?'

'Apparently to put Osbald on the throne.'

'Osbald? But he has no claim to the crown. He's only an ealdorman, not an aetheling.'

'There's worse news, Seofon, and I hate to be the one to bring it to you. I managed to kill Ealdred but Wada and two other men killed both Wulfgang and Uuffa before they fled.'

I had always detested people who showed too much emotion but when I heard that my other son was dead as well, I broke down and cried. To her credit Cynewise did her best to comfort me whilst Eafa stood there looking miserable and helpless. I told her to comfort her son whilst Bernard and Erik helped me back to my bed.

I lay there awake, thinking back to when Octa and Uuffa were boys and I was young Æthelred's guardian. I had loved them all and now they were dead. I felt Wulfgang's loss too.

It was of no comfort to hear that the usurper Osbald's reign had lasted a mere twenty seven days. When he heard that Torhtmund and most of the other ealdormen were mustering an army to depose him he quickly abdicated and fled north to Lindisfarne, of all places.

Higbald came to see me the next day. This time I received him lying in bed. I didn't know it then but I wouldn't leave it again.

'What shall I do, lord. I can't really refuse Osbald sanctuary, but he plotted the murder of King Æthelred and he also slew Beorn, the son of King Ælfwald, by setting fire to the hut in which he'd locked him. He is doubly accursed.'

Beorn's murder had been in 780. I didn't understand at the time why Osbald was never called to account for it. My inclination was to suggest that Higbald hand him over to his enemies. I would gladly hang him for one. But I didn't. There had been enough killing; the throne of Northumbria was soaked in blood.

'I'll send a birlinn across to you. It'll take him to Pictland. Let him take his chances up there.'

And so it was. I lapsed into a coma a few days later but I awoke again to find Eafa, Cynewise and Anarawd by my bedside. I fancied I could see Hilda, Octa and Uuffa too but, of course that must have been my imagination.

'Who's the king now?' I managed to croak, as if that mattered.

'Eardwulf,'

It shouldn't have come as a shock, but it did. He was another usurper. He was ever Æthelred's enemy and I wouldn't have been surprised if he was in on the plot to kill him. 'May God help Northumbria then.'

I was distantly aware that Eafa had asked what I'd said, but it seemed that no one had understood my last words. I had seen ten kings come and go in the seventy two years I'd spent on this earth. It was more than enough. I was ready to depart this life.

THE LORDS OF BEBBANBURG WILL RETURN AGAIN IN

THE WOLF AND THE RAVEN

Book 7 in the Kings of Northumbria Series

AUTHORS NOTE

This story is based on the known facts, but written evidence is scarce and there is confusion in the main sources about dates, names and even relationships between family members. The main events are as depicted, even if the detail is invented. The chronology of events has sometimes been slightly altered in order to suit the story but this is, after all, a novel.

The century after the death of Osric, the last acknowledged king of the House of Æthelfrith, was a turbulent one. Ceolwulf, who followed Osric, abdicated and entered the monastery on the Holy Island of Lindisfarne as a monk in 737. His cousin, Eadbehrt, ruled for nineteen years but faced several challenges for the throne during that time. He too became a monk in 758 and he was followed by no less than ten kings over the next century or so. Two of them were deposed and then restored and three were murdered.

This novel is set during the period from Eadbehrt's election as king in 737 to the death of Osbald – who reigned for a mere twenty seven days - and the accession of Eardwulf in 796. Unlike the previous books in the series, which are written in the third person, this tells the story through the eyes of one man – Seofon of Bebbanburg.

This period saw the decline of the once powerful kingdom of Oswiu, who was acknowledged as overlord by the whole of the North of Great Britain, including Scotland, and even for a time, Mercia. The remarkable thing is that, whilst its military and political power declined, its cultural standing grew, especially in the fields of craftsmanship, missionary work on the Continent and scholarship.

As the eighth century drew to a close the world of the Anglo-Saxons of Northumbria was about to change. The raid by Norsemen on Lindisfarne was not the first contact with the Vikings, as they came to be called. There had been raids on Wessex. Kent and Mercia before 793, notably that of 789 when the Shire-Reeve of Dorset was killed. There may have been mercantile contacts before that because the Norse and the Danes were traders as well as raiders. Perhaps the contrast between the rich pastoral lands of England and the unproductive farmland of much of Scandinavia encouraged these raids as a precursor to settlement.

Although this lay in the future, the internecine struggle for power in Northumbria during the eighth century meant that it was unprepared militarily and politically for the large scale invasion of the Norse and the Danes when it came. Of course, the kingdoms of the south also had to struggle for survival, but survive they did. Not so Northumbria. Its last independent king was Aelle. After that there were a number of Anglo-Saxon kings who ruled as Danish puppets and several Danish kings. In 927 Æthelstan became King of the English and Northumbria became an earldom.

Charlemagne

Charlemagne, meaning Charles the Great, was born on 2 April 742 and died on 28 January 814 aged seventy one. He united most of Western Europe during his reign and the greatly expanded Frankish state that Charlemagne founded was called the Carolingian Empire, named after the dynasty of which he was a member.

Charlemagne was the oldest son of Pipin the Short and became king in 768 following his father's death, initially as co-ruler with his brother, Carloman. The latter's sudden death in unexplained circumstances in 771 left Charlemagne as the undisputed ruler of the Kingdom of the Franks. However, Carloman died in Burgundy, not Frisia as portrayed in this novel.

Charlemagne conquered Lombardy in 774, Thuringia in 774, Bavaria in 778, and Carinthia in 788. He campaigned against Saxony for twenty long years before finally subjugating it in 797.

He continued his father's policy towards the papacy and became its protector. In return Pope Leo III crowned Charlemagne as Emperor of the Romans on Christmas Day in the year 800.

Other Novels by H A Culley

The Normans Series

The Bastard's Crown
Death in the Forest
England in Anarchy
Caging the Lyon
Seeking Jerusalem

Babylon Series

Babylon – The Concubine's Son
Babylon – Dawn of Empire

Individual Novels

Magna Carta
Berwick *(Previously published as The Sins of the Fathers)*

Robert the Bruce Trilogy

The Path to the Throne
The Winter King
After Bannockburn

Constantine Trilogy

Constantine – The Battle for Rome
Crispus Ascending
Death of the Innocent

Macedon Trilogy

The Strategos
The Sacred War
Alexander

Kings of Northumbria Series

Whiteblade
Warriors of the North
Bretwalda
The Power
and the Glory
The Fall of
the House of
Æthelfrith

About The Author

H A Culley was born in Wiltshire in 1944 and was educated at St. Edmund's School, Canterbury and Welbeck College. After RMA Sandhurst he served as an Army officer for twenty four years, during which time he had a variety of unusual jobs. He spent his twenty first birthday in the jungles of Borneo, served with the RAF, commanded an Arab infantry unit in the Gulf for three years and was the military attaché in Beirut during the aftermath of the Lebanese Civil War.

After leaving the Army he became the bursar of a large independent school for seventeen years before moving into marketing and fundraising in the education sector. He has served on the board of two commercial companies and has been a trustee of several national and local charities. He has also been involved in two major historical projects. His last job before retiring was as the finance director and company secretary of the Institute of Development Professionals in Education.

He lives near Holy Island in Northumberland and now devotes his time to writing historical fiction.

Printed in Great Britain
by Amazon

44216980R00180